ABOUT THE AUTHOR

TIMOTHY TRIMBLE is the author of Zegin's Adventures, the Air Born series, and many short stories. He's an author and technologist - basically a geek who likes to write. While he's been a non-fiction writer of computer related books and articles, his true love of writing is in science fiction and young adult fantasy. He lives in the Pacific Northwest, where the prevalence of coffee shops and hiking trails contribute to his inspiration. You can visit him online at www.timothytrimble.com and can follow his constant postings on Twitter at @timothytrimble, or Facebook.com/AuthorTimothyTrimble.

To Zachary.

Thank you for all the love & support.

Enjoy the flight!

T Trimble

Timothy Trimble

EXCERPT

"It has to be the Eighteenth. This is how they operate. They could've been watching for years, looking for a routine, waiting for the perfect moment. I'm suspect they were behind the abduction of her parents as well."

"Then let's go get her. Take her back from them. They did it to us - we can do it to them!"

"If we do that, it becomes a war." Georgeo stood up and began pacing around the table. "If we start a war with them, we expose ourselves. That's just what they want. If we're exposed they can pick us off, one by one. Come on, Torre! There are billions of 'normal' humans and maybe, just maybe, a couple hundred Avitorians." He continued pacing. "That would lead to our extinction. This is not the time to expose ourselves. Humanity can hardly get along with themselves. How can we expect them to understand what we are and accept us as a part of their society if we're different?"

Timothy Trimble

AIR BORN

Do You Dream of Flying?

Timothy Trimble

Second print edition – October, 2016

ISBN-13: 978-1536873290
ISBN-10: 1536873292

Master Editor: Mark Hammer
Cover Design: Russel Calhoun

Moral Support & Sanity Checker: Denise Trimble
Creative Consulting: Azaliah Yadinah

DEDICATION

For Sharon and Cassandra, for virtually adopting this slightly eccentric writer.

CONTENTS

ONE - ALL I WANNA DO

"We do not write our history for fear it would be discovered. Though we cherish our heritage and the gift we have been blessed with, we are to remain vague when it comes to documenting. There are those who seek to obtain what we have, regardless of the cost. Extinction is what we fear - the loss of our beauty, and our sense for peace." (The Guide to Preservation. Author unknown.)

(Year: 1995)

Angela loved the way her hair flowed in the wind as she flew through the pristine and cool night air. “All I wanna do is have some fun…” blared on her earbuds attached to the portable cassette player secured around her upper arm. She slowly drifted through the desert canyon air without glancing at the mountain peaks to her right and left. Her knowledge of each turn, nook, and cranny was permanently burned into her seventeen-year-old subconscious memory. She bobbed her head and silently mouthed the lyrics along with Sheryl. This was, after all, her own personal playground.

“So what if it happened to be in the middle of Joshua Tree National Park?” she had defiantly stated to her older sister, before heading out for the night of flying. “It’s a secluded canyon. The only people who show up are old L.A. hippies looking for a place to get stoned. If they did manage to see me, they’ll think they’re just trippin. It’s no big deal.” She said in defense with one foot out the door.

She shut out the discussion with her sister and gazed at the sky. She enjoyed the stars the most. Moonless nights were always the best - easier to see the millions of pinpoints in the Milky Way, and less of a chance of being seen. She slowly came to a stop and hovered on her back while gazing at the stars, wondering if her ancestors came from the heavens or were just another type of the human species. She had asked her uncle Georgeo during one of his rare visits a few months before. He didn’t know, but he told her that he liked to think they came from the stars. Two Avitorians - male and female - seeking someplace to colonize. Too bad the humans were already here, he would chuckle. He told her they stayed because they saw something intriguing in the humans. Compassion, love, and a thirst for knowledge. The few who spoke of peace and hope out shone those who strive for power and riches. This was what kept the Avitorians on earth. Once they made their decision, the ability to return to their home world or to seek out another place to colonize had been taken away. How or why - he didn't know. Of course, Georgeo reminded her it was just a story and he was not sure if it was really true or not.

Draco the dragon was directly overhead tonight. She traced the shape of the constellation with her finger down past Ursa Minor toward the body of Ursa Major. She drifted her hand from side to side in rhythm with Sheryl Crow's guitar. She rolled over and glanced at the blackness of the ground; she estimated it was a little over 400 feet to the valley floor below. By dead reckoning she triangulated the 3600-foot peak to her right and the 3700-foot peak on her left. With the subtle light from a million stars she could make out the course of the dry creek bed running West to East and another one intersecting from the South straight below. It was a popular intersection for weekend campers, but tonight there was no sign of life below. No campfires, no lanterns, no glow of cigarettes (or joints) as campers would find comfort in a drag of unhealthful smoke. She wondered why anyone would smoke. She remembered the lesson from the blackened tissue on display in last year's biology class. Tonight is Wednesday. *Bah.* I wish I didn't have school tomorrow, she thought.

Drifting West, Angela moved past the creek junction below and the peaks now behind, toward an opening in the canyon. The dry lake bed was completely surrounded by mountains. Three miles long and a mile wide - it was the perfect place for her to hover and soak in the immensity of the night sky. She stopped in her favorite spot and rolled over to face the sky. She really wanted to stay long enough to see the constellation Orion stick its head over the Eastern horizon, but that would mean staying up most of the night, and risking the brightness of the revealing moon rise. She would never hear the end of it from her sister if she did. *Just a few more minutes and I'll head back.* She watched the star Deneb so intently she could sense its movement as it inched across the sky. The clack of Angela's cassette tape player startled her as it clicked off after the last song. She always felt uneasy with even the slightest noise in the middle of such a pristinely quiet night in the desert.

Suddenly, she felt unusually warm. *Now that's weird.* She glanced at the surrounding land marks and noticed that she was starting to descend. Rolling over to face the dry lake bed, she noticed there were new shadows cast by the starlight in a spot where normally there was nothing but sand. She banked steeply to her right and headed toward the Northern cliffs. The warmth was gone and she regained altitude. Her curiosity prompted her to hover feet first and turn, facing the middle of the lake bed. Multiple shadows moved and once again she felt her body get warm. The air around her was still cool, but her body itself was feeling warm - almost like a fever. She felt control of her altitude slip as she again began descending. At the same moment she was blinded by light from below. Bathed in bright white she instinctively covered her eyes with her hands hoping she could get a glimpse between her fingers. She continued descending. She knew if she was forced to go to ground she would not be able to run as fast as she could fly. She could feel panic rising in her chest.

The adrenaline gave her strength to resist the descent. She turned away from the lights and headed for the canyon as fast as she could. *They saw me! Who are they? Why are they here?* Questions flooded her mind as she tried to stifle the panic. Forcing herself to focus, she dove toward the canyon entrance in an attempt to gain some needed speed and momentum. *I've got to get out of here and get safe. Where was the heat coming from and why did I stop flying?* Her mind was racing. She could hear distant shouts and the sound of some kind of vehicle engine firing up behind her. It sounded like a VW - possibly a dune buggy. She didn't want to chance looking back to find out. The lights were still shinning on her, but they were dimmer as she reached the canyon opening. She skimmed the ground barely avoiding the snag of the sage and shadowed brush along the valley floor. With the increased speed and momentum, she shot straight into the night sky and out of the beams of the lights.

"You fools! You frigging idiots! Get the light back on her, now!" The woman screamed at the two men as they jumped to the task and slid into the bucket seats of the four seater sand rail. The woman was crouched in the back gripping the back of a strange looking cannon, in cables and coiled copper wrappings around the barrel. The ribbed balloon tires dug into the sand as the driver gunned the gas. A row of flood lights came on across the top of the roll bar above the driver's head. The man in the passenger seat struggled with the portable spot light as they raced after the escaping flier.

The woman was knocked back into the seat by the acceleration. She quickly stood up and grabbed the twin grips of the cannon, hanging on with all her might as the vehicle bounced along the dry lake bed. She managed her balance and pressed the button on the microphone clipped to her shoulder. "Coming your way." Two clicks over the speaker acknowledged the listener on the other radio received her message.

Angela leveled off at 3600 feet even with the highest peak off to the North of the canyon wall. She glanced back over her shoulder at the approaching buggy with its bouncing flood lights and a single spot light beam searching the sky. Her luck was holding, they hadn't locked her in, at least not yet. Her heart was pounding; she thought it would burst. She turned and along the edge of the canyon as it gently snaked through an S shaped curve. *I've got to calm down and get my senses.* She knew the canyon would straighten out before reaching the creek junction, at least that would give her a vantage point to see the buggy approach. *I could go straight up and just get some distance, but it would be easier to see me. I usually fly East. This time I'll go South. The old creek climbs into the mountains and I can disappear there. No way they can follow me.* She descended toward the creek bed at an angle, building up her momentum.

The sand rail reached the canyon entrance, bouncing and sliding left as the driver dodged the rocks and Joshua Trees. The man with the spot light scanned the sky as he tried to compensate for the sudden movements of the sand rail.

"Crank it up to fifteen hundred, Matt!" The woman stated into the microphone. "Twelve hundred isn't enough." She let go of the mic and grabbed the back of the cannon with both hands. "Try to get us through that S turn without flipping us over," she caustically barked at the driver.

Angela could hear the roar of the buggy entering the turn of the canyon. The sounds of the engine echoed and reverberated off the canyon walls; making it sound like an army of vehicles. She turned and caught a quick glance of the lights flickering on the mountain sides, casting dancing shadows of sagebrush along the sides of the creek bed. Jack rabbits scattered in terror at the sound of approaching vehicles and a once pursuing bobcat turned tail and retreated to the shadows. She double backed toward the straight section of the dry creek bed, skimming a few feet above the sand as fast as she could. She saw the junction of the Southern creek coming up quickly as the light from the approaching buggy caught her while she was preparing to fly toward escape. As she started banking into the turn she glimpsed another vehicle parked just East of her path. Lights beamed from the vehicle blinding her before she could cover her eyes. Realizing she had been cornered she reacted instinctively and shot straight up into the air, flying as fast as her heart and adrenaline would permit.

Immediately she felt the heat again. She darted sideways, gaining altitude trying her best get out of the heat, but it was still there - following her as she flew. The earbuds from her portable Walkman began to bake in her ears. She ripped them out as she jerked the player off her arm, letting them fall away to the ground below. She turned to look at the approaching buggy coming down the straight section of the creek bed. The spotlight from the buggy swung across the sky to meet her. She turned around and saw the converging buggy with lights blaring. She was slowing down and couldn't gather enough strength to continue flying. The heat doubled in intensity and she could feel pain burning in her bones, radiating out into her muscles. She spun around, hoping somehow the maneuver might relieve the pain from the heat, but without any success. She was losing altitude, falling toward the intersection of the creek bed. The pain was becoming unbearable. She was starting to free fall, plummeting the remaining distance to the ground.

Why are they doing this to me? I'm going to die. Confusion and fear filled her thoughts as she continued to fall like a wounded bird to the ground. Just as she braced for impact, the heat disappeared. She hung there, spinning slowly in the air, somehow she had managed to stop her descent. She was just feet from the ground and she was just hovering. She felt the spinning slow and stop as both vehicles converged upon her - their lights blaring, making it hard to see the occupants. The seconds she hovered seemed like hours. Her senses were on full overload, her heart pumping rapidly, and she realized she was hyperventilating; she felt on the verge of passing out.

"Leave me alone! Go away!" She screamed as loud as she could.

What are they waiting for? She wondered. She looked up and saw the star Deneb flickering in the darkness, as if winking at her to tell her everything would be okay. She could hear a woman speaking as the men got out of their vehicles. She started to ascend again, but was instantly hit by the intense heat. Her bones felt like pins of red hot steel, melting from the heat.

"Please. Stop!" she cried out. Curling up in a ball she closed her eyes and fell to the ground. The sand softened the blow. Although the heat had disappeared, she was too weak and exhausted to fly away. She slowly stretched out face down in the sand. The coolness of the sand was oddly comforting. She heard footsteps approaching as she tried to roll over when suddenly, she felt a sharp prick to her neck. All she could think of was *scorpions* as her mind grew fuzzy and she fell into a fitful sleep.

***

(Five days later.)

"We're sorry Miss," the park ranger stated. He removed his cap and wiped at his forehead with a moist hand towel. He tried to think of the best way to break the bad news to the solemn couple standing on their front porch. "We had a chopper and several teams scouring the area where you said she liked to hang out. We even have climbers roping through the crevices in the canyon. Can you think of any other areas that she liked to frequent in the park?"

Faye shook her head, "No. That's where she always went." She looked up at her husband, Torre. Her eyes were puffy and red from days of tears and worry. Torre had his arm around her and gave her a bit of a reassuring tug. "She called it her private play ground," she added.

"We greatly appreciate all the help gentlemen," Torre added. "Would you like to come inside for some iced tea or water?"

"No, thank you, sir." The ranger paused, looked at the ranger standing by the Jeep, then back at Torre. "Um, could we have a moment sir? I'd like to show you our maps and we could let your wife get back into the air conditioning."

Torre could tell by the ranger's eyes that this was not going to be good news. He looked at Faye and gave her the best hopeful look he could. "It's okay dear. It'll just be a few minutes. How about you pour a couple glasses of tea for these guys. I'm sure they won't refuse it."

Faye went inside the house as Torre and the ranger walked to the vehicle. The other ranger held the map on the hood of the Jeep. Magnets held the corners, but he still had to fight to keep the wind from catching it. The first ranger pointed at the circled area of the search. "I'm sorry sir, but after four days of searching, with a couple hundred volunteers, and under these conditions, even I would not be able to last out there without any water." He looked up at the second ranger.

"At this point," chimed in the second ranger. "The only scenarios are she was injured and couldn't make it back to your pick up point, or she was picked up and taken somewhere else. If she was still there, alive or expired, we would've found her by now."

The first ranger continued, "We did find buggy tracks in the creek bed, but we get those all the time from campers and four wheelers." He paused. "Unfortunately, at this point we have to call off the search and turn it over to the authorities as a potential runaway or abduction."

Torre ran his hand through his hair without responding to the rangers. He looked past them at the distant wind farm. The propeller driven generators were in overdrive today. He knew he couldn't tell them his sister in-law had the ability to fly. He couldn't tell them he had been scouring the canyon and the Hexie Mountain range himself, from the air. He couldn't tell them he felt pretty confident she had been abducted. All he could add was, "I understand."

Faye brought glasses of iced tea to the rangers, which they quickly downed. One Ranger folded the map while the other called the dispatcher via radio.

Torre waved as the rangers drove off. Faye, holding the two empty glasses, started to cry.

***

Uncle Georgeo stared at the bright yellow, Walkman sitting on the kitchen table. Torre had contacted him the morning after Angela's disappearance. He wasn't really their uncle, but it's what all the Avitorians called him. The nondescript title was easier to use and didn't arouse suspicion like 'Overseer' would. He was the one and only Overseer of the Avitorians. Personally selected by the previous Overseer to be the communicator and protector of all things Avitorian. He did his best to make sure they kept their ability secret and to uphold the moral and ethical standards they strive to live by. He had been visiting a fellow 'flier' in Costa Rica when Torre called. It took him four days to 'discreetly' fly up to Palm Springs for the emergency.

Torre and Faye stared at the bright yellow, Walkman sitting on the kitchen table. Georgeo broke the silence, "So, you found this in the canyon?"

"Yes," Torre answered. "Right next to the sand tire tracks."

"If you know she was taken why did you contact the rangers?"

"I had to, Georgeo! She was enrolled in public high school. How am I to explain her extended absence?"

"Tell them she's went to stay with a distant relative. Then move. Get yourselves off the information grid." Georgeo responded. "You should have home schooled her, like all the others."

"She's seventeen. She needs to learn how to fit into society. How can she do that if we never let her learn how to be with her peers?" Torre looked at Faye. All she could do was stare at the Walkman on the table. She wanted no part of this conversation. Torre continued, "We've trained her well. She understood the need for secrecy. No one knew. I don't understand how this could've happened."

"It has to be the Eighteenth. This is how they operate. They could've been watching for years, looking for a routine, waiting for the perfect moment. I suspect they were behind the abduction of her parents as well."

"Then let's go get her. Take her back from them. They did it to us - we can do it to them!"

"If we do that, it becomes a war." Georgeo stood up and began pacing around the table. "If we start a war with them, we expose ourselves. That's just what they want. If we're exposed they can pick us off, one by one. Come on, Torre! There are billions of 'normal' humans and maybe, just maybe, a couple hundred Avitorians." He continued pacing. "That would lead to our extinction. This is not the time to expose ourselves. Humanity can hardly get along with themselves. How can we expect them to understand what we are and accept us as a part of their society if we're different? Yeah, it's the nineties. Try and ask any African, Latino, or Asian if prejudice has been done away with. You know what their answer would be." He stopped pacing and sat down next to Faye.

Georgeo put one arm around Faye and quieted his tone. "I'm so sorry, Faye. We just can't expose ourselves or we'll all end up disappearing."

"I know," Faye responded. "It just hurts so bad. She was the baby. It was my job to protect her after our parents…" She couldn't finish. She got up and walked out of the kitchen as she started to cry.

"It's not her fault." Said Georgeo as he looked at Torre. "I know it's painful, but you've got to help her get past this." He reached out and picked up the Walkman - turning it around in his hands. "The authorities need to back off on this. Let them know there was an argument and that Angela most likely ran away to be with her friends. She's almost eighteen. They'll back off and eventually drop it as a runaway case."

Torre just nodded his head while watching Georgeo examine the Walkman.

"I'll go up to Seattle and line up some work for you there." He put the Walkman down and continued. "It'll be a nice change for you. A lot cooler than here and a lot of places to fly without being seen." He paused and extended a thumb to where Faye had exited the kitchen. "Have a kid of your own with Faye. It'll help to take some of the pain away. We all know we need to grow our numbers if we're to survive."

Torre nodded again and added, "You're right, Georgeo. I appreciate you coming on such short notice and helping us out. It's been tough. First their parents, and now this."

"And Eighteenth will come looking for you next. Smooth it over with the authorities and then pull out. I'll find a place for you around Seattle by the end of the week - with new IDs and everything."

"Yes, Georgeo. Thanks. I appreciate it and I know Faye will too - eventually."

TWO - DREAMLAND

Through a wisp of clouds,
I seek to touch the sky in peace.
Misty kisses on my face
reflect the light of the moon.
The wind sings songs of comfort
through the boughs of trees.
I embrace the night,
hearing the wings of a single loon.
(Verbal Poems of the Avitorians)

(Thirteen years later.)

Francie stood at the kitchen sink, giving the appearance of washing a tea kettle. The view out the window was a spectacular glimpse of Mt Rainier. Rarely did the mountain come out for a viewing - usually it was draped by clouds or fog. Today it was crystal clear with a small stack of lenticular clouds above the peak. She was grateful to Uncle Georgeo for finding them this place so they could start over. It seemed like such a long time ago. She liked her new name, her new life, her new environment, and she loved her twelve-year-old son sitting at the table behind her. However, it wasn't enough to clear out all the memories. Her eyes started to tear up slightly as the memory of her sister clouded the view out the window. She shook her head, dabbed away the tear with her sleeve, and finished rinsing the kettle.

"Mom?" Leif asked while wolfing down a bowl of cereal.

"Yes, dear." Francie turned around while drying her hands.

"I had an awesome dream last night. It was so real I could feel it. I think I'll write about it for a school report." He took a swig of orange juice and continued. "I was flying through the hallway upstairs and when I flew into my room there was a bald eagle sitting on my dresser. He kept looking at me and out the window. So, I opened the window and we both flew out over the back yard and up to one of the trees."

Francie felt a pang of panic rise up in her chest. She wrung the dish towel in her hands as she listened. She tried not to sound worried as she responded. "You could fly?

That's funny. Were you in some type of suit, like superman?"

"No mom," he laughed. "I'm not nine anymore. It was just me in my jeans and shirt. We sat in the tree together and then the eagle flew off."

"What did you do?"

"That's the bummer," he paused and slurped down the rest of his cereal and milk. "That's when I woke up. I got real cold and realized dad pulled the blanket down. I wanted to go back to sleep and finish the dream, but dad wouldn't leave until I got up."

Francie gave a nervous laugh. "Well, if you want to write about it, can I look at it before you take it to school?

"Sure mom. I gotta go." Leif grabbed his backpack and headed out the door.

"What? No hug?" she stated as she watched him leave. She knew this moment would eventually come. She started worrying about it when Leif was approaching ten. She was ten when she first flew. Though the girls always seem to start earlier than the boys. But, it starts with the dreams - vivid and real enough to have no doubts it could be possible. They haven't told him yet. Torre, um rather, Ben wanted to talk with Leif years ago, but she wouldn't permit it. Said it was too soon and actually hoped it would never happen. Maybe it would skip a generation or two with Leif. She turned to look back out the window at Mt. Rainier.

***

The middle school hallway was like a freeway on a Monday morning. Everyone scrambling for books, girls refreshing their makeup, or socializing, and the jocks scanned the lemmings, looking for new victims.

"Hey, Leif," came the call from the end of the hallway.

Leif peeked out from behind his locker door to see three of the varsity players strolling down the hallway, looking his direction.

"You get that Myspace page up yet?" One of the jocks jibed as the others laughed along with him. The din of the hallway quieted as the students all looked in Leif's direction - wondering if they were going to see some entertainment before the ringing of the first bell.

Leif closed his locker door and gave the combination lock a spin. He responded back with his best 'in your face' attitude. "No, Dave! You manage to get something higher than a C in math this year?" He turned to face the three as they came within arm's length and stopped.

"Dude, that really hurts man." Dave responded and pretended to be hurt. He reached up to give Leif a high five then yelled, "Yeah, buddy! Dave's got a B plus!"

Leif connected with the high five as the other two jocks gave him a playful shove. The crowd turned back to their normal, loud, activities - disappointed there wasn't going to be a fight this morning.

"Thanks to you man," Dave continued. "That trick you showed me in Algebra made sense. Once I had it I could solve all those other formulas. Coach is glad I get to stay on the team with my improved grade."

The bell for first period rang and everyone started to scatter into their assigned rooms. "Gotta run guys." Leif added. "Halo round tonight?" he asked as he opened the door for his morning home room class.

"Not tonight man. Got practice." Dave answered as the door closed behind Leif.

He scanned the room briefly to see if she was in her assigned seat. *Don't stare,* he told himself as he sat down in his chair. *Does she even know I exist?* He placed his backpack under his seat and fumbled with his notepad, taking a few extra seconds to catch a glimpse of Carina while she was busy writing something. Most likely something for extra credits he figured. She looked up for a split second and he quickly pulled his notebook up and looked back to the front of the class, but not without catching just a split second of eye contact. Enough to connect, but not enough to acknowledge his existence. *I'm such a moron.*

"Class… the sixth period will be fifteen minutes shorter due to a special rally in the auditorium this afternoon," Said their teacher, Mr. Lee. "So, how was everyone's weekend? Max, you can start."

As each student rattled off their boring weekends, Leif thought back to his dream last night. *It was so real. There has to be a way to do it. Why else would I have such an incredible dream?* He gazed out the windows on the left of the classroom. The sky was incredibly clear today and he could see the snow topped peaks of the Cascades in the distance. *I'm sure Carina would notice me if I could fly.*

Leif felt himself drift into a daydream. It started with him slowly rising from his chair. He crossed his legs and hovered a foot above the desk top. The whole class gaped in amazement as he turned to face Carina. He floated over to her desk and held out his hand. She reached out and held it and sheepishly giggled. She rose up from her chair too, as Leif stretched out and headed for the side windows with Carina in tow. He opened a window and turned to look at Mr. Lee. “Permission to be excused, Sir?” Thap! His day dream collapsed around him as the sound of Mr. Lee’s palm slapping the desk brought him back to reality, surrounded by the amused faces of his classmates.

“Excused for what, Leif?” The class erupted in laughter as Mr. Lee’s question.

“Um, nothing sir.” Said Leif as he quickly came to his senses. “I wrote code all weekend, sir,” he added.

“You wrote code?”

“Yes, sir.” Leif paused. “I’m writing a firewall for protocol to prevent jocks or anyone else from hacking into the grades database.”

The class laughed again while Mr. Lee shook his head and moved on to the next student.

Leif laughed and turned to see if Carina was looking. She was. He smiled at her and turned back in hopes she wouldn’t notice how nervous he was. *Score! Now if I could just get up the nerve to speak with her.*

The bell rang and the class quickly bolted for the doors. Leif grabbed his pack, stuffed in his notebook and headed for the rear exit - hoping to get within talking distance of Carina. He looked up just in time to see the back of her head as she headed out the door. He paused for a few seconds then slowly headed for the other door, sadly reasoning if she was really interested in him she would’ve at least given him some sort of sign.

***

The eagle was back, sitting on top of the dresser. Leif hovered above his bed. He rolled horizontally to his stomach and drifted close enough to the eagle to pet it. Subconsciously, he knew he was dreaming, but the recognition he was in a dream state was not enough to make him want to wake up. This felt too good, floating and drifting through the house. He reached out to gently stroke the head of the bald eagle on his dresser. The eagle looked at him and took a couple steps away from his approaching hand. Leif pulled back his hand and paused, admiring the stark beauty of this amazing creature. Strange that it would want to hang out on the top of his dresser.

Leif touched the corner of the dresser and slowly pushed off from it while turning toward his bedroom door. He drifted out the door and into the hallway. The banister for the stairs leading down to the dining room was directly below as he hovered there, silently soaking in the awesomeness of being able to fly. He turned back toward his bedroom and gently kicked his legs, as if he was propelling himself through water. The eagle was no longer on the dresser and the window was open. The curtains were dancing with the air currents flowing in and out of the window. Leif drifted over to the window and could see the white cap of the bald eagle in the top of the tallest evergreen tree in the back yard. Moonlight reflected off the eagle's head and tail feathers as it groomed itself - stopping every few seconds to scan the surrounding trees and the ground for potential meals.

Leif could hear floor boards creaking lightly and footsteps. He heard a gasp from someone at his door. He suddenly realized he wasn't dreaming. He was really floating on his back several feet above his bed. He flailed around as he fell to the bed, bouncing headlong onto the mattress. "What…!" was all he could utter as he quickly looked toward the door, his mom standing there mouth agape. He quickly jumped off the bed and stood up, looking to see if there was some type of contraption below or above his bed that caused him to be suspended above it.

"Leif!" Francie gasped as she ran over to him and threw her arms around him. "It's okay, honey."

"Mom? What are…" he stopped, looked at her and then back at the bed. "What was that? What happened?"

Francie placed her hands on Leif's face and turned him to look at her. "It's okay, Leif. Just calm down and I can explain."

"Explain?" he took a deep breath. "Did that really happen? Was I floating?"

"What's all the commotion?" Ben showed up at the door, rubbing the sleep from his eyes and cinching the belt on his robe.

Francie looked Leif directly in the eyes with the best calm voice she could muster, and answered, "Leif honey. Dear. Yes. You were floating." She looked over to Ben. "And we can explain."

Ben closed the window and closed the drapes, intent on keeping the revelation secret from the neighbors, even if the closest neighbor was two hundred yards away.

"I'm sorry son." Ben stated as he sat down in a chair by the window. "We should have prepared you for this. Please sit down. This is going to take awhile to explain."

Leif slowly sat down on the edge of the bed, testing it out with his hands first to make sure he wasn't going to float above it again.

Ben continued, "What I'm going to tell you, about us, your heritage, and our ability cannot be shared with anyone, under any circumstances what-so-ever. It's a matter of life and death. Do you understand?"

"Ben, dear. Do we really have…" Francie started to ask.

"Yes." Ben interrupted firmly. "He has to know. Not knowing will only make things worse."

Her eyes began to water. "He's all I have left. My parents. My sister." She sat down next to Leif while trying to hold back the tears.

"Mom." Leif put an arm around her shoulder. "Whatever it is. I can keep it secret." He looked back at his dad. "Dad, why is mom so worried?"

"It's because of what we are, son. Her parents and her sister have disappeared, long ago, because of what we are. It's why you have to keep this quiet."

"Okay dad, mom. I promise."

Ben ran one hand through his hair and rubbed the back of his neck as he began. "We are called Avitorians. We have the ability to fly."

Leif interrupted, "I knew it! Just like in my dreams."

"Please son, let me explain. We are exactly like everyone else. Our bodies are the same, we still bleed red blood, we catch colds, and we die of old age - just like everyone else. The only difference is that we have the ability to fly. And, we are very, very, rare."

"Rare? Are we the only ones?" Leif asked.

"No. Our best guess is around several hundred around the world. There might be more than that, but because of our secrecy we just don't know. We know our heritage goes as far back as the ancient Egyptians. We don't know if we came from somewhere else or if we're just a different species of the human race. Uncle Georgeo can fill you in on that if you want."

"Uncle Georgeo can fly too?"

"Yes, Leif. He's not really your uncle. We all call him that. He's really our Overseer of the Avitorians. He keeps us safe, educates us, and is our only communication link with other Avitorians around the world. He'll come by soon for a visit and will answer more questions than I can."

"You can fly?" Leif asked. "And mom too?"

Francie wiped her eyes and announced, "I'll go fix us some coffee."

Leif could feel the weight of the silence as his mom walked out of the room and down the stairs. "Is mom okay?" he asked.

"She doesn't want to fly anymore. It's the danger we all face. What do you think your friends would think if they saw you flying?" Ben asked.

Instantly he excitedly stated, "Man, I'd be the coolest kid at school."

"Do you really think so?"

Leif paused and gave it more thought. He'd never seen anyone fly before, except in the movies. He had managed to fit in with the jocks at school by helping them with their math homework. He also remembered how he was picked on when he was the new geeky kid in school. "I'd be the freak."

"Two things generally happen. One - most people are afraid of what they don't understand. And two - some would want to have what you have, and they would do whatever it takes to get it."

That thought sent a chill through Leif.

"Let me ask you this. Does everyone in the world get along with one another?"

"Not really." Leif answered, remembering recent discussions in world history class.

"As long as that continues to be a problem with humankind, Avitorians will never be safe." Ben paused to let that sink in. "Your mom lost her parents and her sister to people who either hated knowing they could fly or they wanted to experiment with them, to learn how it's done. Your aunt Angela disappeared a little over thirteen years ago. Which is why it hurts her when she realizes you might have the ability to fly."

The thought of being able to fly was no longer as fun as Leif initially thought. The weight of the ability grew heavier with the realization it could put their lives in danger.

Ben could see the burden of the knowledge on Leif's face. He lowered his voice to a whisper and leaned in closer to Leif. "But, when done discreetly, it can be incredibly exhilarating." He added a smile and a wink.

Leif's face full of worry turned into a big smile. Ben rose up off the chair and hovered above Leif's bed. He spread out his arms and legs and slowly spun in a circle. He turned upside down and pretended to walk across the ceiling, his robe dangling down over his face. He quickly flipped back upright, slightly embarrassed his twelve-year-old son just got a good look at his Fruit of the Loom briefs.

Leif laughed and applauded. "My turn Dad. How do I do it?"

Ben lowered himself back to the seat by the window and placed a leg up on one knee. "Well, son, that's the mystery of it all. It could be tomorrow, it could be next month, or it could be five years. Unfortunately, a slight hover while dreaming might be all you get for awhile."

"Ah, man!" Leif's smile quickly shifted back to a frown.

"That's right. Haven't you heard? Good things come to those who wait."

Francie entered the room with a couple cups of steaming coffee and a cup of hot cocoa. As if on queue she added, "You need to wait Leif. You have to give it time. When your mind and your body is ready you will know it, and you have to give me time too, I need time to accept it. You're my little boy. Don't be in such a hurry to grow up."

"Mom, I'm not a little boy anymore. I'm almost thirteen."

"Ah, don't remind me," Ben replied. "We're counting the days." He paused and took a sip from the coffee. "Now that you know the secret, I have a story to tell."

"A story, pray tell. And what would this story be?" Francie asked while sitting down next to Leif.

Ben winked at Francie and began, "The story of how your mother literally flew into my arms."

THREE - UNCLE GEORGEO

Pharaoh Ahmose I, founder and ruler of the Eighteenth Dynasty, is credited as the ruler who re-established Egypt as a mighty nation. His 25-year reign saw the greatest expansion, the greatest construction projects since the Middle Kingdom, and the greatest period of artistic creativity which included the introduction of glass. A little known secret held during his reign was the use of flying humans who would perform intricate visual calculations of dimensions for his massive construction projects. This was discarded as fanciful stories by his successor Amenhotep. (18th of Ahmose, The Sealed Archives)

Although Leif hated to admit it, algebra was his favorite subject. It came easy to him - the logic and the formulas all made sense. His teacher, Mr. McFarland, would always throw him an extra challenge, hoping to make him reach out a little more than the rest of the class. To Leif, it seemed like a video game. The next boss to try and conquer. All he had to do to beat the boss is come up with the right answer. Usually he did. Sometimes he wouldn't, on purpose, just to make Mr. McFarland smile. He had asked his teacher what it was all for - the algebra, that is. Leif didn't understand the need for it in the real world. "It's just formulas and symbols," Leif had stated.

Mr. McFarland's answer was, "Trust me. You'll find a use for it."

Indeed, Leif discovered the power of algebra soon after. The second semester introduced 'Beginning Programming' and his whole idea of algebra and logic took on a new meaning. Especially when it came to designing video games. His new found love of computers and programming also brought a new level of social status. First semester was full of tormenting and ridicule by the jocks and goths. Now he was Mr. Popular. All the jocks wanted to team up with him in nighttime Halo marathons. When asked how he got so good at it, his reply was "It's all in the logic and the math." The goths, well, they still didn't like him.

Unfortunately, sixth period English was the dull time between fifth period algebra and seventh period programming. Today they were covering present tense versus past tense. *I'm way past any tense,* Leif thought to himself while staring out the windows. At least he sat in the back of the room and could get away with being distracted for awhile. He thought about Carina. He saw her again in first period home room. While he managed to get several glances at her without being too obvious, it always seemed to be when she was buried in her books or last minute homework. He knew he was being a 'hopeless romantic' although he also tried to be in denial. He never even knew what denial was until last semester's English Lit 101 introduced him to the painful endurance of Jane Austen's Pride and Prejudice.

I wonder what Carina would think of my being a Avitorian. The thought puzzled him. His mom was one and so was his dad. The story of how they met was puzzling too, how they bumped into each other at the airport on their way to Costa Rica, and then discovered each other over the moon lit waters of Drake Bay. Only the dolphins noticed when his mom sneaked up on his dad and literally flew into his arms. The reality of that was quite amazing. There were only a couple hundred Avitorians around the world and they both discover each other in the same place. *Could a Avitorian fall in love with a regular human?* He would have to ask Uncle Georgeo when he arrives tomorrow. For now, he preferred to think of Carina and of flying.

Leif continued to stare out the windows at the tall evergreens on the other side of the athletic track. He pictured himself, late at night, flying over to the top of one of the trees, standing on an upper branch, and gazing out at the country side. He imagined the view to the Southeast at the snow top peak of Mt. Rainier or out to the Northwest to the glowing lights of downtown Seattle. The city was nice, but he preferred the solitude and stark beauty of the woods and mountains. He could feel his heartbeat increase in excitement as he imagined flying to the top of Mt. Rainier to see the deep crevices of Mowich Glacier and maybe even hover down into the crevices and touch the translucent blue ice. He got a chill while thinking of it.

He remembered the weekend hike with his dad last spring, along the banks of the Van Horn Creek - which was actually more like a river with the spring runoff. They had seen deer, raccoons, coyotes, and even a hungry bear looking for fish after a long hibernation. He remembered his dad going off into the woods for a little while, in the dark, for a small night time hike. More like going off for a flight, now that he knew better. He thought how nice it would be to share those moments with someone like Carina - to fly with her over the top of the river in the moonlight, holding hands, and gazing at each other.

Leif gazed back at the teacher as she droned on about the use of 'active voice' and how the subject must act upon the verb in a sentence. He nodded his head in agreement when she glanced at him. *Okay. Yea. Whatever.* He gazed at the clock. Fifteen long, long minutes before he could bail out and head to Beginning Programming. Looking back out the window and reflecting on being able to fly brought so many ideas to him. Night time whale watching over the Sound, exploring remote areas of the Cascade Mountains, or being able to fly somewhere quicker than having to drive there. *Wow,* he thought. *Could I fly down to California and go to Disney Land and back in a day?* The thought was exciting. Then the questions he wanted to ask started to flow. *How fast can I fly? How high can I fly? How long can I fly? Can I circle the world in a single night?* So many questions he had for uncle Georgeo. He also started to think of the dangers his dad had mentioned.

What would happen if someone saw me flying? Would we be in danger? And very importantly, *would Carina turn me in if she knew I could fly?* He began to understand why his mom had chosen not to fly anymore. It must have been painful to lose her parents and her sister. What would he do if his parents suddenly disappeared? Another chill went down his neck. He looked down at his English book and turned a couple pages without really noticing what was on them.

***

"So," Uncle Georgeo paused and took a sip from his cup of mint leaf tea. He savored the flavor for a moment before continuing. "I hear there was an episode of unauthorized hovering here last week." He put his cup and saucer down on the coffee table and gave a stern look at Leif.

Leif had just sat down, happy he had finally been invited downstairs to sit in on the conversation between Uncle Georgeo and his parents. But with the comment and the stern look, he wasn't so sure. He gave a quick glance over to his parents, trying to get a visual confirmation if he was in trouble or not. Neither one would make eye contact. Leif gulped dryly before answering. "Um, yes sir."

"Well, you sure don't sound too happy about it boy." Georgeo kept the stern look but permitted one eye to give a quick wink.

Leif wasn't sure if he was being scolded and his Uncle had a twitch or if he was being teased. "Uh…"

Georgeo interrupted with a hearty laugh. "It's okay boy. I'm just messing with you." Laughing, he slapped one of his knees with a hand and grabbed his tea cup. "Did it scare you?"

Leaf let go with a sigh of relief. "Only when I woke up," he responded.

"Ah yes, the dreams." Georgeo leaned back into the couch and took a sip of the tea. "Tell me about the dreams."

Leif thought about the dreams before responding. "I had a bald eagle visit. We flew out the window and stood in a tall evergreen out back."

"Excellent. Go on." Georgeo took another sip and closed his eyes - perhaps to picture his own dreams of flying.

"I would always move slowly, drifting through the house. I could move by kicking my legs or pushing off the walls and furniture."

"How about the flight to the top of the tree. How did you do that?"

He had to think about it for a few seconds. It all came back to him, as if really happened. "I pointed my head toward the tree top. My legs were straight and my arms were straight down my sides."

"Good. Good." Georgeo said. He opened his eyes and leaned toward Leif. "How did it make you feel?"

"Calm and peaceful. It was like I was inside a beautiful painting. Me and the eagle, standing in a tree."

"This is the way we are Leif. We are a peaceful people. Flying is a part of our inner being. We were meant to fly. The more we fly, the more we become at peace with ourselves and with the world in general." He glanced over at Francie. He hoped she got the point he was trying to make. "Unfortunately, the world is not ready for us."

"Uncle, where did we come from?"

"And so the questions begin." Georgeo stated with a grin. "We don't know. We might be from here." He spread out his hands. "Or we might be from there." He looked up and pointed a hand toward the sky. "I like to think we came from somewhere else. But, many would argue with me and say we're just a slight variation from humankind."

Leif pondered this for a few seconds before asking his next question. "How fast can we fly?"

Georgeo smiled. "Always, the young ones want to know how fast." He laughed. "Well, the best of us, we figure around two hundred. But only if something special is being worn to reduce the friction. Have you ever stuck your hand out the window while your dad was driving the car on the freeway?"

Leif nodded.

"That is friction from the air. To go fast you have to be slippery. In jeans and a t-shirt you're not very slippery."

"What makes us fly?"

"There are two things which we don't completely understand how, but we are aware of. The first is we can become buoyant. Which is what you were doing when you woke up last week. You were hovering and buoyant. When we are buoyant, we are neutral to the force of gravity. We neither go up or go down. We just float." He paused and took a sip of his tea. "The second is our ability to project a force along the length of our bodies." He held out a hand and straightened it out and pointed it at an angle and pointed at it with his other hand. "When you were flying toward the tree in your dream, you had your legs straight and your arms at your side. This increased the force coming out of your feet and your hands. Mentally, you can control the amount of the force. How? I can't explain. It's just becomes a part of you - the ability to determine how much force is projected. Your dreams are how your body is preparing you for flight."

Leif's mind was a blur with the information. There were so many questions to ask. He had a hard time determining what to ask next.

Francie could see it was pretty overwhelming. "Are you okay?" She reached out and put a hand on Leif's shoulder.

"Yes, mom. I'm just trying to figure it all out." He looked at Georgeo as he asked his next question. "When can I fly again?"

"I wish I knew, Leif. It could be soon. Most likely it will be when you get older and a little more mature. You might hover again a few times before then. If I was to guess, I'd say you might be closer to your late teens before you get the whole process figured out. Be prepared to get a few bruises along the way."

"Ah, man! Can't I speed it up?" He was totally bummed out it would take so long. "That is so far away," he added.

"Sorry. I remember how impatient I was when I was your age. I too was disappointed when I found out how long it would take. However, I am glad I had time to grow up and become more responsible first."

Leif hung his head. Not only was he wanting to fly as soon as possible, he really wanted to try and impress someone.

Georgeo continued. "Leif, I need you to understand something and I need to have your full attention for this." He leaned toward Leif.

Leif looked up and was slightly scared at the serious look on his uncle's face.

"There are very few of us in comparison with the rest of humankind. Only a few hundred compared to billions. I think there might be many, many more of us, but we're outnumbered, and humankind doesn't know how to deal with people who are different. So, we choose to hide who we are, to keep it a secret." He paused to make sure Leif was getting the seriousness of it all. "Your aunt and your mother's parents are no longer with us because someone found out who they were."

A shiver ran down Leif's neck. "Who would want to hurt us, uncle?"

"There is a group of people who call themselves the Eighteenth. They have been around as far back as our history goes. They started with the reign of Pharaoh Ahmose in ancient Egypt. He was able to coexist with us. We helped him with the calculations and positioning of all his great construction projects, including the building of one of the last great pyramids. His successor, Amenhotep did not agree with the use of Avitorians and felt threatened by their ability to fly. He felt if he was to be recognized as a god by his people he either needed to do away with the Avitorians, or be able to learn to fly himself. He founded the Eighteenth as a group to figure out the secret of flight and commanded all his descendants to discover the secret of the Avitorians." He paused for a sip of tea and continued. "The only goal of their people is to take what we have for themselves and they'll do anything to get it. Even if it means killing and dissecting us for their studies. The governments cannot protect us because they are too busy seeking their own agendas, and they have not yet learned how to exist peacefully among themselves. We fear they might have even been involved with abducting our people. Until humankind can learn to live with us in peace, we cannot let the human race know we exist." Uncle Georgeo reached out and caressed Leif's face with one hand. "Do you understand? You cannot tell or demonstrate your abilities to anyone who is not an Avitorian."

"Yes uncle, I understand." He was almost shaking from the fear.

"You must swear to me and to your parents, you will never, ever, reveal who we are to humankind unless you are directed to do so by your Overseer. You cannot fly when or where others can see you. You cannot tell anyone about the Avitorians. You cannot even mention the name or imply in any way that you are different from other humans." He paused to let it sink in. "Do you promise?"

"My overseer?" Leif was confused. "What is an overseer?"

"I am your Overseer, Leif. It is my job to watch out for the protection and guidance of the Avitorians around the world. I am not your real uncle, but that is what you can call me. Now, do you promise?"

Leif now understood he would never be able to tell Carina he was different. He would never be able to show her he could fly. He would never be able to fly for her or take her with him as he flew. This special gift he would have, would be locked away for his own personal self and for the safety of all Avitorians. The weight of being twelve years old was heavier than he imaged it would ever be. With one tear in his eye he looked up at Georgeo. "I promise, uncle."

“Good, good.” Georgeo responded and rubbed Leif’s hair with one hand. “You are a good boy and I know that you will turn into a fine Avitorian man. Listen to your parents, study hard, and one day you will be a fine example for all Avitorians. Maybe in your lifetime you will see humankind find peace where we will be able to coexist openly among all. Until then - do not forget who, you, are!” Georgeo emphasized strongly each of the last three words.

Leif looked over at his mom and noticed her eyes had teared up. He stood up and stepped over to give her a hug. “It’s okay mom. I understand.”

***

“I think it is time to change our paths, Matt.” Dr. Suzanne Corellis stood in the middle of the Cryolab. Matt was sitting at a computer desk surrounded by panels full of various gauges, dials, displays, and buttons.

“Yeah. I knew you were going to come to that conclusion. I’m amazed the guardians - um, the gents, have given you this much time already. They’ve been leaning toward particle physics since before Joshua Tree.”

“They like me,” she stated bluntly. “They know the knowledge we’ve gathered here has been of benefit. It’s not going to waste, and they know that. I had to be sure, beyond any doubt, this wasn’t biological.” She walked over to a one of the cryotubes. The circular viewport revealed the face of a middle aged man, or at least what was left of the face. The forehead stopped just above his eyebrows and various biopsy divots could be seen in his cheeks and the temples behind his closed eyes. The nameplate below the viewport said ‘Mr. Rowley - 1985’. She continued, “At least aside from their genetics. We’ve pretty much confirmed it’s hereditary.”

“The Rowleys are pretty used up.” Matt added. “I can make sure they’re taken care of.”

“Yes.” Suzanne stepped over to the next cryotube. The nameplate said ‘Mrs. Rowley - 1985’. “It was good of Dr. Morley to provide them to us when I took over. But,” she paused while dwelling on Mrs. Rowley’s cryotube. “They have served their usefulness and we still have Angela. I’ve been saving her for the particle studies.” She turned and walked over to Matt.

“I have some candidate facilities. The gents have provided a list of locations in New York, Sweden, Nevada, and Seattle.” Matt stated while gazing at his computer. “They’re going to let you decide where you start. They’ll provide the appropriate credentials and grant funding.”

“I’ll need to review the capabilities at each facility. Though, I can pretty much count out Sweden. Way too cold for my taste.”

“Agreed.”

FOUR - A LONGING

Into the night air I dance
and breathe in the star's radiance.
Yet, I still hunger.
Eagles soar by light of the moon
and heat thermals of mid-June.
Yet, I still hunger.
Clouds cling to reaches of Earth
and distant glow leads the sun's birth.
Yet, I still hunger.
Yet, still, I hunger.
(Verbal Poems of the Avitorians)

(Eight years later.)

The two kayaks drifted slowly along the shore of Burrows Island - smooth wakes radiated out from the back of the kayaks through the water and formed a large M where they met. Puget Sound was unusually calm this morning. A light fog hovered along the distant coastline of Lopez Island to the west. Leif gently dipped a paddle into the water and smoothly pulled it through. Lifting it out at the end of the stroke he laid the paddle across his lap and leaned back in his seat. "Is it whale sign dad?"

Ben's kayak drifted off to the right and slightly behind. He held a pair of binoculars to his eyes and scanned the water to the northwest. "Nah, it's just a couple seals." He turned and pointed the binocs at a large dried out tree extending from an outcropping of rocks along Burrows Island. Two bald eagles peered out from the tallest branch. One scanned the water for any fish daring to hover near the smooth surface while the other one groomed its wings. "The eagles look nice though."

Leif turned and looked up at the treetop. Normally the sight of the majestic birds would bring a sigh of awe, but not this morning. They only reminded him of his own longing. He uttered a condescending "yeah", lifted his paddle, and gave the water a graceful stroke.

Ben stowed the binocs under his buoyancy vest, grabbed his paddle, and stroked the water to match his speed with Leif's kayak. "Yah know, if I wanted this much quiet I could've come out here by myself this morning."

Leif really didn't feel talking about it, but he knew his dad wouldn't let it go until they talked.

Ben stroked the water then turned the paddle sideways to stop from passing Leif. "Isn't the new job working out?"

The job? Leif thought. *Dad never could read me the way mom does.* "The job's great! I'm writing physics routines."

"Physics? I thought you were working on a game?"

"I am." Leif responded with a slight chuckle. "It's a game in space and I have to calculate the movement of objects through space based on mass and velocity. It's actually pretty generic mathematics."

"I never could handle that part of math. Flowing electricity I can handle." He paused while giving the water a gentle stroke with the paddle. "So, the job is great. I know you're making good money. You've got a nice set of wheels and a pretty cool pad." He smiled at himself for trying to sound hip. "So, what's with the mood?"

He looked around to make sure there were no fishermen or someone within hearing distance. "I hovered again last night."

"That's great, Leaf!" he replied while looking around as well.

"No, it's not great." Leif replied. He reached down into the water and let his hand drift through the water. "That's all I ever do. I wake up hovering. I can stay there but as soon as I try to do anything I fall back down. I'm getting tired of waiting, dad."

"Ah," was all Ben replied with. He never spoke without giving his brain a chance to formulate first. "You never met your grandparents." He paused. It was not a topic he would generally bring up due to the pain it brought to Francie. “Your grandfather didn’t fly till he was twenty-four.”

“Whoa! Twenty-four?!” He didn’t like the thought of having to wait another four years. “I’ll be old and gray by then.”

“Hey!” Ben used his paddle to splash some water at Leif. “I might be a little gray, but I’m still far from old. I mean, look at Georgeo. Now that guy is old!”

Leif laughed while wiping water off his sunglasses. “Yeah. Uncle Georgeo is old.”

Ben took advantage of Leif’s distraction with the sunglasses. He dug in with his paddle in a strong and smooth stroke through the water, followed by another on the opposite side of the kayak. Left side, right side, left side, right side - he managed to get a good five strokes before Leif could get his glasses situated and the paddle back in his hands. While his dad had smoothness and finesse with the kayak, Leif had the strength of youth. It didn’t take long for him to match Ben’s speed. He followed along in the wake of his dad’s kayak - looking for an opportunity to try a pass.

Ben continued to pour on the consistent paddle strokes through the water. His kayak kept a straight line through the water without any rocking from side to side. Leif didn’t care about smoothness. He leaned into each paddle stroke, rocking the kayak from side to side, and swinging the bow in a zig zag as he plowed through the water. It wasn’t very graceful, but he was closing the distance quickly. Ben took a quick look over one shoulder at Leif. Ben stretched his strokes out behind him while keeping the paddle gripped aerodynamically along the length of the kayak. He bowed his head down toward the front of kayak, almost touching the brim of his ball cap to the surface of the kayak. The speed of the kayak increased slightly and added more distance between him and Leif.

"Hey, that's cheating." Leif called out.

Ben laughed and sat back up. He stabbed the paddle into the water to slow the kayak and to turn slightly for blocking Leif's approach.

Leif dug his paddle into a reverse stroke on the left side and managed to slide the right side of his kayak alongside Ben's kayak. "No fair flying your boat there mister," he laughed.

Ben took his cap off and dipped it into the cool water, shook it off, and placed it back on his head. "Okay, okay. You caught me."

They both paused to catch their breath and to take in the scenery. Leif figured they were about a hundred yards off the coast of Burrows Island. It was just enough to pick up the northerly current flowing up to Rosario Strait. The water was still pretty smooth. There wasn't much wind for creating any chop to the water. The fog was starting to burn off the coast of Lopez Island to the east.

"Well, that was fun." Leif stated. "But it's going to be…"

Ben looked at Leif and interrupted him. "Shush!" He looked around and put his arms out while scanning the water around the kayaks. Shallow plumes of water appeared in a circle around the kayaks. "Quick, grab on!" Ben grabbed his paddle and stuck it out for Leif to grab onto.

As soon as Leif managed to grab the paddle Ben thrust one hand toward the front of his kayak. His kayak lurched suddenly into reverse. Leif had to tighten his grip on the paddle with one hand while trying not to drop his own paddle. Suddenly a large grey fluke of a whale appeared in the spot where the kayaks had been just a few seconds earlier. The whale rolled and slapped it's fluke in the direction of the kayaks. One huge eye of the whale appeared to be watching them as Ben tried to get farther away. The top of the whale's head rose several feet above the water and a huge plume of water whooshed from its spout with a tremendous rush of air.

The spout of water poured on Ben and Leif as they struggled to get their kayaks several lengths away from the cresting whale. It's head dove back into the water followed by it's huge curving back. Ben 'flew' his kayak along the water, dragging Leif's along as he tried to gain more distance. They both kept their eyes on the arch of the graceful beast as it's back narrowed into the tail. The horizontal slab of it's tail rose up out of the water and poured a trail of water off as it curved and gently entered back into the water with hardly a sound. Several waves of water rocked the kayaks as Ben and Leif both stared in amazement at the restless whirlpools and vortices of water left behind by the beautiful grey whale.

"Did you see that?" Leif shouted. "That was amazing!" He let go of Ben's paddle and shook his own paddle in the air. "Whoo hooo!"

"Wow," was the only thing Ben could utter as he pulled off his cap and ran one hand through his hair.

"You okay dad?"

"Yeah," he replied while putting the soaking cap back on. "That was close."

"How did you know?" Leif asked. He remembered the look on Ben's face when he told him to shush.

“I could feel it. The electricity.” He replied while looking around to see if there was anyone who might have seen their narrow escape. “I don’t know if it was from the friction through the water or from the whale itself. It was just a mass of power directly below us.”

“Wow.” Leif laughed. “I’m impressed.”

“He’s heading north. Looks like he wanted to get a closer look at us. See if we’re edible,” Ben joked.

“I don’t know. I think we’re a bit too crunchy and bigger than a shrimp.” Leif added with his best Monte Python accent.

“Well, whale watching doesn’t get much better than that. How about breakfast at the marina?” Ben asked while turning his kayak toward Anacortes. He dug in with the paddle while adding, “Last one to the marina buys.”

***

The bald eagle was back and staring at Leif from the top of his dresser. Everything was the same as before. The window was open and a cool breeze was making the moon lit curtains dance along the sides of the opening. Leif drifted over to the eagle and reached out to stroke its head, knowing he would never make contact. The eagle moved to the edge of the dresser and gave out a piercing call while looking at Leif. It spread out its wings and coasted over to the window ledge.

Leif’s heart raced with anticipation of what he would get to see next. Just like the hundreds of times before, he drifted over to the window. He watched as the eagle took off. Its mighty wings stroked the crisp night air with a whoosh. It flew to the top of the tallest evergreen tree in the back yard. Leif drifted half way out the window to get a better look. His breathing almost stopped as he gazed at the blonde haired girl standing in the top of the tree next to the bald eagle. She reached out and stroked the head of the eagle while gazing back at Leif.

Would this be the moment? Leif knew he would eventually break the curse of this dream. He drifted further out the window. He tried to will himself to look back at his feet, but he couldn't take his eyes off of Carina. Her long blonde hair drifted with the wind as she continued to stroke the eagle's head. She signaled with one hand for Leif to join her and the eagle. He boosted himself out the window only to suddenly catch one of his feet on the side of the window sill. He cursed as he tried to lift his foot high enough to clear the sill, but the harder he tried the heavier his foot felt. He looked back at his foot as he began to fall from the window. It was once again the same as before. He fell backward toward the bushes surrounding the back of the house. He rolled his head back to see Carina standing in the top of the tree. There was nothing else he could do. He braced for the landing in the bushes that would never come.

Leif suddenly awoke to find himself hovering a few feet over his bed with his blanket draped over him. He looked like a human tent as he hovered there in disgust. He knew he could stay in that position all day if he wanted, but as soon as he tried to move he would fall back down to the bed. He shifted slightly and fell with all his weight back onto the bed. He threw the covers off, swung his legs over the side, and walked over to the bedroom window. Spreading the curtains slightly, he gazed out at the traffic on the street below and Lake Union just beyond. Kayakers were slowly meandering along the shoreline. Normally it would be a peaceful and scenic view, but Leif couldn't get the lingering image of Carina out of his head.

***

"The particle projection application programming interface can be accessed with a single collection of parameters passed to the object class. As long as the objectmass property is set to the location of the grouped particles. In this example…" The instructor continued to drone on while pointing out computer source code projected on the movie screen in the large conference room.

Leif was having a hard time paying attention. The frustration of not being able to fly combined with the empty hole he felt inside, and the droning monotone of the instructor was not making it easy to get involved with the presentation. *Besides*, Leif thought, *this would all be in the online documentation anyway*. With over fifty employees in the room he figured he could get away with working on a picture he had been drawing on his computer tablet. He feared he would someday loose the image he had of the blonde hair girl from his middle school class who continued to haunt his dreams. The drawing he produced had taken countless hours and multiple false starts with different software packages until he found one that would suit his needs. Carina was never close enough in his dreams to get the image of her face correct, so he relied on what was left from the memory of a single day in home room back in middle school. He felt she'd looked into him, deep into his soul when he glanced back at her. The look of her face was haunting and mysterious. Her smile, barely perceptible as her pale blue eyes pierced Leif, making his heart stop. It was like she was asking ‘When?’ Her look both scared and enticed him. Of all the times he had gazed at her in school - this was the one image burned into his very being. He gave up trying to forget. He couldn’t. It would be there forever - tormenting him.

“She’s pretty,” the whispered statement from the co-worker sitting next to him startled him.

“Huh, what?” was all he could muster as he came out of his tormented trance while turning to look at the young lady sitting to his right.

“The picture you’re drawing. She’s pretty.” She pointed at Leif’s tablet. “Girlfriend?”

Leif looked around to make sure their discussion was not drawing the ire of the instructor or other employees in the room. “Ah, no. Just someone I knew.” He glanced back down at the tablet and closed the drawing program.

“Sorry.” She whispered. “I didn’t want to stop you. You’re quite good.”

“Good?” he took a second to get his senses. “I just dabble at it.”

“Well, for dabbling, it looked pretty good. Maybe you could do one of me sometime.”

Leif let out a short chuckle at the idea of someone actually asking him to draw their portrait. The instructor gave him a look while spewing on about collision detection algorithms.

“Jewels,” she stated while holding a hand out for a shake.

Leif took her hand and gave it a short shake. “Leif.” He recalled seeing her in the office before. Her slim figure was attractive while her long black hair and matching eye liner gave the slightest hint of a Visgoth without being too obvious.

"Leif," she repeated with a hint of recognition. "I've heard good things about you," she whispered while giving him a slight bump with her shoulder. "Don't tell anyone I told you this, but the boss is pretty impressed with your programming. Says you have a good grasp of the math."

He could feel a slight blush coming on, though he wasn't sure if it was from the complement about his programming or the shoulder bump. "Thanks." He noticed another glance from the instructor. "I think we better give this guy some attention before he comes over here with a death look."

Jewels gave a slight snicker. "Alright. Maybe we'll talk more later about my portrait." She gave him another shoulder bump.

Leif gave her a smile and a look without expecting her to be looking directly back. Her deep hazel eyes caught him off guard. If there was any doubt about her interest in him from the shoulder bumps, it was now pretty obvious from thc dircct cye contact. He was glad the only light in the room was from the programming source code listings on the movie screen. He could feel the warmth of embarrassment flush his face as he gave her a silent nod and turned back to pay attention to the instructor.

FIVE - MATURITY

“From the first glance I knew it was you. We said hello as if we were two eagles, soaring on the same thermal, circling almost wingtip to wingtip, watching each other yet not touching. The thermal ended and we both flew off in our own directions. Yet, I continue to see your face, your eyes, and your smile. I catch a whiff of your perfume among a crowd of people and my heart stops as I look for you, but you’re not there. I’ll continue to search, to seek your smile, your smell, and your eyes. Until we meet again…” (Anonymous letter found in a sealed glass bottle on Mt. Rainier.)

Leif madly typed away on his computer. He was in the 'zone' - that place where programmers go when they have thirty different numbers and symbols stored in their head while writing code fast enough to get the logic working without forgetting what they wrote fifty lines of code earlier. It was almost a zen state. Tens of hours could fly by without straying from the monitors while in this mode. With headphones on to drown out any disruptive noise from the huge cubicle farm in the Amzoft, Incorporated offices, Leif was on a three hour stretch that started at five a.m. He leaned back in his chair, ran his hands through his hair, and complemented himself on completing a significant piece of physics code for plotting the course of slowly drifting debris caught in the rings of a planet in space. He leaned forward and scrolled through his code, stopped, and satisfied with it, he pressed a key on the keyboard and waited while his computer 'compiled' his code into a completed routine and automatically merge it into a master program containing over a million lines of code. He realized it was going to take a while to compile as he watched the slowly advancing progress bar on one of his monitors.

While thinking about the movement of objects through the vacuum of space in a video game he started to think of his dreams of Carina, standing in the evergreen tree with the mighty bald eagle. A small pang of longing jumped through his gut. He wanted to fly so bad it hurt. The constant hovering was starting to bring on anxiety attacks as he awoke each morning. He felt it would be better if he just tried to forget it all - quit wanting to fly, quit thinking about Carina, quit trying to be something he wasn't. Maybe he was a freak of the Avitorian race -

unable to really fly. Maybe he was more human than Avitorian. He was growing tired of the disappointment.

The progress bar on the monitor showed ten percent completion. Leif placed his elbows on the desk and his head in his hands. He thought of the beautiful sunrise he saw on his way in to work. The snow on the top of the peaks of the Olympics glowed a bright orange as the sun had crested over the top of the Cascades. The sunlight bounced off the bottom of scattered clouds in a shower of pinks and orange along the bottom of the clouds. If only he could touch those clouds. He could almost feel the moisture of the clouds in his hands as he dwelled on the image. He pictured himself reaching into those clouds, feeling the moisture, and letting himself disappear into the dense fog. His heart skipped as he felt his butt rise up off the seat of his chair and the top of his legs pressed against the bottom of his desk.

Leif grabbed his headphones and stripped them off his head while exclaiming, “Whoa!” He fell back down into the seat of his chair. A fellow worker in the next cubical popped her head up over the cube wall and asked, “What’s up, Leif?”

“Ah, nothing, Marie.” He quickly gathered his senses. “Just surprised my code is compiling without any errors,” he responded.

“Alright,” she replied as she disappeared back into her cubicle.

“Wow,” Leif quietly mouthed to himself. *Did I just do that?* He closed his eyes and focused back on the clouds and his floating up to touch them. Again he rose from the chair and up against the top of his desk. He laughed out loud and quickly silenced himself as he fell back down into the chair. He looked behind him, through his cubicle opening, to make sure no one was watching or passing by. This time he decided to just think of hovering above his chair slightly. His heart accelerated as he slowly lifted off the seat of his chair. He couldn't help but smile the biggest smile possible as he hovered between his chair and his desk. Knowing the extension of his hands and legs could affect the force, he slowly extended his fingers of one hand toward his monitors and thought about moving backwards. The extended force caused him to lean back in his chair while still hovering slightly above the seat. He couldn't help but laugh out loud.

"What's so funny, Leif?" Jewels asked, standing at the entrance of his cubical.

Leif was startled by the question and landed hard in his chair, throwing his balance backward. He managed to catch his feet below him as he stood up and the chair crashed to the floor. He turned to see Jewels standing there looking puzzled. "Um, nothing really," he stammered and looked back at his monitors, the progress bar was at twenty-two percent. "I'm just glad my code is compiling without any errors."

"Well," Jewels exclaimed. "You've been in the code a little too long, I think." She gave a sly smile and a short laugh.

"Yeah, I think you're right." Leif replied while picking his chair up off the floor and sliding it under his desk. "I've been at it for a while and I think I need some coffee."

"I thought you'd never ask. How about McNallies, across the street?"

"Why not downstairs?" Leif asked while glancing at his monitors, trying not to show his embarrassment at being startled.

"Too many visits from," she looked around. "The mangers who don't really have much to do, so they pop into the cafeteria for coffee and to spy on who's wasting time."

Leif laughed nervously at her comment, thought about it for a moment, then responded, "Okay. Sounds good to me."

***

Jewels brought two coffees to the table as Leif stared out the window at the Amzoft building across the street. He found it interesting when people constantly streamed in and out of the rotating doors. But, with over nine hundred people in the same building, it was bound to be busy. He felt grateful such a prestigious software company was interested in having him as an employee. It had been over a year since being employed and he felt he was in it for the long run. Jewels noticed his distant gaze at the building.

"What cha thinking Leif?"

"Ah." he blinked a couple times to clear the fog of deep thought and gave a small chuckle. "Just thinking about how glad I am to be working for Amzoft. Amazed I've lasted this long."

"Really?" she replied in disbelief. "You're like the master math whiz of the whole building. I hear the managers talk about you all the time - how you saved their butts by completing your code way ahead of schedule and adding code that makes the game run smoother." She pulled her dark hair back out of her face and tucked it behind her ear. "I wouldn't be surprised if you're up for a promotion when you get your review."

Leif could feel his face flush with embarrassment as he looked down at his coffee. "Well, it's really not that big of a deal. It just comes easy to me, I guess." He turned his cup a couple turns before picking it up for a sip.

"Wow," Jewels replied. "Smart, cute, and humble." She stated more to herself than to Leif.

He wasn't quite sure if he heard her correctly and decided to let it pass while he took another sip. He felt a bit awkward at the lack of his response.

"You're certainly a mystery, Leif." She took a sip while watching him intently.

Leif chuckled. "A mystery? How so?"

"I did a web search for your name. It came up blank. You're not on any of the social media sites. All I could find was a profile on BizLinks saying that you worked here since last year. No selfie pictures, no postings, nada, zilch!"

He wasn't sure if he should be intrigued by her efforts or afraid. "So, you're trying to stalk me?" he replied with a smile.

"No," Jewels laughed. "Well," she paused, "maybe just a little." She looked down at the cups sitting on the table and rolled her eyes up to make direct eye contact with Leif. "You're very different from anyone else I've met before. I'm curious, and I guess," she paused again. "I guess I'm just trying to know you a little better."

Leif was flooded with a thousand different thoughts all at once. He felt honored that someone as pretty as Jewels would be interested in him. Though, at the same time, he felt conflicted. Would he ever find Carina again? Maybe he could be attracted to Jewels. He just wasn't sure. He just didn't know what to say.

"Leif, did I scare you?" She gave a nervous smile - hoping she wasn't too forward in her approach.

"Ah, no." He smiled back. "I'm just not sure what to say. I'm flattered." He paused and looked out the window at the building across the street. He was trying to find the right words to not dissuade her, but also not lead her on. As he was gazing, he noticed a man leaning with his back to the Amzoft building, next to the rotating doors, staring directly back at him and Jewels. He thought it was odd someone from across the street would be watching them. He didn't recognize the man. He wore jeans and a flannel shirt. He had jet black hair with pointed bangs and his eyes were hidden by dark retro sunglasses. The man pulled out a cell phone without breaking his stare then turned and walked away. Leif looked back at Jewels, realizing she was waiting to hear more. "Sorry, I was distracted. Um, I'm flattered, and speechless."

"Speechless is good," Jewels replied with a smile and a nod.

Leif looked back out the window. The man was gone.

"You see someone?" Jewels asked while glancing out the window as well.

"Nah. I thought I saw someone, but he's gone." He looked back at the same time as Jewels. "Well, maybe we should get back."

"Big hurry to see if your code compiled?"

Leif laughed. "Yeah, I guess so." He paused, gulped down the rest of his coffee. He gathered up enough guts to make the next move. "Coffee again Monday? Maybe I'll let you ask me some questions and take care of that curiosity."

Jewels smiled glowingly. "You're on. Monday it is."

***

"Come on!" Leif barked at the slow traffic. The rest of the day at work had been a major struggle. His discovery he could hover at will, Jewels expressing her interest in him, and then being watched by the stranger outside the coffee house - it was all overwhelming. He spent the rest of the day staring at the same section of computer code on his monitor with no progress at all. He felt relieved to leave the office. He called his parents to ask if he could stop by for the evening.

He felt more relieved when he finally got off the main roads crazy with traffic and onto the rural road that ran toward his parent's house. It was a joy to be able to throttle up his Audi S5 as he wound through the last few miles. The thick evergreens flew by as he pondered how he would break the news to his parents. *Maybe a demonstration would be the way to go,* he thought. He was grinning as he pulled into the driveway. His parents were already outside the house, taking advantage of the summer evening daylight to squeeze in some yard work. They stopped what they were doing and walked over to the car as Leif stepped out.

"I could hear you coming a mile away," Ben joked as he pulled off his gloves and gave Leif a hug.

Francie wasn't quite as jovial. She hated having to wait for news - always anticipating it would be unpleasant. She gave Leif a hug with a "Hello dear."

"So, what's the exciting news?" Ben asked.

Leif took a quick look back toward the street to make sure no one was walking by. The rest of the property was secluded from prying eyes with thick evergreens, ferns, and mulberry bushes. They allowed the prickly bushes to grow on the edges of the property line without encroaching into the yard. Thorns were a good deterrent to trespassing. When Leif was satisfied no one else was watching he added, "I need to show you something." He closed his eyes and straightened his arms down along his sides. Slowly he lifted a couple inches off the ground. He opened his eyes and hovered for another couple seconds till one of his legs slipped out to one side. He felt like he was on invisible ice as he flopped around and flailed his arms, trying to regain his balance.

Francie muffled a squeal, startled to see Leif hover above the ground and flailing about. Ben reached out and grabbed one of Leif's arms to help him regain his balance.

"Whoa, boy. That's a crazy dance you have going on there." Ben stated while gazing around, making sure there were no onlookers. He kept ahold of Leif's arm. "Okay. Straighten your arms down by your sides. Not too stiff, but relaxed."

"Umph, okay." Leif replied while regaining his composure. He was able to steady himself, he lowered his arms back down to his sides and continued to hover a bare few inches above the ground.

"You got it? Ready for me to let go?"

"Yeah, I think so." Leif nervously replied.

As Ben released his grip, Leif continued to hover. He was a little twitchy with his hands and legs as he tried to keep his balance.

"Spread your stance just a little. That will help." Ben offered.

Leif spread his feet about a foot apart. His balanced improved and he started to relax a bit.

Ben backed away to give Leif more room and to admire his son's new found ability. "You know, when they train helicopter pilots, they start by teaching them how to hover. Just keep practicing that and getting your balance before you start trying to move anywhere or go higher."

Francie wasn't sure how to feel. She could see the huge smiles on Ben and Leif. She didn't want to ruin this for them. Thoughts of her parents and younger sister flooded her. A small tear gathered in the corner of her eye and she brushed it away before anyone could notice. "Guys, I think we should take this inside."

Leif dropped back to the ground and absorbed the impact with a slight bend of his knees.

"I 'spose you're right dear." Ben replied while giving the surrounding area a quick glance.

Leif placed an arm around Francie as they all walked to the house. "It's okay mom," he softly stated. "I'm not going to let anything happen to me." He tightened his arm around her shoulders as they walked into the house.

***

The evening was full of non-stop talk and excitement as Leif got them caught up on how things were going at work, with his new car, his crazy neighbors by Lake

Union, and finally about the cute girl at the office. The dining room got suddenly quiet at the mention of Jewels advances.

Leif wondered what the big deal was while he noticed 'the look' between his mom and dad - their way of silently agreeing on something with a single look before they expressed their feelings. It was the same look they gave each other before they gave him the sex talk when he was eleven and the 'Being Responsible' talk when he was fifteen. "What?" he asked.

Francie put on her 'I just want to be helpful' face. She knew Leif was a man now and could make his own decisions, but this was a topic she and Ben wanted to make sure Leif fully understood. "Do you remember our talk when you were eleven?"

"Really?" Leaf laughed. "I think I remember the sex talk pretty clearly. Plus, it was a big topic in middle school."

"It's not about that son." Ben added with a chuckle. "It's about the bonding."

"Bonding? You mean commitment? I get that. Whoever I end up with is who I'm committed to stay with." Leif could tell by the looks on their faces he was missing something.

"Commitment is good," Francie added. "I'm sorry if we weren't more clear before. Bonding is much more. It only happens with our kind. When you meet 'the one' you just know it. It becomes an instant bond. Sometimes we might pretend it's not there." She looked at Ben with a grin. "But, it always becomes a eternal, lasting bond. There's no desire for anyone else." She looked back at Leif. "Is that how it is with Jewels?"

Leif understood now. He did have it wrong all along and instantly his thoughts went to Carina. "Nope. Not with Jewels." He stared blankly at the kitchen table while thinking of that blonde haired girl in school. The same one who haunted him in his dreams from the top of the evergreen tree. Looking up at his parents he asked, "Is it possible to bond with someone in middle school?"

"What? Middle school?" Ben stated more than asked. "I, I don't know." He looked at Francie who just shook her head and shrugged her shoulders. "Maybe Georgeo would know. I' was going to shoot him a note anyway, to give him the good news."

"Dad. Mom. I need to try something." Leif stated while standing up. "Let's go to my room."

Ben and Francie looked confused as they followed Leif up the stairs and to his old bedroom. Leif flung the door open and stood in the threshold. It was almost a year since he had seen it last.

"I thought you were going to use this for your paintings?" he stated to his mom while gazing inside.

"I will," she replied while placing a hand on his shoulder. "Once I get enough time."

Leif walked into his bedroom letting his mom's hand drift off of his shoulder. His parents were still not sure of what this was all about. They stayed just outside the doorway while Leif slowly ran one hand along the top and front edge of his old dresser. He visualized the image of the bald eagle standing there gazing at him and then looking out the window. He walked over to the window and spread the curtains apart. It was darker now, the sun had set almost an hour ago while they were having dinner. A small sliver of the moon was showing just to the right of the tallest evergreen tree. He visualized Carina standing in the tree, petting the eagle, and gesturing for him to come up.

"What is it son?" Ben asked. He stepped into the room and gazed out the window to see what Leif was staring at.

"I have to do this," Leif replied. He unlocked the window and slid it fully open. He turned and sat down on the window ledge and swung his legs around to hang them outside.

"Leif, honey." Francie rushed into the room and placed a hand on Leif's shoulder. "You don't have to do this now. You're not fully ready yet."

Ben knew his son was going to do what he wanted to do. He just stood back, ready to leap out the window if he needed to help.

"It's okay mom." Leaf stated while patting his mom's hand. "I've got this." He leaned out the window and pushed off the ledge with his hands. He stood straight up as if there was a floor outside the window, but there wasn't. He was hovering next to the second floor window of his parent's house. He kept his feet spread slightly apart to maintain his balance. He swirled his arms slowly as if he was floating in water, to turn himself around to face his parents. Both of them were leaning out the window. Francie was afraid and fearful for Leif. Ben was grinning ear-to-ear.

"It tingles." Leif stated. "I can feel pressure under my feet and in the palms of my hands." He turned his hands around to look at them. His body turned and moved as he turned his palms to face different directions. He giggled at the sensation. "I can feel it flow through me."

“That’s the dark matter.” Ben added. “At least that’s what Georgeo has told me. Something in our body attracts it. We can feel it flow and as we get more sensitive to it we learn how to control it for our movement. Looks to me like you’ve got a pretty good start.”

“I’m going to go to that tree and stand in the top of it.” He pointed to the top of the tree. “That’s where I see her in my dreams. Carina, the blonde hair girl from middle school. She’s my bond. I’m going to find her, but before I do, I’m going to go stand in that tree.” He turned slowly to face the tree. He raised both arms to a point above his head and stroking down with his hands he slowly thrusted himself up to the tree top. He realized he could increase or decrease his speed by the position of his palms and how much surface of his palms he exposed. Just when he thought he had the speed controlled he extended his fingers down along his legs and quickly discovered this increased his speed instead of slowing him down. He arrived at the tree top much quicker than he expected. He reached out to grab the top of the tree, but found that extending his hands caused him to drift farther away from the tree. He closed his eyes for a few seconds to concentrate on the flow of the energy through his body. Taking a deep breath, he calmed down and stood vertical with his feet spread for hovering. He opened his eyes and saw that the tree top was only a few feet away.

“You okay?” Ben asked while hovering between Leif and the house. Francie was still leaning out the window - almost in tears from watching Leif fumble around the tree top.

“Dad! I’ve got this!”

"Okay, okay. I just want to make sure you're safe. I'll stay right here. You know," he nodded back toward Francie and continued, "you're giving your mom a heart attack."

Leif slowly slid over to the treetop, stepped onto a branch and gripped the thin trunk with one hand. He relaxed and let himself move with the top of the tree as it swayed in the breeze. He closed his eyes and listened to the wind, the rustling of the leaves, and the creaking of the branches. It was comforting knowing Carina could be out there somewhere. She had to be. He felt the bond and he knew it was real - now that he understood it was more than just commitment. He opened his eyes and gazed up at the stars and the wisps of clouds slowly drifting by.

Ben was hovering next to the second story bedroom window with one arm around Francie's shoulders. He was busy composing a message with his other hand on his smartphone.

Georgeo. The boy has matured!

SIX - AIR BORN

Bonded on a cloud
Transfixed I am by your eyes
I hover nearby - Avitorian Haiku

The elevator doors opened up on the eighteenth floor of the high-rise business building. Matt stepped out and stopped for a moment to admire the view. The entire floor was wide open, exposed concrete floors, steel support columns covered with sprayed on insulation, and various pipes, cables, and HVAC ducting along the ceiling. Matt's attention wasn't on the rough interior, but rather on the incredible view through the thick, tinted, plate glass windows. The western corner of the building faced out toward the Olympic Mountains. The setting sun was just starting to touch the peaks and the northern corner of the building revealed the famous Space Needle awash in the bright orange reflection of the setting sun. The echoed sound of typing on a computer keyboard reminded Matt why he was here. He walked over to the source of the noise as he added his own echoes from hard soled shoes on a concrete floor to the facility.

Dr. Corellis was too busy typing to even notice the stark beauty of the scenery. Her L-shaped desk was the only one on the floor of the building, sitting next to several racks full of computer and networking gear. Several bundles of cables stretched from the equipment into various conduit openings in the ceiling. She glanced at a world clock map display on one of her three monitors, checking to make sure Matt was arriving on her pre-defined schedule.

"I think I have a candidate," Matt stated rather nonchalantly as he approached her desk.

"You think?" Dr. Corellis stated without looking up from her computer display.

"I want to do a little more observation to make sure."

Dr. Corellis looked up from her computer, removed her glasses, and gazed at Matt while pondering the implications of his statement.

"What?" Matt asked.

"That's fine," she stated while putting her glasses back on and returned to looking at her computer display. "We still need a little more time to get our cover settled. The university has accepted my credentials along with the grant from a generous contributor. We should be able to move in and get settled before the fall semester."

"That's excellent news. Which facility?"

"University of Washington, CENPA," she replied.

"Ah, perfect. The Center for Experimental Nuclear Physics and Astrophysics." He paused while watching the last of the sun settle down past the mountains. "Excellent computer system there. I'm sure we'll put it to good use. What about logistics?"

"I've acquired some space in the lower levels of the bio building. It's close enough that we can get Angela into the facility with a boat." She paused and looked up at him. "I'll coordinate it. The team will be here in a few weeks. You just stay focused on your candidate and keep me posted."

"Sure thing doctor." He leaned down over the desk and gave her a quick kiss before heading back toward the elevator.

***

Leif spent most of his day hovering throughout his condo, getting his balance and stability while trying not to leave too many marks on the walls. He remembered what his father told him the night before, about the training techniques used for helicopter pilots. They hover, barely above the ground, focusing on balance and stability. In the back yard at his parent's house he had the wide open spaces between the house and the evergreen tree. It was easy to just point in a general direction and go. But, as he quickly discovered when he got close to the tree, it was important to have control over his position in relation to other objects. His bruised knees reminded him his landings needed a lot of work as well.

Most of his living room furniture had been moved to the walls, giving him as much room in the center as possible. If anyone came for a visit, they would clearly think he had been practicing dancing or aerobics. The smell of sweat from all of his exertion would complete the image. He figured exercise would be his excuse if one of the neighbors stopped by to see what all the wall thumping was about.

After spending most of the morning practicing his vertical hovering he decided to focus on horizontal. He started vertically and slowly moved to a horizontal, face down hover over the center of the living room. He laughed at himself, thinking about the many "planking" pictures he had seen on the internet. He focused on the tingling of his skin from the forces being projected from his body to counteract the force of gravity. By making slow and smooth movements he discovered he could change his height and position by thinking about the tingling and where he wanted the tingling to move. He learned he had the most control through his hands and feet with movements reminding him of swimming. He slowly drifted in circles around the room, raising and lowering himself over the terrain of the furniture along the walls. Occasionally he would touch a wall or a piece of furniture and push himself off in a different direction. It didn't take long to figure out he didn't need to touch the surface of a solid object - he could just think of the tingle in his hands or feet and the propulsion force would flow toward the surfaces. He played around with the intensity of the propulsion until he slammed a shoulder into the door frame toward the hallway. He grimaced from the sharp pain and cursed himself for getting clumsy. *Great, another bruise.* He straightened into a vertical position in the doorway, letting himself drop to the floor and landing on his feet with a thud. The loudness of his landing startled him. "I gotta work on those," he mumbled.

Leif peeked out from the closed living room blinds at the dimming twilight over Lake Union. It was slightly past nine p.m. and the sky was still too lit up to even consider flying without being seen. Even with the lights of the city he wasn't sure if it would be secure enough to launch off in this area. He pondered if he was really truly ready. *What if I misjudge my landing and kill myself?* Leif's phone vibrated two short pulses on his belt clip, indicating he had received a text message. He pulled the phone from its clip, gazed at the screen, and smiled at the text message from Uncle Georgeo.

Want to go practice?

"How in the…" Leif mumbled to himself. He started to type a reply when there was a light knock at the door. He quickly typed out 'sure' and pressed Send while walking to the door. He was certain it was one of the neighbors wanting to complain about his bumping around. He opened the door and was startled to see his uncle Georgeo standing there.

"Uncle Georgeo!" Leif gave him a hug and invited him inside. "You are indeed a sly one," Leif laughed while closing the door.

"It's good to see you again. Your father says good things about you." He paused while examining the disarray of the living room. "Is that your shoe print halfway up the wall over there?"

Leif blushed. "Um, yeah."

"If I was your neighbor, how would you explain it?"

While the critique stung, Leif knew it was for the best. "I was exercising?" He replied, half knowing it wasn't a very plausible excuse. *The training has begun already,* Leif realized.

Georgeo laughed. "Well, let's get that cleaned up and then go flying."

"Alright," Leif responded while heading to the kitchen for the cleaner and a rag.

***

Leif stepped out of Georgeo's Jeep, stretched, and took in a deep breath of the cool night air - full of the scent of evergreens, ferns, and moss of the forest. It was refreshing, and much needed after the hour long drive and information dump from Georgeo. All the reminders about secrecy, protection, being alert to surroundings, to be wary of those who want to get close, and the need to be unseen when flying. It all made his head spin. He watched as Georgeo walked back down the dirt road they came in on -

checking to make sure there was no one following or watching.

They were on a secluded trail surrounded by thick evergreens, hilly slopes on one side, and a high tension power line path a hundred yards off. Leif could hear the sound of a flowing river off in the distance. He took another deep breath to try and calm his nerves - a combination of excitement and anxiety about flying with uncle Georgeo. He felt close to Georgeo. Even though he wasn't really a true uncle to Leif, he felt like family. Leif felt privileged to be receiving his training from the one and only Overseer of the Avitorians. It sure seemed impressive when he thought of it that way. But, then again, it was just uncle Georgeo.

"Looks clear," Georgeo stated while walking toward Leif and the Jeep. "Take your shoes and watch off and put them in the Jeep. Wait here. I'll be right back."

"My shoes?" Leif asked, but was startled to see Georgeo suddenly shoot straight up into the night sky. He tried to see where Georgeo went, but it was too dark. He took his shoes and watch off, put them in the Jeep, and waited just as Georgeo asked. The moisture from the ground started to soak into Leif's socks, but he didn't care. It actually felt kind of refreshing. There was a slight breeze blowing through the trees creating a soothing whisper. Leif imagined the trees were talking to one another. *What are the humans doing here? Can't they see we're busy. Tell them to go away and leave us alone.* He chuckled at the thought.

Georgeo appeared just as suddenly as he had left. "Are you ready?" he asked.

"Um, yeah. I guess. Why the shoes?"

"If you are to learn how to land without killing yourself or breaking your legs, you need as much sensitivity as possible. Taking your shoes off gives you more feeling for the flow of the energy and the position of the ground. Just as airplanes experience what is called 'ground effect', you'll be able to sense when you're getting closer to the ground or to other objects."

"Ah, okay, but what about my watch?"

"Silver strap easily reflects light. What if you're tempted to hit the button for lighting it up to check the time?"

"Ah, gotcha. You're right." Leif realized he needed to be more aware of the things that could make him visible while flying.

"So, ready?"

"Um, yeah."

"Okay. I want you to just hover for a bit. A few inches off the ground. I want to make sure that you're stable and able to hold your position."

Leif lifted off around six inches from the ground and held his position there. He felt pretty confident about his hovering after his practice time at the condo. He even rotated around both directions just to show Georgeo he had control over his movements.

"That is pretty good." Georgeo commended. "I want you to go straight up and stay at the level of the top of the trees."

Leif increased the flow of energy through his legs and out his feet. He quickly ascended to the top of the trees and past them. Realizing he had gone too far he backed off on the flow and descended to the tree tops. Georgeo came up to meet him at the tree tops.

"Good job. A little sloppy, but actually very impressive for your first time out in the wild." Georgeo added with a smile. "Take a good look around and make sure you don't see any potential for being spotted."

Leif slowly spun around and gazed in all directions, looking for any lights or indications that someone might be close by who could see him. He increased his altitude another fifty feet to get a better look above the tree line. Georgeo rose up to match his altitude.

"Very good. I'm impressed. Now let's see how you do with orientation. I'm going to spin you around into a different position and I want you to right yourself back into vertical."

"Okay." Leif added.

Georgeo reached out and grabbed ahold of Leif's shoulders. He spun him around in different directions and different angles. He let go and let Leif's kinetic energy continue drifting at an unnatural angle. "Okay, straighten out."

Leif thought it felt pretty weird to be in a strange angle - slightly upside down and around forty-five degrees' angle toward the trees. He got his senses and straightened himself into a fully horizontal position in front of Georgeo.

"Excellent." Georgeo smiled and patted Leif on the shoulder. "See the clouds above?"

"Yes."

"Follow me into the bottom of the group of clouds directly above us." Georgeo started moving before he was even done speaking.

Leif followed. He could hear the wind whistling past his ears as he accelerated to catch up with Georgeo. As he entered the bottom of the cloud mass he could feel the additional moisture on his skin. He slowed down and stopped as he saw Georgeo hovering in the fog of the cloud.

"Excellent." Georgeo reached out and grabbed Leif by the shoulders. "Now I want you to close your eyes and to reach out with your senses."

"Um, okay." Leif closed his eyes and tried to listen and feel for anything out of the ordinary.

"We have the ability to sense the flow of electricity when we focus." Georgeo added. "It takes practice, but you'll soon be able to detect the flow of masses of electrons in various directions from your position. It's very difficult when we're down on the surface. We're bombarded by so much from computers, communications, machinery, automobiles, and life in general. But," he paused and then continued. "Up here, it's easier. We're in the air and surrounded only by clouds when they are here. Tell me what you feel," he asked.

Leif tried to reach out with all his senses to try and feel what was out there. With his eyes closed he started to detect the flow of something distant yet elongated along the south of them. "I sense something, like a string, off to my right. It's vibrating, kind of like a string on a guitar or violin."

"Very good," Georgeo added. "That's the high tension power lines off to the south. Anything else?"

Leif kept his eyes closed and he listened to the silence. He reached out with all of his feelings and senses. He spread his arms and his legs, thinking these would improve his ability to receive whatever was out there. "I sense a blanket below us, pulsating and constant, extending out for as far as I can sense."

"Those are the trees and the plant life. All living things have electrons flowing through them. When we're up here, it's easier to separate what is where." Georgeo responded. "You need to perfect your ability to sense the flow of these electrons. This will keep you safe when you are flying. If there are planes or machinery nearby, you will sense it. If the clouds are stormy and full of lightning, you will sense it. Stay away from those. They can have a major effect on your ability to sense direction and on your flying. Same with the high tension power lines. The radiated energy can disrupt your flying. If there are cars or people below, you will be able to sense it. All life is full of energy. As you become more adapted to your senses and what you can feel, you will get better at knowing what is out here, just by feeling."

Leif slowly rotated with his arms and legs spread out, trying to sense as much as he could in all directions. As he started to feel the various sensations of the power lines and the trees below, he could tell he was more sensitive to these feelings. As he continued, the sense of the energy was almost overwhelming - as if he was trying to listen to multiple radio stations at the same time. It all became noise and he had difficulty separating the different sensations.

Georgeo sensed that Leif was becoming overwhelmed with the different sources of energy he was feeling. "Open your eyes, boy," he added while shaking Leif's shoulders.

"Wow!" Leif opened his eyes. "That was amazing. I had no ideas this was possible." He did a flip in the air with his excitement.

Georgeo laughed at Leif's exuberance. "Take your time. Come out here as much as you can and feel the environment around you. You'll find it might be a little overwhelming when you're down below and surrounded by everything. But, it'll get better. You'll learn how to shut it out when you're on the surface and when to utilize it when you're air born." Georgeo released Leif and added, "Do you sense where the Jeep is?"

Leif closed his eyes again and reached out with all his senses. He directed his feelings toward the blanket of trees and life below. Among the blanket he was able to detect a single pinpoint spot where there was something different than the rest of the environment. "Yeah. I think I've got it. It's different than everything else below."

"Excellent. So, now that you know how to find your way back, go and fly. Be free and feel the exhilaration of what it's like to be an Avitorian."

Leif opened his eyes, took a deep breath, gazed above, and extended as much force as he could muster toward flying straight up into the air. He passed through the top of the clouds and could clearly see the thousands of stars above. He stopped and slowly rotated as he absorbed the enormous view of the Cascade mountains off to the east, Mt. Rainier off to the south, the lights of Seattle off to the west, with the bountiful peaks of the Olympics beyond. He could see a line of aircraft lined up for approach into SeaTac airport - the distant blinking of strobe lights on the wings. A glow in the clouds to the south showed where Tacoma was and off to the north were various glows of lights into the clouds for Belleview, Redmond, and Everett. A half-moon was hovering above the Cascades and was reflecting off the snow covered peaks. Mt. Rainier was the closest and the glow of the snow topped crater sent chills through him and made the hair stand up on the back of his neck. It was at this moment he felt the proudest he had ever felt about being privileged enough to have been born as an Avitorian. No longer a curse as he had felt while in school, or while waiting for his abilities to show. He had truly become what he had always dreamed about and had desired. He was, as his uncle Georgeo had stated - truly Air Born.

***

Amazing, was all Leif could think. He hovered barely above the top of the clouds and gazed at the full moon rising slowly over the top of Mt. Rainier. It was so bright it almost hurt his eyes. In the three weeks since his first flight with Georgeo, he had managed to fly almost every night. Each night he had stated to himself it was the most beautiful night of all. But this night, “this takes the cake,” he mumbled to himself. He rose slightly from the cloud top to get a better view of the glowing white blanket of clouds stretched out around the mountain. He didn’t want to test his abilities, see how fast he could go, practice landings, or try to sense where the closest airplanes are. With this stunning of a view he just wanted to soak it all in. The moon slowly climbed higher as he continued to watch. He figured it was a good test of his abilities - being able to hover in a stationary position for a longer period of time.

After what seemed like an hour or more, Leif stretched out his arms, closed his eyes, and slowly spun around. Reaching out with his senses, he could feel the forest below. Stopping suddenly, he thought he felt something different. Something at his same altitude and not too far away. He turned toward the direction of the sensation. He slowly opened his eyes while trying to maintain his sense. Right away he saw it. His heart jumped into a rapid pulse when he realized it wasn't a thing or machine, but rather, a person. At first he thought it was Georgeo trying to sneak up on him, to test him out. But Georgeo didn't have long, blonde, hair, and he sure wasn't a female. She was hovering in the clouds, facing away from him. He guessed she was about fifty yards away. Far enough that he couldn't see any other details other than the back of her head. Her hair danced with the fluctuations of the light breeze. He didn't know what to do. It was as if all his senses, his muscles, and his mind, had instantly shut down.

Should I say something? Should I get closer or should I just watch from a distance? Does she know that I'm here? The thoughts bombarded him and none of them with any clear answers. His heart skipped a beat when she rose up slightly out of the clouds. She wore a flowing white blouse which made it appear as if she was a part of the cloud itself. She reminded him of the tales of mermaids who would briefly make an appearance above the waters to entice the sailors away from their ships. As quickly as that mental image came to him, she plunged down into the clouds, disappearing into the blanket of white.

"Wait!" he shouted without even thinking. He quickly flew over to where she had entered into the cloud, but she wasn't there. Closing his eyes and extending his arms, he slowly spun around - trying to get a sense for where she went. All he could sense was the forest below. His heart sank into his stomach. He felt like he could die of stupidity - for not even saying hello. For the next few hours he flew through the clouds, above the clouds, below the clouds - looking for any indication of where she could be or had flown off to. There was no sign or sense of the girl with the blonde hair. The moon climbed higher and a faint glow of a approaching sunrise appeared on the eastern horizon. Leif was devastated. He didn’t even know if she knew he was there. He slowly fell to the forest below while gazing up at the glow of the moon through the clouds and hoping to catch a glimpse of the mystery girl.

SEVEN - FOUND

Out from among the clouds you came to me. Truly a dream I thought it must be. For how could one of such beauty and grace be real. Yet as I floated in the glow of the moon, above the mountains and below the stars, you were there. As real as the air you took from my lungs and the beats you took from my heart. You were there. Will you ever be real to me again? - Leif's letter in the wind.

Leif never considered himself a stalker - to find and follow someone he had seen. A complete stranger. This was different. It was only a few weeks ago since he had seen the blond haired girl, floating in the clouds. The memory of her haunted him in his sleep and when he was awake. He hardly ate, he barely slept, and he couldn't focus on his daily work. His once shining reviews by his bosses had become looks of unspoken questions. He knew it was only a matter of time before someone pulled him into their office for a reprimand about his performance.

He continued to return to the same spot night after night, but she was nowhere to be found. His gut ached with the thought he had lost her forever - she would never return to give him the chance he had thrown away when he first saw her. Each night was no different from the next as he hopped from cloud to cloud, searching for any sign she had been there. He looked for the slightest wisp of cloud and fog streaking in a direction contrary to the wind. He looked into every gap with the hope she had just passed through, leaving a trail for him to follow. As with each night before, when the horizon started to glow, he would return home feeling devastated and exhausted.

Regardless of the lack of sleep and the stress from work, Leif had a hard time waiting for the darkness to settle over Seattle. He thought about trying other locations, thinking maybe she would fly to other remote spots to enjoy the peace and serenity of the night. There were too many places to look. The forests and mountains outside of Seattle were too vast to cover. He considered enlisting the help of his parents, but felt too embarrassed by his lack of initiative on that first night. His excuse of their advancing age made it easy to not include them; at least, not yet.

I'm panicking, Leif thought while driving to a secluded spot at the base of Mt. Rainier, close to where he had seen the blond hair girl. *I have my favorite spots, remote and away from prying eyes. She has to have her favorite spots as well.* He reasoned this would be the only location where he would be able to find her - the same location where he saw her. She had to eventually return, even if it was weeks, months, or years later. He was determined to not let her slip by again.

Leif waited for the darkness to settle. At this time of the month, he knew he would have an hour of complete darkness before the moon showed itself over the horizon. When the time was right he launched into the cool night air. Distant city lights painted a faint glow against the clouds around Mt. Rainier. Fog was starting to form and drift through the thick forest below. Stars were peeking through openings in the clouds. There was a slight wind bringing more cloud cover in from the Puget Sound. Leif flew to same place he had been searching every night for the past few weeks - his best approximation of where he had seen the long, flowing, blonde hair in the clouds. He slowly rotated while rising above the clouds, scanning every possible nook, wisp, crevice, and gap in the clouds. He closed his eyes, extended his arms, and reached out with his senses - seeking anything that felt different from the normal flow of energy through the plants, animals, and distant power-lines below. He felt nothing unusual.

He opened his eyes and continued to scan the cloud tops and the horizon while rising slowly above the clouds. He took a deep breath to calm his nerves and the ache of emptiness in his gut. *I have to see her again. Patience. I can do this.* He stopped gaining altitude and continued to turn while scanning. The crispness of the air was helping him to relax. He always enjoyed the serenity of the mountains and the forests. Even when he was grounded - walking through the many trails and along the rivers, he found he was most at peace and happiest when he was here. He stopped turning and gazed at the distant glow of light on the peaks of the Cascades. The moon was rising and would soon provide more light.

Leif heard a sudden rush of air above him. He looked up, expecting to see a flock of birds, a stray seagull, or a graceful eagle. There was nothing. He slowly turned around, looking up, hoping to catch a glimpse of flapping wings against the backdrop of the mountains or the distant city lights. Another rush of air passed under him, startling him to a verbal, "Whoa." He quickly flipped upside down, trying to see what had flown under him. He thought he made out the movement of something rapidly flying away, but it was too dark to tell and he couldn't sense anything. He quickly followed in the same direction, but stopped when he couldn't detect any further movement. *I'm chasing ghosts.*

His heart was beating rapidly. He wasn't sure if it was the excitement or the fear of not knowing what was happening. Something or someone was out here with him. *Could it be her?* He slowly turned around looking for any possible movement while listening for any change in the light wind. His senses didn't seem to be picking up anything. Maybe his anxiety combined with his exhaustion, and frustration was dulling his senses. Or maybe the movement was too fast for him to sense. He stopped to try and calm down enough to determine who or what was up here with him. He felt the moon rising and he turned to watch it's cresting above the ridge of the Cascade mountain range to the east. The clouds continued to move below him, rolling in from the northwest, providing a base to reflect the moonlight and provide protection from prying eyes below.

"I've been watching you." The soft voice came from above and to the south.

Leif quickly turned to look in the direction of the voice. There she was - hovering in the distance and being softly caressed by the clouds encircling Mt. Rainier. Leif could hardly contain the beating of his heart. He could hear it pounding in his ears and was afraid his heart would just fall out of his chest and kill him before he could utter a single word. He could tell she was smiling as she hovered among the clouds. The glow from the rising moon washed over her. She was wearing jeans and a flowing loose jacket over a t-shirt. Her hair moved with the wisps of the clouds and would occasionally fall to her elbows as she hovered with her hands on her hips. Her posture seemed to imply it was Leif's turn to respond.

Leif took a deep breath and blew it out slowly. He smiled with a bit of a chuckle, realizing while he was hoping to be the one to find her, she had in fact, found him instead. He paused and took another breath before responding. "You've been watching me?"

She drifted closer as she responded, "Yeah. For like the past month." She paused and looked off toward the lights of Seattle and continued. "I had to strike a pose for you before you saw me."

"Wow. I've been blind for a whole month, eh?" Leif responded with embarrassment. "And here I didn't want to be perceived as a stalker if I found you again."

She let out a small laugh. “Well, I guess I’ve been stalking you, Leif.” She replied.

“What? You even know my name? I admit, you really have me at a great disadvantage.” Leif responded as he slowly drifted closer to her.

“Sorry,” she replied while looking down and letting her hair drift down over her face.

Leif’s heart almost stopped when he got close enough to get a clearer look at her.

She looked back up and her hair parted to each side of her face. “I’m …”

“Carina.” Leif interrupted her. “The girl from school.”

“Yeah. I was wondering when you would come up and say hello.” She drifted close enough reach out and touch him. She stopped a few feet away.

“Wow.” Leif responded. He searched for what he always wanted to say to her if he ever got the chance to see her again. But he couldn’t remember the words. All he added was, “I’ve missed you.”

Carina drifted closer and took his hand. “Nice to see you again too, Leif.”

The touch of her hand was calming to him, as if it was always meant to be. He smiled after a long pause and finally asked, “Would you like to talk and catch up over a cup of coffee?”

“I would love to.”

***

“…and when Mr. Krazinski found my missing page he decided to change my D to a B plus. I was so stressed out over that." Carina paused a few seconds to catch her breath and continued. "I knew I turned it in, but he insisted it was incomplete. It was such a relief when he found it and he actually apologized for misplacing it in his briefcase."

Leif hung onto every word. He was listening, but he was also watching. Trying not to be too obvious he would sneak a glance into her eyes at every opportunity. They were a cross between blue and hazel with a refreshing glow of excitement and radiance. Fortunately, she was so wrapped up with reminiscing about their days in school, she hardly noticed his intense gaze. Though once she made direct eye contact when she asked Leif about an incident in home room. Her pause and glance caught him off guard. He responded, "Um, yeah. That was pretty funny." He quickly recovered and watched as she continued.

"Look at me." Carina chuckled. "I think I've been babbling about school for a solid hour and you've hardly said anything."

Leif smiled. "It's okay. I'm enjoying it. It sure brings back a lot of memories." He paused and looked down at his empty coffee cup, then he gave the nearby tables a quick scan to make sure no one was listening to their conversation. The droning noise of grinding coffee, background music, and other conversations were loud enough to drown out any conversations farther than a few feet away. He leaned closer to Carina and spoke in a lower volume. "I wanted to talk to you there," he paused, "back in school. In home room."

Carina smiled slightly. "So, why didn't you?"

"Shy, nervous, afraid of making a fool of myself. I didn't want to get the cold shoulder." Leif sheepishly replied.

"I figured."

Leif laughed. "You figured?"

"Yeah. I wanted you to come and talk, and I got the sense you wanted to. But," she stopped and gazed around with her eyes, trying not to show she was scanning the room. She continued in a lower volume, "I didn't know you were one of us. Uncle Georgeo never told me."

"Georgeo?" Leif sat back surprised. "You know Georgeo?"

"Don't we all?"

Leif shook his head and laughed. "Yes, we do!"

"He helped me when I started. I just didn't think you might be one of us."

"When did you start?"

Carina held up all ten fingers.

"What?" Leif responded a little louder than he intended. He gazed around and was glad to see he didn't draw anyone's attention. Getting quieter, he added, "Ten years old. That's just not fair."

"Why?" Carina asked. "How old were you?"

"Um, it was almost two months ago." He held his head down in embarrassment.

Carina placed her hand on Leif's, on the table. "Don't feel bad. Georgeo told me I was special. He had never seen anyone start as early as I did. In fact, it scared me. I thought I was some kind of freak or something."

"What about your parents? Didn't they help you?"

Carina paused. The glow and excitement previously in her eyes faded as she reflected on her experience with her parents. She gazed down at her coffee cup before replying. Carina tried to choose her words carefully, in case someone was listening. "I woke up screaming the night it happened. They came in and told me it was normal, but they were concerned it had happened so soon. That was when I found out they were, um, capable, but they had decided not to - participate. They discouraged me from trying to make it happen." Small tears started to appear in the corner of her eyes.

Leif reached up with a napkin and dabbed at one that rolled to her cheek. "I'm sorry. I didn't mean to make you remember such a sad time."

She continued, "I ignored them. It felt natural - like I was supposed to be, um, participating. I tried to be careful, but my mom caught me a couple years later. She didn't scold me like I thought she would. She just slumped to the floor and cried. Uncle Georgeo showed up the next day and gave me the full 411." She looked up at Leif, patted his hand a couple times. "It's okay." She wiped at the other tear. "He taught me well."

Leif didn't know what to say. He placed his other hand on top of Carina's and rubbed it. He just gazed into her eyes and she gazed into his. He smiled and gave her a wink. She smiled back, comforted by Leif's concern. It seemed like forever and neither one wanted to break the moment. They both already knew and felt it - the Avitorian bonding was starting.

***

Matt and Suzanne stood in the center of a room surrounded by racks filled with computer equipment, cables, and electronics. Matt looked around to see if anyone else was in the room. He watched as a university student technician left the room and he listened for the door to click to a close. He gently grabbed Suzanne by the waist and pulled her toward him. Gazing into her eyes he spoke slightly above a whisper. "Well, doctor. It looks like everything is going according to plan."

"Feeling frisky today, are we?" she responded.

He chuckled. "Just glad we're able to get into this facility and move on to the next step. I'm feeling pretty good about this candidate and I think I can bring in a good specimen as soon as you're ready."

"Really? Well, that IS good news. The facility is ready. We moved Angela in last week. And I start teaching astrophysics for the university next week." She gave him a quick kiss then pulled away, not wanting to have someone walk in on them. "Do you need the team and equipment?"

"Nope. I want to keep it small, quiet, and simple. I'll let you know when I'm ready to deliver."

She nodded in agreement and pointed at the equipment and spread her arms. "This is ATHENA!" she stated proudly. "One of the most highly advanced computer clusters in the world for working on advanced astrophysical research and below ground is the Van de Graff particle accelerator. Between these two, we have the ability to finally determine, once and for all, the source for the ability of Avitorian flight." She turned to face Matt and gave him another kiss. "We - you and I - will gain full control of the Eighteenth and will learn the secrets of Avitorian flight. The royal lineage of Ahmose will rise again, with abilities that rightfully belong to us.

***

Leif was writing programming code like a mad man. He was on a euphoric high since meeting Carina and nothing could get in his way. It didn't matter he was only getting between four and six hours of sleep per night. Thankfully, with the fall season coming, the nights were getting longer. They were able to start their nightly flights earlier each evening. She had taught him a lot during the past few weeks. How they could fly faster in the colder weather and how being under stress or a sickness could affect their ability to sense the flow of electricity. A big no-no was the use of electronics such as cell phones or music players which could block being able to sense anything. When Carina discussed this with him he remembered what his parents had told him about the disappearance of his aunt Angela and the tape player left behind.

His project manager had noticed the increase in productivity as well. Every now and then he would pop his head into Leif's cubicle and give him a "Atta-boy" and a pat on the back. The kudos were nice, but Leif was more concerned about getting his work done and then heading out for some quality time with Carina. He had been in the "zone" most of the day and was looking forward to leaving soon when Jewels stopped by and startled him out of his mental web of algorithms.

"Hey Leif!" She had managed to sneak up right behind him.

"Uh, hi Jewels," he responded while finishing up a couple code statements on the computer. "What can I do for you?"

"Actually, you can help me get my source checked in. I'm stuck on the compile with the new libraries and you seem to be a pro at getting the new routines to integrate."

"I would love to help out, but I have plans for this evening. Can't you get McCreaddy to help out?"

"His wife went into labor this afternoon and this is the build we have to deliver tomorrow."

Leif felt his heart sink with the realization he wouldn't get to meet up with Carina this evening. "Okay. Give me a few minutes to get my code checked in. I'll come over to your desk."

"Thanks Leif." Jewels squeezed his shoulder and added, "You're a pal."

Leif started his code compile then pulled out his phone. He texted Carina:

Bad news, have to work. Miss you. Maybe later?

He tapped the 'Send' icon and stared at the phone, hoping to get an immediate response. *I hope she doesn't think I'm blowing her off. Of course she doesn't!* He argued with himself. His computer beeped in acknowledgement of completion of his code compile. He stood up and put his phone back into his pocket with a sigh. On his second step toward her cubicle his pocket vibrated. He looked at the phone and smiled.

:(Sorry. I'll wait

Leif spent the next four hours glued to the computer keyboard and monitors on Jewels desk. Though Jewels sat next to him, she hardly interrupted his intense concentration. She watched the monitors in amazement while he installed code modules, wrote configuration code, and tested each process as he continued. She tried to understand the processes he was performing, but she gave up trying to keep track a few hours ago. That's when she went for coffee and microwave pizza from the break-room vending machines.

Leif kept checking the time on his phone every chance he got. The four hours felt like eight. He so desperately wanted to be flying around with Carina. Every now and then, during a brief code compile, he would text Carina to let her know his progress.

"There!" Leif stated with a press of the 'Enter' key. "That should do it. We just have to wait and see if the code compiles this time."

"Wow. You're amazing." Jewels responded with a hand on his shoulder. "I don't think I even helped past the first ten minutes."

Leif watched as the progress meter on the monitor moved to ten percent. "It's just a knack I have. The math and logic comes easy to me," he replied humbly.

"Obviously. Or," she paused, "did you get help from your friend?" She chuckled while nodding at Leif's phone on the desk.

"Ah." Leif picked up the phone and stuck it in his pocket. "That was just a good friend of mine. We had plans and I was just letting her know my progress."

"Her?" Jewels was surprised. "A girlfriend? I thought you seemed to be glowing more the past month or so." She smiled.

"Well, I, um." Leif wasn't sure why he was getting so embarrassed over it.

"Is it serious?"

Leif peeked at the progress bar on the monitor as it moved to fifty percent. "Not yet, but there's promise."

"I'm so disappointed," Jewels responded with a frown.

"Disappointed?" Once again, Jewels caught him off guard. "How so?"

Jewels scooted her chair a few feet away and gathered up her notes from the desktop and arranged them into a neat stack. "You were supposed to be this lonely computer geek who always ate alone, played video games, and would eventually come around to my whims and advances. I would wrap you around my little finger and we would wink at each other while working at the office." She looked up and gave him her best mischievous smile.

Leif wasn't sure if she was joking or serious while trying to make it look like a joke. "You're messing with me, right?"

She laughed and stuffed the papers into her laptop computer bag. "Yeah, for now." She stood, pointed at the monitor, and continued, "Because it looks like we're done for tonight."

He glanced at the monitor as it showed the progress bar at one hundred percent. "Alright!" he responded with a fist pump and turned back to Jewels.

"Tell the girlfriend I said hello, and be sure to get the lights on your way out." Jewels gave him a wink, grabbed her bag, and walked out of the cubicle.

EIGHT - WATCHERS

The secrets of flight belong only to royalty and thus it shall be enforced as so. (Ancient writings of Pharaoh Amenhotep, held sacred by the 18th of Ahmose.)

Leif never thought he would ever experience the pure joy he was having at this moment. Here he was, hand in hand with Carina, skimming across the top of the thickest fog he's seen in Seattle in the past ten years. Even Sea-Tac airport was shut down - departures were canceled and arrivals were being diverted to Portland. An eerie glow of orange, yellow, and white lights from the city of Seattle lit up the cottony texture of the blanket of fog.

"Wow," was the only word uttered by Carina as they flew toward the Olympic mountain range to the west. The sliver of a crescent moon hung barely over the top of the Olympics, giving them an unreachable target to fly toward.

Leif loved that Carina had a deep admiration for the stark beauty of the skies, the mountains, the waters - all of nature in general throughout the great northwest. She was raised here too, yet she didn't take it for granted.

The skies above the fog were crystal clear. Bathed in the light of the half-moon and the thousands of pinpoints of the milky way. Leif wondered if the theory about Avitorians coming from another planet was actually true. It was plausible. Why else would they have this ability and the rest of the human race did not? He also considered maybe mankind was meant to fly, but throughout the ages most had forgotten and lost their focus by dwelling on what was on the surface of the earth. Also plausible. He hesitantly released Carina's hand and rolled onto his back to gaze up at the stars.

"Do you think it's true?" he asked Carina.

She was momentarily confused by his question until she saw he was focused on the stars above. While rolling over to face the sky she reached out slowly and slid her hand against his, intertwining their fingers. "I'm not sure," she replied. "I like the idea of venturing out among the stars, but I also think we're here for a reason." She paused for a few minutes while contemplating. "There's just so much to see and experience here. How could we ever have the time for anything else?"

Leif grinned from her response. It wasn't a simple answer - it indicated her complex reasoning and the love she felt for the earth. "Good answer," he replied while giving her hand a squeeze.

"But," she added.

As Leif waited for her to finish, he quietly watched her while they continued to slowly fly above the fog covered waters of Puget Sound. He was surprised to see she was looking at him instead of the stars. She flew up and turned to face him. Leif reached up with his free hand to take hold of Carina's free hand. They flew together, hands held together, staring into each other's eyes. Leif didn't want to blink for fear of losing a precious split second of this remarkable moment.

He could tell she was searching for words, so he prompted her with, "But?"

Carina grinned and replied, "But, would you want to travel to the stars?"

Her question caught him off guard. He thought about giving her the answer he thought she wanted to hear. *Not if it means leaving you.* He knew she would see right through it. It was too cheesy of an answer and would show he was only trying to please her instead of revealing his true self. He knew she wanted to hear his truest thoughts and feelings, and he wished for nothing more than to share them.

He gazed past her at the flickering stars and replied, "If given the opportunity? Yeah. I think I would like to give them a visit." He was being honest and hoped she wouldn't be discouraged by his answer.

Carina tilted her head up to glance at the stars and looked back down at Leif. "Well, I guess I would go with you."

Leif laughed from the surprise answer. Carina just declared she was willing to stay with him if he ventured off to the stars. He added, "But, as far as I know, no one is going to give me a rocket ship any time soon."

"Yeah, I guess not." Carina added.

She released one of her hands from his and reached out to caress his face. Leif felt his heart rate double with Carina's touch. She slid her hand slowly toward the back of his neck and gently pulled him closer. She gazed into his eyes and looked at his lips.

"Carina?"

She stopped her advance as he called her name. "What?" she asked.

"Ever since I first saw you in school…" he paused, as he brought both his hands up and gently cradled her face. "I have always wanted to kiss you." He drew her closer and softly pressed his lips to hers. It was only a few seconds - long enough to show how he felt, tender enough to show he cared, and short enough to not be overbearing. He slowly drifted back while stroking her face with his fingers, gazing at her face, he watched her reaction.

Carina smiled, grabbed ahold of Leif's jacket collar, and pulled him toward her. "And I, have always wanted you to kiss me." She kissed him just as long as the first, followed by a gentle kiss on his cheek. She drifted up into the night air, slowly spinning with her arms spread wide then put her hands together over her head, and dove down to skim the top of the blanket of fog.

"Where are you going?"

"Oh, I thought I would get a head start."

"What?" Leif responded and was startled by Carina's sudden departure toward the Olympic mountains.

"Race you there!" Carina laughed - her voice trailing off as she cut a path through the fog.

***

Leif would have flown his car to work if he could have. Every chance he could, he zipped into an open lane and past any cars that were moving too slow for his bundled up excitement. Even though he only had a few hours of sleep, he felt like he had enough energy to fly to the moon and back. He tried to not let his thoughts of flying to the mountains and back with Carina last night distract him from his driving. It was tough when he got stuck in stopped traffic however, or held up at a red light. He dwelled on Carina's kiss. He skipped brushing his teeth and washing his face this morning for fear of losing the memory of her lips, the taste, and her smell - a mix of perfume and nervous sweat. His heart beat increased with just the memories of the night. *Man, I've got it bad!*

A blaring horn behind him reminded him the light had changed to green. "Sorry!" he yelled out and waved as he hit the gas and chirped the tires. He managed to get another chirp from the tires as he hit second gear and angled toward the freeway. He was all smiles as he entered the onramp and the speedometer hit seventy-five before he was on the freeway. He backed it down to sixty with the memory of the expensive ticket he managed to get a year earlier for reckless driving and excessive speeding, not to mention the major ding to his insurance.

He checked his rearview mirror to make sure he didn't draw the notice of local law enforcement. Just a black Chrysler 300 with smoked windows. Leif couldn't see the driver but imagined it was either some old retired executive or a young meth dealer. He could hear the 'whump, whump' of excessively loud bass speakers as the windows of the 300 would vibrate in a synchronous beat. *Meth dealer,* he thought and turned his attention back to his own driving. He decided to pick up the speed a little and put some distance between him and the annoying noise.

The 520 floating freeway over Lake Washington was busy with traffic, but not enough to prevent Leif from weaving between the two lanes to get around some of the slower traffic. He liked being able to hop on the freeway early enough in the morning to not get stuck in the bumper to bumper rush hour traffic. His Audi S5 digital speedometer showed he managed to get over seventy while dodging through the traffic. He saw his normal exit off into Bellevue was coming up and he slowed to sixty and merged back into the right lane.

Leif could still hear the 'whump, whump' of the loud bass speakers. *No way!* He looked in the mirror and saw that the Chrysler was still on his bumper. He turned on his turn signal and exited off the freeway. Glancing backward, he saw the Chrysler follow him down the ramp. He wondered if the driver was just playing with him - trying to show the smoked up 300 was just as beefy as his Audi.

Normally he would veer to the right side of the exit and turn right into the residential neighborhood past the local golf course before turning toward the work offices downtown. This time, he wasn't sure what the intent of the 300 driver was. He kept going straight and through the green lighted intersection and onto a road running parallel with the freeway. The 300 continued to remain on his tail.

Traffic was light and Leif took advantage of it and gunned the Audi. In just a few seconds he was up to ninety. He just hoped no one would pull out in front of him before he got to the next intersection. He glanced into the mirror and saw that the 300 was lagging and loosing distance. He smiled, knowing the excessive weight of the 300 took away from its acceleration. He rapidly slowed as he approached the intersection.

"Stay green, stay green, stay green." Leif repeated as he took a left, sliding through the intersection at a much higher speed than normal. He quickly checked to make sure there was no oncoming traffic and took another glance in the rearview mirror. The 300 was still at a distance, but he could tell it was accelerating. Once through the turn he laid on the gas and veered onto an onramp of the freeway. He glanced back at the 300 to see it fishtail through the intersection and almost hit another car as it corrected the slide. Leif's heart rate climbed higher as he realized the driver of the 300 was intent on catching up to him. With two hands on the wheel he focused on the top of the onramp as it merged onto the freeway. He was doing over one hundred when he merged back onto the freeway. Several approaching cars veered left and slowed down as they saw him.

Leif's mind was racing as fast as his car. *Why is he doing this? Is it just some game or is he drugged out?* A quick glance back showed no black 300's at the top of the ramp yet. *Good!* He kicked the car up to one twenty as the freeway made a slight turn to the right. He knew there were cameras at key locations for monitoring the amount of traffic, but he didn't care. He would rather deal with the fines than let the maniac driver in the 300 catch up with him. He could explain the situation and hope the cameras could see the 300 as well. Another glance back showed the black 300 around a quarter mile behind and the distance was increasing. Leif noticed a semi-truck ahead in the right lane of the freeway. He rapidly passed the truck and slowed down to sixty to match the speed of the truck as he pulled as close as he could in front of the truck. He was hoping his timing would pan out for the next exit ramp off of the freeway.

The 300 was accelerating and had moved to the far left lane of the freeway. Leif watched the car in his left side mirror as he kept pace with the semi-truck behind him. He didn't want to make the truck driver mad by slowing down, yet he also didn't want to be seen by the rapidly approaching black Chrysler 300. As the 300 approached the left rear of the semi-truck, Leif slowly moved to the right shoulder of the freeway. He could see the next exit ramp approaching and he slowed down to let the truck stay between him and the 300. He matched the speed of the truck as he stayed on the right side of the truck cab. He watched the wheels and lower half of the 300 as it passed along the left side of the truck. He was sure that if the 300 driver was alert that he would be able to see the back of Leif's car through the undercarriage of the semi-truck. With the speed of their vehicles and the approaching exit ramp, there was not much the 300 could do without slamming on the brakes.

Leif veered onto the exit ramp and rapidly accelerated through the curve and onto the southbound thoroughfare toward downtown Bellevue. He was doing eighty when he exited the ramp. The suspension of his Audi held up through the turn as he tensely held the steering wheel - not wanting to make any slight mistakes which could lead to his losing control of the car. The wheels squealed as he finished the turn and flew down the street. He jammed onto the brakes and rapidly slowed down and came to a stop behind several vehicles at a red lighted intersection. His heart was pounding and his shirt was wet with perspiration. He looked in the rearview mirror and was relieved to see that the 300 was nowhere in sight. He kept staring at the mirror while waiting for the light to change. Still no sign of the black Chrysler. He took a couple deep breaths to calm himself as the light changed and the traffic continued.

Leif headed back to his office while keeping a vigilance on the rearview mirror. By the time he pulled into the underground parking garage he was confident that the drug crazed driver of the 300 was gone and that it was just a isolated incident. Still, he couldn't squelch the uneasy feeling in his gut. The whole situation was unnerving. He hoped that there was nothing more to it than just some crazy dude in a hopped up car wanting to flex his testosterone. He couldn't help but think of Carina and wonder if she was okay. He pulled out his cell phone and gave her a call as he walked toward the garage elevator.

"Hey, how you doing?" he asked - trying to sound as cheery as he had felt before his encounter with the 300.

"I'm great, aside from being tired." She replied. "Why the call?"

He didn't want to make her worry. He felt it would be best to keep the incident to himself, at least for now. "Oh, just wanted to tell you I had a wonderful evening. How about dinner tonight? Some place quiet?"

"I'd like that. Sounds great. And," she paused. "I had a wonderful time as well. Too bad you lost the race." She chuckled.

"Well, we'll talk about a rematch tonight. Catch you later." Leif added before ending the call.

***

Leif was glad they were able to get a quiet table in a back corner of the quaint Italian restaurant. He wasn't his usual self tonight. He spent the entire day pouring over the big chase of this morning. Part of his brain told him it was just some random incident with a crazy driver. But a warning bell kept going off in his head about the Eighteenth. He remembered the warnings he received from Georgeo and the details his parents told him about his aunt Angela's disappearance. If this was them, he should take Carina's hand and leave - get out of town and disappear without a trail. Georgeo would help. If it wasn't the Eighteenth he was just being paranoid - letting himself get all worked up for no reason.

He hid behind the dinner menu, trying to decipher the fancy Italian words while trying to hide his composure from Carina. *What the heck is Filetto di Manzo?* He hoped it was the steak in the picture next to the entry.

"What are you having?" Carina asked while trying not to hide behind the menu.

"Steak, I think."

"Really? Where did you see that?"

"The File to die Man Zoo."

Carina couldn't help but laugh. "Not up on your Italian, eh?" She added. "I'm aiming for the Conchiglie de Mare," she pronounced with a perfect Italian accent.

Leif looked up over his menu. "I'm impressed." He looked around nervously. "You've been holding out on me. Where did you pick up the Italian?"

"Oh, it was a hot summer fling a few years back." She joked.

"What?" Leif was totally caught off guard - not knowing if it was a joke or not.

Carina put her menu down and focused intently on Leif. "What's going on? You're not you tonight."

He put his menu down and gave the room another look. The closest patrons were at least three tables away and the soft music would help to cover their conversation. He leaned closer, reached across the table, and held her hand.

Carina raised her eyebrows. "Little soon for a proposal, isn't it?"

"What do you know about the Eighteenth?" Leif asked just above a whisper.

"Whew! You had me worried there for a minute." She gave the room a quick scan and replied in a softer voice. "Just what I learned from my parents and Uncle Georgeo."

"Something happened this morning." Leif paused then recalled the entire incident with the black Chrysler 300.

"Sounds like a guy who just wanted to show off his car against yours." She put on her best 'I'm not worried' face. "I think you're reading too much into it."

"Yeah. I guess you're right. But,…"

"What?"

"If it IS something. Maybe we should just be extra careful for a while." He gave her hand a squeeze. "You're," he paused while looking for the right words. "I care about you - about us. I just don't want anything to happen…"

Carina smiled, leaned over the table, and gave Leif a kiss.

Almost blushing from the kiss, Leif was a bundle of mixed feelings. He cared so much for Carina. She was right - he was just being overly cautious.

The waiter had been waiting at a distance for the right opportunity and decided to approach as he saw Carina sit back in her seat. Knowing humor usually resulted in a better tip he added, "Ah, a kiss usually means appetizers are next, yes?"

***

The black Chrysler 300 was parked in the shade next to the university boat house on Lake Washington. The driver stood outside and leaned against the hood of the car while tapping on his smartphone. A dark green Jeep Rubicon slowly pulled up next to the car. The smoked driver side window on the Jeep lowered, showing Matt was at the wheel.

"What were you thinking?" Matt asked the 300 driver.

The driver continued to tap and slide his fingers on his smartphone while replying back. "It was nothing man. He got a little spooked so I had some fun with him."

"Deek, you were supposed to be invisible. Just keep a tail on him. Not show him what your wheels looked like."

"It's all good man." Deek didn't look up from his phone. "I'll flip to ma non-descript vehicle for the next shift."

Matt stepped out of the Jeep, grabbed the phone out of the Deek's hands, and heaved it into the lake.

"Hey man! What cha doing? You didn't have…"

Matt grabbed the driver by the top of his jacket, under his throat, and pushed him up against the car, almost lifting him up off the parking lot. "Now you listen to me and you look at me when I'm speaking to you."

Deek had no choice but to stare into Matt's angry eyes. "Man, It was nothin."

Matt tightened his grip and lifted a little more. "I gave you a job to do and I told you exactly how to do it. WE don't tolerate stupidity." He paused to make sure his words sank in. "Am I clear?"

"Yeah. Clear," Deek choked out.

Matt released his grip and climbed back into the Jeep. "Go get your phone and don't come back to work until you can deliver it to me.

"What?" the driver exclaimed. "That's impossible."

"Are you telling me you can't do what you're told?" Matt asked coldly.

Deek thought for a few seconds before responding. "No sir. I'll take care of it."

"Good. We can't have loose ends or data devices out in the wild. If I don't see you Monday, you're a loose end." Matt raised his window and drove off, leaving the befuddled driver alone in the parking lot.

NINE - FALLING

Air born apart. Held together by love.
Two hearts in the air.
Eternal hearts. Bonded from above.
We are one. We are here.
Forever in love. Forever to fly.
In gray or in blue.
Forever in love. Together we fly.
(Vows of Avitorian Love)

Leif was surprised to receive the text message from Jewels, asking him to meet her at the coffee shop across the street from the office. Through the elevator ride and the walk across the street, he was formulating his responses to Jewels continued advances. He lost count of the number of times her innuendos were cast his way while working. He would've figured it as a game for her if it wasn't for the fact he was the only one receiving so much attention from her. His usual response was laughter followed by, "You crack me up, Jewels." His planned defenses disappeared as soon as he saw her sitting with an older red haired lady, engaged in deep conversation. Jewels didn't even notice him as he walked up to the table with his mug of freshly brewed vanilla latte. She was busily talking while the red haired lady was the first to notice Leif's approach.

He smiled at the lady and spoke up to get Jewels attention. "What? No colorful invitation for wine and dinner at your place tonight?"

Jewels stopped mid-sentence. "Leif! So good to see you. Grab a seat. I want to introduce you to the new physics professor at University of Washington., Dr. Corellis."

Leif shook the doctor's hand and sat down. It was a warm and firm handshake, not quite like a manly shake, but it exuded confidence and determination. She made direct eye contact with a look of friendly interest, much like the same look he got from Jewels every morning at the office. Leif started to give a greeting, but was quickly interrupted by the doctor.

"Jewels has told me a lot about you, Leif. She says you have the best grasp of physics and math of any programmer at Amzoft."

"She did?" He looked at Jewels as she placed her chin on the top of her hands and batted her eyelids at him. He laughed and responded, "Well, I enjoy doing it and I've always been good at the math. I'm just a humble geek."

"What type of math are you working on?" Dr. Corellis asked.

Leif took a sip of coffee while deciding how technical he should get with a physics professor. She was sure to find flaws with his calculations if he got into the details. Such is the bane of any programmer. Always afraid someone else would know a better algorithm. He decided to provide an overview. "I developed a physics engine which the rest of the development team uses for object movement. Since our core product is a massive, multi-player, video game based in space, we deal with having to calculate movements of planetary bodies, asteroids, spaceships, and projectiles in a spacial 3D environment. I provide an A.P.I., an application programming interface, for calculating those movements based on mass, velocity, and near-by gravitational forces." He looked at the doctor, expecting to see the normal glazed over blank stare he received whenever he provided details on what he does for work. Instead, he was met with her deep, intensive look of understanding and interest.

"How involved are your calculations for the near-field gravitational forces?" she asked. "What distances are we talking about?"

"Um, well, solar system wide."

"Mass and density?"

"I calculate mass only. I wanted to include density types. The core materials and their mass, but the project managers felt it would be too in-depth and not really necessary for the game environment. You see, gamers like to think they're in a complex and real-world type environment. But what they really want, is to not think about effects on their trajectory when they're trying to blow up the spaceship, or asteroid in front of them."

Dr. Corellis continued to stare at Leif for an uncomfortable few seconds. She finally responded. "We could use those talents at the astrophysics lab. I have some great programmers and some great mathematicians, but what I could use is someone who can do both."

"Um, Doctor. I appreciate your offer, but I already have a job and I really don't have any plans to find another." He looked over at Jewels who just smiled and gave him a wink.

Dr. Corellis laughed. "It's not a job offer, Leif. You'll still continue working for Amzoft. I know the board members. I'll provide interns and fresh programmers from my physics classes in exchange for your services to the university. In exchange, Amzoft gets to say they provide the most realistic space flight environment for their gamers due to their relationship and knowledge exchange with the University of Washington's Astrophysics Lab, and you'll get to add those core material density calculations to your programming engine for our use."

This was an unexpected turn of events for Leif. He came for coffee and ended up becoming a programmer for the UW astrophysics department. "Wow. It sounds like it's all arranged." He wasn't sure if he was comfortable with the offer. "Do I have a choice?"

"I'm sorry Leif. I assumed you would want to jump at the opportunity. Am I wrong?"

Now he felt bad for bringing it up. “Well, I guess working on real science instead of a game would be a great opportunity.” He paused. “Sounds like a good deal.”

“Awesome. We’d like to bring you in and get you oriented next week. But, before that, we’re hosting a private astronomy party at the observatory tonight. It’s out past the Cascades, but we would love to have you visit, and bring a guest.”

Jewels chimed in, “Oh, I finally get to meet the girl in the drawing?”

“I suppose so.” Leif answered.

***

The long drive from Seattle to the observatory was a mixed blessing. It was tough for Leif to be in the car for that long, being pinned to the earth, subject to its gravity and wrapped inside a steel container. Although, the last half hour of the tight mountain curves, with only the Audi’s headlamps to lead the way up the mountain side, was exciting. The time with Carina was great for reminiscing about their days at school and sharing their childhood memories. Leif took the opportunity to tell her about his aunt Angela’s disappearance before he was born. There was a long uncomfortable silence after that, followed by a discussion about The Eighteenth and if they were still a threat. They both shared some of the wisdom learned from Georgeo, about being discrete in their conversations and actions, especially when flying. She started to tell him about her parent’s fear of flying, but she found it too hard to talk about, even with Leif. He tried to diffuse the tension, recounting his experience with his own mom. He could feel Carina relax as he continued to explain. She felt better and smiled as they pulled into the parking lot of the observatory.

"That was a long drive," she said, while stepping out of the car and stretching. She subconsciously scanned the area to see if anyone was within listening range. There was a half dozen vehicles, but she didn't detect any radiating energy outside the observatory, aside from a possible family of raccoons nearby. She lowered her voice and added, "I bet we could've been here in fifteen minutes."

"I agree, but it would've been a little tough explaining the lack of a car."

Carina giggled. "And descending out of the night sky." She looked up and took pause at the incredible clarity of the stars.

Leif handed Carina her coat, helped her put it on, and took her hand while gazing up at the stars. "Tempting, isn't it?"

Carina responded with a squeeze of his hand as the sound of an opening door came from the observatory. Someone with a red lens flashlight walked toward them.

"Hey guys." It was Jewels voice. "The party is inside." She stopped and directed the red light along a path they could follow.

"This is Jewels." Leif introduced her to Carina as they got closer. He felt the stress of being there with Carina and Jewels at the same time. He hoped Jewels would refrain from any sly propositions while Carina was there. That would be difficult to explain.

Inside the observatory, Leif and Carina were greeted by shadows of strangers bathed in red light, standing around several tables of hors d'oeuvres and drinks. Jewels handed a glass of Champagne to each of them. She stepped to the side of Carina and quietly stated, "You look just like your picture, only a little older."

"My picture?"

"He hasn't shown you the drawing?" Jewels asked while giving Leif a look of surprise.

Leif was thankful for the red lights as he felt his cheeks glowing with embarrassment. Only a few minutes in the door and Jewels has started up the drama already. Looking at Carina he added, "Um, I'll explain later."

Carina smiled coyly back at Leif.

"The big show is upstairs," said Jewels as she pointed to the spiral stairs leading up to an entryway into the main observatory.

They heard a female observatory guide speaking as they entered the observatory. "Please stand to the side of the dome as we move the scope to our next target, the Orion Nebula."

The room was bathed in a dim red glow, making it hard to see anything except the massive structure of the telescope and the metal roof of the observatory dome. The curved roof rotated slowly as the telescope tracked the slotted opening to the night sky. The guide stopped the rotation of the dome with a hand-held control. She released the control box and let it swing back on its tethered spring next to the telescope. Reaching for her jacket pocket, she stepped toward the dome opening and pointed a green laser beam into the sky.

Leif and Carina joined the twenty or so observers as they gazed out at the stars in the distance.

The guide continued, "The hourglass of Orion is one of the largest constellations in the late fall and winter night skies." She moved the green beam along the outlines of the shape, making it easy for everyone to see how large it really was. There were gasps and muffled discussions from the observers in the room.

"Amazing, isn't it?" Dr. Corellis whispered from behind Leif and Carina.

Leif responded while turning around. "Doctor. Thank you for inviting us to this. The telescope is amazing."

"Yes, it is," the doctor replied. "It's one of my favorite parts of being a physics professor. Learning how our physical universe is a part of our own physical essence." She looked past Leif to the stars in the distance as the guide continued to describe the night sky to her enraptured audience. "From the most minute particles of the atom to the immense structure of the galaxies, we're all entwined with a great design." Doctor Corellis paused while contemplating the view. "Ever hear of Fibonacci?" she asked.

"Of course," Leif answered. "I use his number sequence for determining the curvature of the spiral arms of galaxies in our game.

"Excellent. You're going to fit in nicely with our group of programmers." She paused and looked over at Carina. "And this must be the object of Leif's admiration, Carina." She reached out and patted Carina's shoulder.

Carina smiled, nodded, looked at Leif, and gently embraced his arm.

"The girl in the picture." Jewels added.

Leif was glad the domed room was so dark or Jewels might have noticed his blush, and look of irritation.

Dr. Corellis interrupted the difficult moment. "Would you like to actually view the Orion Nebula?"

"Absolutely." Leif replied.

"Come this way." The doctor turned and headed toward a set of metal steps attached to the superstructure of the telescope. The observatory guide continued speaking in the background, describing the various features of the Orion Nebula with her laser.

"Here." Dr. Corellis guided Leif up the steps and she showed him the eyepiece of the scope. "Don't put your eye directly on the lens. Let your eyebrow barely touch the rubber cup around the lens."

Leif looked into the opening, barely touching the circular rubber surrounding the lens. It took a moment for his eye to adjust to the view and the magnification of the lens. "It looks like a greenish cloud. Kind of like a bird's wings." He reached out to take Carina's hand and guided her up to the eyepiece. "I thought it would have more colors," he added while letting Carina look.

"Most of the pictures you see in the magazines and on the web were taken with color filters on the lens. These filters help to enhance the details of the nebula. There are various gases in the nebula that respond differently depending on what filter is being used. Currently, you're looking through what's called an O3 filter attached to the lens. This enhances the view of the oxygen atoms contained in the gas of the nebula and gives it the green tint."

"Wow." Carina replied after taking a look.

Jewels next took a look through the scope, followed by Dr. Corellis.

Leif and Dr. Corellis descended the stairs together, followed by Jewels and Carina. The doctor gazed out past the end of the telescope toward the night sky and asked, “Did you know that the ancient Egyptians were the fore-bearers of the science of astronomy?”

“I’ve heard that.” Leif added. “Something with the position of the pyramids, right?”

“Right, and they provided us with the calendar days of the year based on the movement of the stars in the sky. This is how they were able to predict the annual flooding of the Nile river. Many lives were saved by their ability to use the position of the stars.”

Leif felt a chill as Carina reached out to him and grabbed ahold of his arm. He remembered a discussion he had with uncle Georgeo, about The Eighteenth of Ahmose, and how they originated with the ancient Egyptians. They used Avitorians for deriving the measurements of the pyramids. He then reasoned he was just being overly suspicious. *Of course any study of astronomy and astrophysics would include a history of the Egyptians.* He noticed Dr. Corellis was intently looking for a response from him as he squeezed Carina’s hand on his arm. “I remember from school history they were really good at math and geometry. Someday I’d like to visit the pyramids.”

Dr. Corellis smiled and turned to direct the line of observers up the metal stairs.

“Wasn’t that amazing?” Jewels stepped off the stairs and bumped into Leif while misjudging where the stairs ended and the floor began. Leif reactively reached out and steadied Jewels with his hand on her hip. She regained her balance and paused for a moment to enjoy the closeness.

"Humm, thank you," she whispered. Leif quickly withdrew his hand and put his arm around Carina's shoulders. Jewels turned toward the back of the line. "What's next doctor?"

For the next few hours they repeated the process of getting in line, going up the stairs, and exclaiming in awe while gazing at the next magnificent object in the night sky. Pleiades, the Veil Nebula, Pollux, and various galaxies and nebulas filled the eyepiece. Leif didn't mind that Carina had latched onto his arm for most of the evening. He no longer cared about the images in the telescope. His entire focus was on Carina, how she smelled, her warmth when she held onto his arm. He watched her face intently as she described what she had seen through the telescope lens. Whenever Jewels got close, Carina's grip on his arm would get tighter. She was sending a signal to both Jewels and Leif. He enjoyed the attention and the look on Jewels face.

***

Leif had a difficult time with staying focused on the road back to Seattle. The star filled sky hovered between the massive evergreen trees, above the winding freeway through the Cascades, like a sparkly ribbon close enough to reach up and touch. Carina had fallen asleep in the passenger seat. Leif would sneak a glance at her peaceful face in the yellow glow of a passing lamp post and the occasional passing headlights. She seemed to be smiling slightly. *Must be dreaming of me,* Leif thought and chuckled to himself.

Carina shifted in her seat and opened her eyes. She tugged on one of her earlobes for the change in air pressure while yawning, and she sat up. "Where are we?"

"Good morning sleepy head," Leif responded. "We just passed North Bend. It's two in the morning and we're about an hour away from Seattle. I'm glad it's Saturday."

Carina was silent for a few minutes while admiring the view of the night sky, the evergreens, and the light dusting of snow. "So, what is this drawing I keep hearing about?" She asked.

Leif chuckled nervously. "Um, well. I drew a pencil drawing of your face, from when I knew you in school. Jewels saw me working on it one day and she asked about it."

"You drew a picture of me from school?"

"Yeah." Leif's heart almost skipped a beat from the moment of silence. He finally responded. "I drew it from memory."

"You drew my face from memory, from when we were in school?"

Leif glanced over at her and tried not to be too distracted from his driving. Her eyes gazed directly at him, seeking answers. He was exposing his inner soul and thinking - and his desire to love the girl he met in school. He loved her so much, he could remember every line and curve of her face, and draw it out on paper, many years after seeing her. He felt so exposed to her gaze. "Yeah. I did," was all he could muster.

She continued gazing at him while he drove. She visually traced the shape of his face, his eyes, and his lips. He would gaze back for a few seconds and smile while trying not to forget he was driving. "What?" he asked.

"Can we go flying?"

"Now? Two a.m. in the morning, in November? It's going to be cold."

"I don't care," she added. "I need to be in the air, with you."

Leif pulled off the freeway at the next opportunity and drove into the Tiger Mountain State Forest. He was familiar with the roads since he often had gone hiking and fishing there with his father. He picked a dirt road that he knew would dead end part of the way up the mountain and would be surrounded by massive evergreens, shielding them from any curious onlookers.

As soon as they were both out of the car and had donned their coats, Carina grabbed Leif's hand and launched up into the cold, night air. They cleared the trees and she headed for a small wisp of clouds hovering near the top of the mountain. The moon had crested the Cascades off to the East and was lighting up the sprinkling of clouds as they formed along the mountain tops, as moist air would rise from the forests below and gather in the cold, like a group of wolves huddling against the weather.

Carina pulled Leif along into the cloud and she stopped as they were surrounded by the foggy mist. She grabbed him with both arms and pulled him close enough to see his face in the haze of the cloud. He couldn't help but laugh at her exuberance of wanting to fly and to be in the cloud.

"Okay. We're here now. You and me." Leif whispered.

"What did you draw first?" Carina asked.

Leif placed his hands gently on each side of Carina's face and gazed deeply into her eyes. He slowly spun around, twirling both of them like a cork screw up through the cloud until their heads cleared the top. The stars, and moon, reflected a soft glow upon them. Their faces were damp from the moisture of the clouds. Leif finally answered, “Your eyes. I drew your eyes first. Deep and beautiful as they are and I didn’t have to correct any errors as I drew them. As perfect as they are, my drawing could not even come close to what I’m seeing right now.”

Carina’s eyes started to tear up as she pulled him closer to her. “Oh, Leif.” She paused and then gently kissed him. She gazed into his eyes and added, “I have fallen fully, and hopelessly, in love with you.”

Leif smiled, caressed her face, and added. “Carina, I have been in love with you since the day we met.”

TEN - UNCERTAINTY

The device, although bulky and power hungry, performed well during testing. We were able to utilize it for capturing a specimen. We feel the cooler night air during the capture contributed to the success. A direct correlation between lower atmospheric temperature and induced beam temperature affects the efficiency of the beam at greater distances. Higher atmospheric temperatures require shorter distances for effectiveness. This is the same physics at work as when an aircraft becomes more efficient in colder temperatures. (Field science notes from Dr. Corellis from specimen capture event on September 19th, 1995.)

Matt stared at the wet phone in the sealed plastic bag on his desk. It's owner, dressed in his best black suit, thin black tie, neatly trimmed beard, and yellow lens aviator glasses, stood at the front of the desk, nervously awaiting a response.

"I knew you had it in you Deek. You just had to extend a little effort and realize how important it is to follow instructions, no matter what." Matt stated while throwing the bagged phone in a brown plastic tub behind his chair. A yellow sticky note with "Destroy" scribbled in black marker ink was on the front of the tub. "Call your crew. We need a pick up, as soon as possible." Matt pulled a letter size manila envelope from the top drawer of his desk and slid it toward the front of the desk. "I'll be going with you. This has to be clean and pristine."

Deek opened the envelope and removed two stacks of hundred dollar bills and a photograph. "Not what I expected. I thought you were going for the boy."

Dr. Suzanne Corellis spoke up from the other side of the lab. "I plan to use him. The girl we use for motivation, if it comes to that." She walked up beside Deek and placed a strange looking weapon on Matt's desk. It almost looked like a double barrel shot gun, except for the extra wide dual tubes, which were flared slightly on the business end. Small tubing was coiled around the back half of each barrel and extended to a black, round, cylinder extending below a four inch wide shoulder butt. Two finger width cables exited from the bottom front of the shoulder butt and entered the back of a sliding trigger, mounted below and in the middle of the two barrels. A black hand grip hung below the barrels, closer to the front of the weapon.

"Is that what I think it is?" Deek asked.

Matt grabbed the black hand grip with his left hand and hefted the bulk of the weapon up to his right shoulder. He slid two fingers into the sliding trigger and flipped a switch above it with his right thumb.

"Matt!" Dr. Corellis uttered in surprise. "Wha…"

Multiple sounds emanated from the device. A low, lingering hum, and a solid tone rose up to a high pitch and peaked out slightly above normal hearing. Matt swung the weapon around and pointed the barrels at Deek.

"Hey, man! I thought we were cool." Deek stepped backward, away from the desk.

"Hold still!" Matt calmly stated while pulling the sliding trigger back.

Deek stared down into the barrels, pointed at his upper chest. He noticed the ends of the barrels held small, oblong, dish shaped antennas. He felt relief with the realization that projectiles would not be blasted into his chest. The high pitch tone of charged capacitors dropped to a gyrating sound of electricity jumping between circuits. He felt his chest become warm and then increasingly hot to the point where he thought his clothing had caught fire. "Ouooo. Hey!" he yelped and instinctively stepped aside from the invisible beam from the weapon. He patted his chest and looked at his tie to see if it was on fire.

"You're okay Deek." Matt chuckled while shutting down the gun. "Just a little cooked." He examined the weapon and bounced it in his hands a couple times. "This is a lot lighter than the last model."

"Well, I guess we don't have to test it now," Dr. Corellis added while shaking her head and grinning at Matt.

***

Leif sat staring at the monitors on his work desk, but he really didn't see anything on the displays. He was so energized from spending the weekend with Carina. The smell of her perfume still lingered on his clothes from her hugs while flying most of the night. Sleep was not even a consideration after dropping her off at her condo. The clock on his monitor read 6:00 a.m., he couldn't focus on any programming. He grabbed his mobile phone typed out a message to Carina:

Great weekend. Can't sleep. At work. Love you.

He paused a few seconds, wondering if it was too early to send the message. She would still be sleeping, especially after getting home at two in the morning.

"Wow. You're in early for a Monday." Leif was startled as Jewels voice came from his cubicle entrance.

He pressed the 'Send' button before turning around. "Yeah. I couldn't sleep and I have some programming to wrap up before I leave for the university."

Jewels chuckled. "I can tell." She nodded at his computer displays, the screen saver was active and showing images from the Hubble telescope.

Leif turned to look at his monitors then laughed. "Okay, I guess I'm just a little distracted."

"She's cute - your girlfriend, Carina. How serious is it?"

"It's headed in the right direction." He answered with a hint if irritation. "You don't give up, do you?"

Jewels smiled. "Some goals are worth pursuing, and I've learned that persistence pays off."

"Even if the goals are out of reach?" He didn't return the smile, hoping she would back off."

"Things change. People change." Jewels paused. Her smile changed to a smirk and she added, "But, I understand. It's all fresh for you. I'm glad you're happy. You just be sure to let me know when you're not." She turned and walked off.

Leif shook his head in frustration and checked his phone. There were no new messages. He tapped the spacebar on his computer keyboard and entered his password. The displays revealed the lines of code he previously ignored. "I got this," he reminded himself and he dove into his programming.

***

The phone vibrated on the night stand next to Carina's bed. Normally, she would sleep so soundly that she wouldn't notice it. However, she mentally floated between dreaming and consciousness. The night spent flying with Leaf had been incredible, if only the images of it could last forever, just floating through the clouds next to Mt. Rainer. She wanted to remain there, in his arms, in his kiss, hovering in the moonlight. While trying to hold on to Leif and the clouds she knew in her dream her phone had vibrated. Part of her wanted to stay in the clouds, to remain in Leif's arms, but another part of her wanted to check to see if her phone held a message from him. She reluctantly let her dream slip and blindly reached for the phone. She plopped the phone on the side of the bed, tilted the screen toward her face, and slowly opened one eye to read the screen. The brightness of the screen was overwhelming and she had to blink a few times before she was able to focus on the text message. She saw it was from Leif and she opened both eyes to read.

Great weekend. Can't sleep. At work. Love you.

She smiled at the message and placed the phone over on its face to kill the brightness of the light. Closing her eyes, she hoped to find the dream again and embrace the images of the night before, but instantly her mind snapped awake. A clear and distinct sound captured her attention. The scratch of wood against concrete was unmistakable. It was the sound of her painting easel shifting ever so slightly across the floor. Her heart skipped a beat as she listened intently for any further noise. She knew exactly where the easel was. There was no reason for it to move on its own. She reached out with her senses. Her heart raced as she felt the flowing energy of three distinct life forces in her condo. Two downstairs and one slowly coming up the stairs to her loft. She quietly took a deep breath and slowly blew it out to try and calm her heart.

The entity on the stairs reached the top and slowly crept toward her bed. She felt the obvious intent. Fighting back the fear in the pit of her stomach she let him edge closer to her bed and waited for the moment to arrive. As she felt him center his energy for the attack, she sprang into action. Carina took hold of her blankets and in the same instant flew to the ceiling, hovered and dropped the heavy fabric, entangling the surprised assailant.

The quiet morning erupted into pandemonium and chaos as the assailant misjudged the movement and dove for the now empty bed. Carina flew to the peak of her gabled ceiling and dropped her full weight onto the back of the man face down on her bed. His shout turned to a scream of pain as his ribs cracked from Carina's weight. The wooden frame of the bed split apart, sending her phone to the floor, followed by the bounce of a heavy metal object. Carina tumbled sideways and rolled off the bed. She instinctively reached out and grabbed her phone and what she thought was a gun. Fumbling with the device she flew back up to the ceiling and quickly located the grip and trigger. Instead of a gun barrel, it had a stubby injector with a small cylinder underneath.

"Up now! I'll cover!" came the shout from the studio below.

Carina decided her best option was to get out of the condo as quickly as possible. The closest windows were at the top of the vaulted ceiling of the studio. She flew to the railing of the loft and quickly glanced at the men below. She saw the point man began moving up the stairway. Both were wearing black, but without any insignia usually worn by the police. The laser sights of their weapons swept the room as they methodically covered and moved up the stairs.

"Twelve high!" shouted the lead as he pointed at her.

A high pitched hum emanated from something the man below was holding. Carina knew she needed to get out quickly. She flew past the rail and toward the windows. They were all closed.

"Matt, windows!" the man on the stairs shouted. He turned and bounded back down to the studio.

Carina let go of the injector gun, letting it bounce off the studio wall to the floor below. She grabbed the frame surrounding one of the windows and reached for a lever lock at the top of the window frame. It had a large metal circle on the crank end that allowed operation from below with a pole. Carina's adrenaline was raging. She ripped the entire lever lock off the frame. She pulled at the window, flipping it open toward her, but the gap was too narrow. She stuffed her cell phone into a pocket and gripped the top of the window with both hands, pulling violently and jerking it at different angles to try and rip it from the hinges. "Come on!" she shouted.

Matt pulled the beam rifle up to his shoulder, focused on the hovering Carina, and pulled the trigger.

Even though the air rushing through the window was cold, Carina felt an intense heat in her back. Her weight grew heavy as she felt her ability to hover slip from her control. She held tightly to the window frame, but she started to fall backward. She couldn't understand why. The window popped from its hinges as she fell toward the floor. The intense heat stopped and Carina felt her power return. She stopped in mid-air, turned, and flung the broken window toward the men below.

The two men jumped away from the flying window and let it crash to the floor. Glass shards exploded across the concrete floor at their feet. Matt quickly refocused the beam on Carina as she flew toward the opening where the window used to be.

She felt the intense heat hit her again as she reached out to escape. "Aaaahg!" she screamed as she once again fell backward.

Matt kept the nozzle of the rifle aimed at Carina. He had given her a full blast of the beam at the start and then backed it off to keep her from falling full force onto the floor of the studio. “The injector!” Matt barked.

“Got it.” The assailant jumped toward her, trying to guess where she would land.

Matt backed off the power of the beam and stopped Carina’s descent several feet above the floor.

She righted herself with her feet down and turned to face the men. She swung out with a round house kick with her right leg, but was not close enough to make contact. “Who are you? What do you want!?” Carina screamed as her momentum spun her around.

“Now!” Matt calmly stated as he pulled the trigger to full power on the rifle.

Carina squealed in pain as the intense heat surged through every fiber of her body. She pulled her knees to her chest as she dropped fully to the floor. The impact knocked the wind out of her. She gasped for air and she felt a stab of sharpness to the side of her neck. She felt a booted foot roll her onto her back. The two men stared at her as she felt the drug of the injected narcotic take effect.

“Well, Deek, that was exciting.” Matt exclaimed as he removed the knitted hood that obscured his face.

Deek pulled off his hood and flipped on the lights to the studio. “I think she messed up Isaac,” he stated as he bounded up the stairs.

Matt looked around the floor of the studio. He then turned his attention to Carina and searched her pockets. He pulled out her cell phone.

Deek reached the bed in the loft and threw the covers off their companion. Isaac laid lifeless, stomach down, across the bed. Deek placed his hand on Isaac's neck, searching for a pulse. "His pulse is weak and he's out."

"Roger." Matt replied while examining Carina's phone. He grabbed a hand mic to a walkie-talkie attached to the inside of his black jacket and keyed it. "Package is ready. Bring in clean-up, and we have a man down." Setting his focus back on the cell phone, he found the icon for text messaging and selected it. The last message from Leif appeared. "Awe. Isn't that cute." He keyed in:

Me too. Gonna chill for the day.

He pressed the send button as a group of people entered the studio.

***

The local coffee shop was packed, but Leif didn't care. The longer the line, the longer he would get to stay away from his desk. He was having difficulty staying focused on his programming, either from the lack of sleep, the distraction of Carina and her last text message, or a combination of both. He spent the last few hours wondering about the intent of her message. It sounded a little distant from her normal self, like she was distracted. Or maybe she wasn't feeling well, due to the lack of sleep. Late night flying, combined with the colder weather, can be tiring. *Maybe I'm over thinking this.* He decided to finally reply.

I understand. See you tomorrow.

He pressed the send button and stuffed the phone into his pocket.

"So, um, are you in line?" a voice from behind him asked.

Leif suddenly realized the line had moved up without him, leaving a significant gap between him and the person in front of him. "Uh, sorry," Leif replied. He turned to look at the person behind him. "Oh, Dr. Corellis. I didn't realize you were here." He was surprised. "You come all the way from the university to get coffee here?" He smiled to break the tension he was feeling, wondering why she was there.

"I had a meeting with the CEO this morning. We're arranging for more collaboration between the university and Amzoft."

"You met with the CEO of Amzoft? Wow, I'm impressed," Leif added while moving up in the line.

"Well, I did have to get his signature on your transfer papers. You all ready for tomorrow?"

"Absolutely," he nervously replied.

Dr. Corellis laughed. "You don't sound too convincing." She patted him on the shoulder. "It will be great. You'll love the computer. It's the fastest calculator in Washington State."

"Nice. I'm looking forward to it."

Leif stepped up to the counter and placed his order. He felt awkward standing next to Dr. Corellis while waiting for his coffee. Wanting to look occupied, he pulled out his phone and checked for new text messages and emails. He was disappointed there were only a few work emails.

"Leif…" Dr. Corellis was interrupted by her vibrating phone. "Yes?" she answered while walking to a far corner of the coffee shop.

Leif continued to mess with his phone while watching the doctor from the corner of his eye. He couldn't hear the conversation over the noise of the customers and the baristas making espresso. The doctor glanced up at him a couple times during her conversation, but would quickly look away. He wasn't sure if he was a topic in the conversation or if she was just checking for her coffee. Based on her expressions he hoped he wasn't part of the conversation. She didn't look happy. His drink order came up quickly followed by the doctor's. He held up her drink for her to see and she signaled him over.

She muted the phone as he got close. "Thanks Leif. Something came up at the lab that I have to deal with, but I'll see you tomorrow."

"Sure thing. Bye," Leif added and headed for the door. The doctor waited a few seconds before getting back to her call.

Leif paused outside the door of the coffee shop and checked his phone for new messages - there were none. Discouraged, he gazed up at the Amzoft logo on the building across the street. He had mixed emotions about his transfer to the university, he worried about Carina's sparse messages, there was a bunch of programming to complete by end of the day, and he felt there was something a little odd about Dr. Corellis. *I'm being paranoid, over-thinking it, and I'm stressed.* He took a deep breath, blew it out slowly, then headed for the building. "I can do this," he mumbled as he crossed the street.

***

It was after 9 p.m. by the time Leif drove out of the Amzoft parking garage. He had a major struggle with staying focused on his programming tasks during the day, and the only way he could get through it was to turn his phone off and stick it in his laptop bag. Since Carina wanted to chill for the day he figured he would quit thinking about her and let her chill. But now, it was late, and not hearing from her was killing him. He pulled up to a red light and took advantage of the time to pull out his phone and turn it on. The light turned green by the time the phone booted up and received a signal. Leif glanced in the rear view mirror while hitting the gas pedal. *Good, no cops to see me checking my text messages.* While dividing his attention between the phone and his driving, he checked for new messages. By the time he reached the freeway entry ramp he saw there was one new message, but it was from Jewels, wishing him good luck on the new project tomorrow. He tossed the phone onto the passenger seat, disappointed there was nothing new from Carina.

Once on the freeway, Leif floored the gas pedal until the car hit ninety, passing several cars in the process. He checked the rear-view mirror again to be sure he didn't attract any attention of the local law enforcement. Realizing his emotions were affecting his driving, he backed off the gas and let the car drift back down to the speed limit. *I've got it bad.* Leif chuckled at himself. He couldn't think straight, his stomach was in knots, and he was letting himself get worked up over a lack of text messages in less than a full day. "Wow," he said out loud.

Leif grabbed his phone off the seat and scrolled through the screens to a weather application. The map showed the usual cloud cover for this time of year. *Can't sleep. Might as well go flying.* He turned off on the next freeway exit, and got back on, heading the opposite direction. After checking all the mirrors, he kicked the car up to just barely under eighty. He figured as long as he wasn't a full fifteen miles per hour over the speed limit he wouldn't get the added 'reckless driving' citation if he got caught. The drive to Tiger Mountain didn't take very long, at least it didn't seem like it with the stereo blaring and the wind rushing in through the sunroof at seventy-nine miles per hour. Leif pulled off the freeway and headed for his favorite 'hidden' dirt road toward the top of the mountain. Instead of taking the road all the way to the summit he turned off onto a forestry service road which came to a dead end.

When Leif turned off the car he was plunged into total darkness. He stood beside the car for a quiet fifteen minutes to let his eyes adjust to the darkness. As he stood there his inner senses came alive to the sensations from the trees, plants, and animals surrounding him. He smiled as he sensed a few rabbits huddled together in the brush, not more than twenty feet away. His sensing of the flow of energy was usually suppressed due to the overload of electricity flowing through practically everything in the city and neighborhoods. The longer he stood still quietly, the more he was able to detect, and at greater distances. He could sense the electricity flowing into the towers at the peak of the mountain. There was someone up there, no doubt working in one of the structures, but far enough away that he could remain out of sight if the person came outside. Leif felt a small pang of discomfort in the pit of his stomach. He had grown accustomed to the flow of energy in Carina as she flew with him, her unique signature. She wasn't there with him and he felt the emptiness in his heart.

The clouds hovered just above the tips of the evergreens. Leif grabbed his coat from the back seat of the car. The dome light of the car lit up the forest around him and he noticed a set of coyote eyes gazing from a safe distance. He closed the door, swung on his coat, and lifted off the ground while still stuffing his arms into the sleeves. He slowly navigated through the branches and then hovered for a few minutes at the top of the trees. A slight red glow in the clouds could be seen from the radio tower at the summit. The tower was buried in clouds and would be a flight hazard if Leif wasn't careful. He could detect the height of the tower from the electricity flowing through it and the pulsing of signals emanating from the antennas at the top.

Leif bounded up into the clouds. Aside from the faint red glow in one direction Leif couldn't see anything else. He was surrounded by thick clouds heavy with moisture. It didn't take long for his hair and face to get soaked. Water dripped from his ears, nose, and chin as he continued to fly straight up through the clouds. By the time he finally reached the top of the clouds he was thoroughly soaked, but he didn't care. The cold and the wetness helped to numb his loneliness. He stopped above the cloud tops and slowly twirled around to take in the scenery. A half-moon hung over the horizon to the West with a thick blanket of city lit cotton just below it. Another layer of wispy clouds raced higher up in the night sky, obscuring the stars, creating a tunnel of reflected moon and city lights between the two cloud layers. Mt. Rainer was nowhere to be seen. It was hidden in the clouds, behind an approaching wall of rain from the south. The snow on the Cascades to the east still showed a slight glimmer of reflected moonlight with the peaks enshrouded in lenticular clouds. It was a once in a lifetime view, one that he would've liked to share with Carina. *I'll tell her tomorrow, what she missed.* He tried to put off the emptiness and to reflect on the beauty of the night.

ELEVEN - UNIVERSITY

"For our next agenda item, our newly appointed Director of the Nuclear Particle and Astrophysics facility, Dr. Suzanne Corellis, has managed to garner additional funding for continued particle physics research. The Sands Research Foundation has generously contributed a grant of three million dollars and a future scheduling of continued grants based on progress. While Dr. Corellis has stated the Sands Foundation is a conglomerate of various interested parties, we can only assume our own government might be contributing funds. Regardless, we are quite pleased with the progress we've been seeing since the appointment of Dr. Corellis." (Dean of U.W. Operations at the monthly Board of Academics meeting.)

Giant Bald Eagles flew in a perfect circle above Leif as he hovered in the air. The sunlit sky was crystal clear and bathed in a blue almost as deep as the distant waters of Puget Sound. A full moon could barely be seen in the center of the circle of eagles. One of the eagles screeched loudly, pulled in its wings, and dove from the formation, heading directly toward Leif. His pulse raced as he looked around for someplace to hide, preferably a dense cloud, or trees would be perfect. There was nothing except the distant ground below. He could see the cone of Mt. Rainer, a small circle of jagged snow, thousands of feet directly below him. He looked to the horizon and spun around. There were no clouds as far as he could see. Mt. St. Helens, Mt. Adams, the Olympics, and even Mt. Baker were showing peaks were above the curve of the distant horizon. *How can I even breathe?*

A shadow suddenly appeared over Leif as he impulsively flinched and looked up in time to see the eagle extend its talons toward his head. He flew backward, watching as the eagle pulled in its claws, and stroked the air with its massive wings. It turned and gazed at Leaf with one eye as it took another stroke of the air and climbed back up toward the circle of eagles. Leif continued to fall backward. He no longer feared the eagle, recognizing the attack was just a show of force. Mirroring the eagle's graceful flight Leif let himself fall through the sky. It felt good to stop exerting himself against the pull of the earth below. The wind whistled in his ears and his hair rapidly fluttered against his forehead and face. He smiled as the eagle slipped back into formation of the flying circle above. They continued as if there had been no intrusion into their space.

Leif rolled over to face the ground and Mt. Rainer directly below. He continued to let himself fall through the air, spreading his arms and legs in the typical skydiver fashion. The crater of the mountain below grew in size. He lowered his legs, placed his arms at his sides, and focused his energy toward the ground. Nothing happened as he continued to fall. His speed increased. It was difficult to keep his legs together from the force of the rushing air. He attempted to cross and lock his ankles together, but as he pulled one foot forward the wind caught his leg and flipped him over. He started to tumble and spin from the momentum. Extending his arms and legs he managed to stop the tumble, but now he was on his back, facing up. He slightly pulled in his left arm and leg which rolled him back over to face the ground. The circle of the Mt. Rainer crater was much larger. *I wonder if I can get a bullseye,* Leif chuckled to himself, strangely not afraid of not being able to stop his descent. He was more afraid of being seen. *I'm a black dot in the sky, falling like a meteor, about to smash into the center of the crater.*

The sound of the rushing air past his ears stopped. He was still falling, but he could no longer feel the wind or hear it. A peacefulness fell upon him as he watched the crater get rapidly closer. He pulled himself into a ball and started to tumble. A shadow of blackness engulfed him and he caught a glimpse of claws as they wrapped around him. The end points of the claws pierced into his chest and legs and were suddenly gone as quickly as they had appeared. Leif felt himself fall into the mattress of his bed and rudely out of his peaceful dream. The bounce back off the bed caught him off guard. He had no idea he had been hovering so high above it. He opened his eyes and grabbed onto the blankets to keep from falling off, but it didn't help. They draped over his shoulders as he slid off the side and ended up sitting on the floor with his legs straight.

"Wow," Leif said while shaking the sleep from his head. He reached out for his cell phone from the bed-stand and checked the display. No new messages received. He selected Carina from his contact list and tapped on the 'Call' icon. Three rings and then voice mail. He couldn't leave a voice message. There was no way he could convey in a voice message how he currently felt. *Maybe she's still sleeping,* he tried to convince himself, but he felt something wasn't right. *Did I scare her off?* It didn't make any sense to him. He was certain Carina was just as in love with him as he was with her. *Why is she ignoring me? Maybe something is wrong.* He decided to send a text message for her to see when she woke up.

Going through withdrawals. I need a fix. ;)

***

"Suzanne, I think she's waking up," Matt stated.

Carina's eyelids fluttered slightly. Black retaining straps held her securely on a wheeled gurney. She was on her back with a strap running across the top of her chest and over her arms, below the shoulders. Fur lined straps held her wrists and ankles. Another wide strap ran across the top of her legs, just below her pelvis. Several tubes extended from her mouth and were taped to the side of her cheek, and a IV drip line ran into one of her veins in the middle of her left arm. Electrode sensors were attached to each of her temples and a finger clip sensor dangled from the tip of her left ring finger.

Dr. Corellis walked over from her desk to the gurney where Carina was strapped down. She examined the monitors on stands behind the gurney. “Vitals look good and heart rate is coming up.” She stood beside Matt at the side of the gurney and gently grabbed Carina’s hand.

Carina tightened her grip on Dr. Corellis’ hand as she slowly gained consciousness. The memory of the struggle she had in her condo with the men in black washed over her like a cold bucket of water. She opened her eyes wide in fear and saw Dr. Corellis and a strange man standing next to her. Her adrenaline spiked, greatly increasing her heart rate. She tried to scream, but no sound would come out - only air wheezing past the tubes in her throat.

Dr. Corellis glanced at the monitors and back down at Carina. “It’s okay dear. We’re going to take good care of you.” She gently squeezed Carina’s hand. “We paralyzed your vocal cords for now. It’s for the best.”

Carina tried to pull her hand away from the doctor’s, but couldn’t due to the straps around her wrists. She violently shook her body against the gurney restraints, her hair flailed in all directions, and she almost shook loose the sensors attached to her head.

“Please dear, don’t do that.” The doctor calmly stated and patted Carina’s arm. “We’re not going to hurt you. If you act like this, we’ll just have to sedate you again.”

Carina stopped shaking and stared angrily at the doctor. She mouthed and whispered “Why?”

“We just need to do some studies and perform some experiments. You have a special talent dear, and we just want to understand it better." She paused and gently moved Carina's hair away from her eyes. "And I'm sure Leif would want us to take good care of you as well."

Carina's eyes became wet with tears with the realization Leif could be in danger as well.

"We have him close by and he's working his magic programming for us. If you don't cooperate with us I'm afraid we'll have to turn our attention to him. Do you understand dear?"

One tear streamed from Carina's eyes as she closed her eyelids. She nodded her head and whispered "Yes" hesitantly.

"That's a good girl, Carina. We'll make sure you're comfortable." Dr. Corellis winked at Matt. "All we want is a little cooperation."

Matt pulled a cell phone out of a pocket and smiled as he noticed a text message showing on the display. "And we'll make sure Leif knows you're okay," he added. He entered a reply to Leif's message:

I understand. Need more time to think. Txt you l8r.

"Ah, the angst of young love," Matt stated as he pressed the send button.

Carina opened her eyes and stared at him. She recognized his voice as one of the men in her condo when she was abducted. She raised her head and threw it back with a thump into the thin pillow of the gurney. Once she knew she had his attention she locked her gaze with his. She mustered a look of as much hate and distain as she could without being able to speak.

Matt chuckled, “She’s feisty. This will be…” he paused and looked at Dr. Corellis, and continued, “interesting.”

***

Leif managed to wake up, scarf down an energy drink and a microwaved breakfast sandwich, showered, dressed, and reached his car in under thirty minutes. He tossed his laptop backpack into the back seat as he felt his phone vibrate. Pulling it out of his pocket, he quickly read the message from Carina as he sat behind the wheel and started up the car. “More time?” he stated while tossing the phone onto the passenger seat and backing out of his parking spot. He pulled into traffic and grabbed the phone again, hoping he could get a long red light at the next intersection. It didn’t happen. The next three lights were green as he headed for the Amzoft office.

“Duh!” Leif exclaimed when he remembered he was supposed to be heading for the University of Washington campus instead of the Amzoft office. He almost stopped at a green light as he thought about making a u-turn. A car behind him honked. He waved at the driver behind and accelerated to the next intersection. Checking all his mirrors, he noticed a man in a mini-van on his right who looked familiar. The man was wearing thick rimmed retro sunglasses and had jet black hair styled into various angled points along his forehead and down past his ears. The exact same man he had seen outside of the Amzoft office over a month ago, when he was having coffee with Jewels. The man looked back at Leif for a second and then sped ahead as Leif quickly made a u-turn.

The sight of the man in the sunglasses sent a chill down Leif's neck. He checked his rear-view mirror as he now headed in the correct direction toward the UW campus. He felt relief as he saw the back of the silver mini-van heading away. The next light turned yellow, then red as Leif approached. He stopped and took the opportunity to check the message from Carina on his phone again. He quickly typed out:

Miss you, but understand.

What else am I going to say? You say you love me and then disappear for two days? Leif shook his head and hesitantly pressed the send button before the stoplight changed back to green. Tossing the phone back onto the passenger seat while accelerating, he checked the rear-view mirror and noticed the silver mini-van was back and heading his direction, with five or six cars between them.

"Really?" Leif stated to the mirror. Instead of running and trying to lose the tail, Leif decided he would drive normally and keep an eye on the mini-van - even though he made direct eye contact a few minutes ago.

Leif continued driving to the UW campus at a slower pace than normal while keeping one eye on the tail. He almost lost him by accident when a stoplight caught the mini-van driver after Leif made it through the intersection. The driver managed to catch up again a few minutes later, still keeping his distance of four or five cars behind. Leif laughed and figured this guy was either very bad at tailing someone or just didn't care about being spotted. "Why are you even tailing me?" Leif asked the reflection in the real-view mirror. Twenty minutes later Leif, and the mini-van driver, arrived at the university campus.

The campus was a mix of red brick buildings with grey stone accents surrounded by lush landscaping and plenty of benches and grass for lounging students. It was everything Leif had previously imagined as a typical college campus. Even the air seemed to smell intellectual as he slowly drove through, looking for the Astrophysics facility. Both students and faculty staff were on the move to their classes. He checked the rear-view mirror and noticed the driver in the silver mini-van was no longer there. Tapping his brakes, he slowed to a crawl while looking around for the mini-van, but it was nowhere in sight. A student on a skateboard took advantage of the near stop and crossed the street in front of Leif's car.

Leif quickly lowered his side window and called out to the skateboarder. "Hey, excuse me. Can you tell me where the Astrophysics Center is?"

The skateboarder didn't even look back as he pointed behind and to the left of Leif's car. Leif turned to look and saw the sign on a nine story, red brick building - 'University of Washington C121 Physics-Astronomy Building'.

"Thanks!" Leif responded loudly, but the skateboarder kicked-jumped from the street to the sidewalk and kept on rolling. Leif found a nearby parking garage, parked, threw his backpack over one shoulder, and tried not to look like it was his first time on campus. He kept glancing around for any sign of the man with the jet black pointy hair and dark sunglasses, to no avail.

***

A security guard watched Leif approach the double glass doors and buzzed him in. As Leif walked up to the lobby counter where the guard was sitting, an elevator door opened with a ding. A woman's voice could be clearly heard, echoing off the marble floors and walls of the lobby. "It's just the way she looks at me when I'm calibrating the …" A man and a woman, appearing to be in their mid-twenties, in white lab coats exited from the elevator and halted their conversation as soon as they saw Leif standing at the guard's desk. Leif gave them a quick glance and turned his attention back to the guard.

Leif could hear the couple walk behind him and out through the doors. He thought it odd that they didn't continue their conversation, but just walked past quietly.

"Can I help you?" the guard asked.

"I'm Leif Anderson, here to see Dr. Corellis." He was surprised to see the guard was an intimidating mid-thirties something with a holstered side-arm instead of an aging retiree with the typical can of mace. A walkie-talkie was on the guard's belt with a wired microphone clipped to a button downed flap below his left ear.

"I need a picture I.D., your signature, and time of entry on the sign-in sheet. Put your pack on the counter and unzip all pockets and compartments."

Leif obliged as the guard typed into a computer, ran Leif's driver's license through a scanning device attached to the computer, and performed a rudimentary search of the backpack.

"Take a seat," the guard stated while handing back the driver's license and pushing the backpack back to the front of the counter. "The doctor will be here in a few minutes."

Leif sat down by a corner table with scattered magazines and technical journals on physics, astronomy, a Scientific American, and a couple entertainment periodicals with the latest gossipy celebrity on the cover. Leif grabbed the astronomy magazine and started to thumb through it when the elevator dinged and Dr. Corellis exited. The guard placed a clip badge on the counter for the doctor as she walked past. She grabbed it and give it a quick glance while walking toward Leif. He stood and threw his backpack over one shoulder.

"Hello Leif," Dr. Corellis stated. "Welcome to CENPA, the Center for Experimental Nuclear Physics and Astrophysics. We're very excited to have you joining us here at the university." She handed him the clip badge. "You can clip this to your shirt. Just don't lose it or you won't be able to get any of the doors to open for you."

"Thanks." Leif noticed the badge had his picture from his driver's license on it, a started date, a QR bar-code, and a light blue square on the bottom right corner with a dark blue dot in its center. A small strip of 10 colored boxes ran along the left side of the badge, starting with light blue and ending with a dark blue square at the bottom. Tiny white numbers were on each square, with 0 on the light blue and incrementing 2, 5, 10, 25, 50, 100, 200, 400, and 1K on the dark blue square. He could feel a small square bump in the middle of the badge, below his picture. He assumed it was an RF chip for door scanners.

"Did you have any trouble finding a parking place?"

"Nope." Leif responded while following the doctor and studying his new badge. "You have tighter security than we did at Amzoft," he added as they stepped into the elevator.

The doctor scanned her badge across a small black panel below the elevator buttons. Leif was startled when the elevator started moving down when he was expecting to go up. He glanced at the floor number indicators above the doors and noticed there was a 'B1' to 'B3' to the left of 'L', and 8 floors to the right. The elevator continued to descend.

"How far down is the basement?" Leif asked.

"Far enough." Dr. Corellis answered. She gave him a small grin. "We have very sophisticated measuring equipment, a bubble chamber, and a small particle accelerator. Aside from being away from surface vibrations we also have to keep the lab contained in case something goes wrong."

"Wrong?" he nervously asked.

She chuckled, "It's okay. It's perfectly safe. The underground protection is more for government standards than anything else. We have to play by the rules to keep our funding."

Leif nodded as the elevator stopped on B1 and the doors opened. They stepped into a small room with a single empty desk, a couple chairs, and a single steel door. A panel with a speaker, numeric keypad, and black scanner box was left of the door. "Let's see if your badge is working." She held out her hand.

Leif handed her his badge and she waved it in front of the black scanner box. A light above the door handle changed from red to green and sounded a short beep. "Excellent," she stated and handed the badge back.

"I guess the students won't escape too easily," Leif chuckled, trying to calm his nervousness.

They entered a corridor with various doors, each with an access panel and a number. He followed the doctor till they reached door '9'. The doctor stood to the side and pointed to the panel. Leif waved his badge in front of the black scanner panel and waited for the beep and the green light. The light turned green and a computer generated voice stated, "Leif Anderson access granted," and the door clicked. Leif opened the door and was surprised to see a brightly lit laboratory with white granite floors, concrete walls, the ceiling twenty feet above, steel tables with equipment, pipes and cables running to various locations, computers, several racks of electronic monitoring equipment, and a dozen people in white lab coats busily working. A low vibrating hum from a ventilation system permeated the room. A glass enclosed room was on the opposite side of the lab with a small ramp leading up to the glass doors. Multiple racks of black computer servers formed several corridors within the glass room. The left side of the lab revealed a circular tunnel with a long steel table against one side holding a pipe several feet in diameter, covered with wires, hoses, and tubes, extending far into the distance within the tunnel.

"We call it the cave." Dr. Corellis stated. "It holds our miniature particle accelerator and all the equipment for measurements. We have wave and particle detectors at the far end of the tunnel as well. Over here," she pointed toward the glass room, "is where you'll be working."

Leif followed Dr. Corellis up the small ramp to the double wide glass doors of the computer room. She pointed to a black scanner panel off to one side of the doors. A small red light glowed in the middle of the panel. Leif waved his badge in front of it and the light turned green as a single beep and a click of the door locks indicated he was allowed to enter the inner computer sanctuary of the U.W. Astrophysics laboratory. He wasn't sure if he should be excited or afraid with such a privilege. *What if I trip over a cable and shut the whole system down?*

Once inside the room Leif noticed there were no cables to trip over. The floor was comprised of square tiles, approximately two feet on each side, with hundreds of tiny holes for allowing cool air to flow into the room from underneath the floor. Leif remembered seeing the same type of floor in the main server room at Amzoft, but only through the windows since he had never been permitted into the room. Dr. Corellis led the way through a maze of towering server racks with tinted glass doors, each rack connected with perfectly bundled cables, busy with red and amber status lights. Leif could feel the heat emanating from the equipment and he understood the need for the raised floor air conditioning system. He noticed small circular cylinders mounted to the ceiling with downward facing nozzles, spaced every ten feet. "Is that halon above the racks?" he asked.

"Yes. Which is why you take a deep breath and head for the doors if the fire alarm goes off."

They turned a corner and came to an open area with two rows of computer desks. Each desk had between two and three monitors on it, and one or two keyboards. There were two men and a woman busily working at some of the workstations. All the desks faced a wall with six, large, flat-screen monitors mounted in two rows of three across. Graphs and numerical values could be seen on each, along with several camera views of the particle accelerator. The cameras switched views every fifteen seconds to keep a watchful eye on other equipment within the laboratory every fifteen seconds.

"This is ATHENA, our super computer cluster," the doctor provided.

"Wow." Leif exclaimed. "You have your own mission control down here."

"Indeed we do." Dr. Corellis responded with a look of satisfaction. "We perform very serious work here. Rocket science, if you will. Our research fund comes from very influential people with very deep pockets." She paused for a few seconds, grinning slightly, then turned and pointed to one of the workstations. "Your desk is at workstation 15. You can sign in with 'leifa' and a password of 'new42'. It will prompt you for a new password and the system will step you through our standard set of orientation tutorials. It will take you most of the day to get through it all. Just get comfortable and settled. Tomorrow I'll give you your first work assignment."

Leif nodded his head and placed his backpack in the chair at his workstation. "I'm excited about being here. But…"

"A little overwhelmed?" the doctor added.

"Yeah. I mean, I'm a video game programmer and a bit of a math hack. How can I help with particle physics?"

Dr. Corellis crossed her arms and stared intently at Leif for a few seconds before answering. "Ever hear of Einstein's Equivalence Principal or Newtonian inverse-square law?"

The question caught Leif off guard. He wasn't expecting to be suddenly thrust into the scientific aspects of what he would be working on. His mind began racing from the question. Scientifically, he was familiar with both of the theories, due to his intensive research shortly after he discovered he had the ability to fly. His biggest question back then was 'How does this work?' He responded as quickly as he could, not wanting to show that her question had startled him. "Um, yeah. They are theories having to do with the movement of mass and how it's affected by gravity." He hoped his answer was enough.

The doctor smiled slightly. "Sorry if I caught you off guard. Your programming for Amzoft had to deal mostly with the effects of the mass of planets and other spacial bodies on the gravitational forces which were exerted on the player's space ship, right?"

Leif was afraid of where this might be headed. He suddenly became aware his interest in programming and knowledge of the math for gravitational forces might potentially expose him - something Georgeo had warned him about in the past. He had sloughed it off with Georgeo as being overly cautious. Now, he wasn't so sure. If he kept his focus on the video gaming, it might detract from a hint of his abilities. "Yes. That's right. I thought it would be more realistic for the players if we had various levels of gravity affect their movement, based on the mass of the nearby planets or suns."

"Excellent! Well, we want to use that knowledge of yours and the associated math, to determine if, and how, sub-atomic particles, might be used for manipulating those forces."

Leif glanced away, staring at the ceiling with a tilt of his head. It gave the impression he was deep in thought. He was buying time to keep himself calm, to not give away any revealing details, and to give himself a moment to gather his thoughts before responding. He decided to ask, “So, to affect the forces of gravity?”

“Exactly!” Dr. Corellis responded. “What if you could help invent the first, true, hover-board?”

Leif forced himself to chuckle at her question. He knew there was more to this assignment than just hover-boards. What he wasn’t sure of was if the doctor was truly involved with anti-gravity research, possibly for the government or other corporate sponsors, or if she was with the Eighteenth and was trying to uncover the secrets of Avitorian flight. He felt a chill on the back of his neck as he wondered if she already knew that he, himself, was an Avitorian.

TWELVE - INTO THE NIGHT

There are many ancient Egyptian carvings which depict the workers utilized for the building of the pyramids, but there are rarely any that depict the pyramids themselves. I personally was able to see the three tablets of 'ta dehent' over thirty years ago. An unusual feature of all three tablets was the scrape marks from stones above the carvings of the pyramids, as if something was removed that was previously there. We were preparing to use specially prepared x-ray imaging equipment to determine what might have been carved into the stone before they were damaged. However, during transportation to the University of Gaza (where the equipment is available), the truck carrying the tablets was involved in an accident, and the tablets were stolen before help could arrive. We can only assume they are now in the hands of private treasure collectors, or with individuals who also have an interest in ancient UFO's. (Excerpt from the book, "Ancient Alien Builders of Egypt" by Associate Professor of Egyptology, Dr. Willheim Grolsch.)

Are you there?

Leif sent the text message to Carina and tossed his phone onto the passenger seat. It wasn't safe to be so distracted with his phone while driving. "Come on!" He shouted at the car in front of him. Fortunately, the windows were all rolled up and no one could hear him, and it was too dark to read his lips, or see his facial expressions in a rear view mirror. The last thing he wanted was an altercation with another driver. The drive to one of his secluded launching spots on Tiger Mountain took longer than he really wanted. Maybe it wasn't longer than normal, but his impatience made it seem too long. It was all he could do to limit himself to yelling and staying off the horn when other drivers slowed him down.

He finally reached the dirt and gravel road, skidding to his spot and sending rocks flying into the woods. He wasted no time driving to the end of the road, hidden deep in the thick of evergreens and ferns. Once out of the car, he paused and took a deep breath of the oxygen rich, moist forest air. He sat on the front of the car and stared at his last message to Carina on his phone. It was a poor conclusion to his first, uncomfortable, day in his new job at the University physics laboratory. The lack of response was unnerving, and with the comments Dr. Corellis made before his day of training, his inner gut didn't feel right. There was something wrong about this entire situation. *I have to do something. This is killing me.*

Leif reached out with his senses into the surrounding area. Only animals and plant life returned their slight pulses of electricity. One large animal, about the size of a bear, was rummaging around in the ferns a fair distance away. Leif made a mental note to check for the bear before landing back at his car. He zipped up his coat and pulled the hoodie out and pulled it down over his head. Sensing a pair of rabbits hopping out from around a tree and stopping to nibble on the undergrowth, he asked, “Keep an eye on the car for me, okay?” The rabbits were startled at the sound of his voice in the darkness and the sudden whoosh of his launch into the cold night air.

Fortunately, there was no moon up yet. Unfortunately, Leif was headed to a heavily populated area in Lake Forest Park. Carina’s two story condo was across the road from the waterfront of Lake Washington. Most people did not expect to see someone flying through the night air. They would be busy with their normal activities of life, driving, walking, or staring at their phones and tablets. At least that’s what Leif was hoping. It was chilly outside, it was past ten p.m., and most people would be indoors. It was still a big risk, one that Georgeo would highly disapprove of. Any potential awareness of their capabilities could be detrimental to their race. Leif continued to wrestle with the risk of exposure versus his desire to see what is going on with Carina. There were some clouds at four thousand feet, but not thick enough to completely hide his approach.

Upon reaching the airspace above Carina’s condo, Leif hovered at a couple thousand feet. He closed his eyes and tried to sense if anyone was outside in the area. It was difficult due to the interference from all the electrical power-lines and high frequency radio devices in the area. His shivering from the cold air didn’t help much either. He opened his eyes and took note of the various streetlights close to the condo, but they were the energy saving LED bulbs, projecting the light downward and not up into the sky. He remembered the skylight windows along the top of Carina's roof and decided it would be the best target for his descent. A slow descent would put him at more risk of being seen. He dropped feet first, reached terminal velocity, and tried to judge the distance to the roof, in the dark, while shivering, and trying to sense if anyone was around. He realized, almost too late, his approach had to be halted to prevent slamming into the top of the roof and possibly breaking some bones, and making a whole lot of noise in the process. He managed to come to a complete stop several feet above the roof and slowly dropped to the roof while doing a quick glance around to make sure he wasn't seen by anyone.

A terrier mix at the next house over started barking and scratching at the wooden fence. *Dang dogs!* Leif shook his head slightly in frustration. He took a deep breath and slowly blew out, to calm his nerves and try to reduce his shaking. The dog finally quieted down after its owner whacked the bedroom window. Leif saw the curtains in the window part slightly, but no one would be able to see him hunched down in the shadows on the roof. He waited a few minutes to make sure all was quiet before looking at the windows on Carina's roof. It was hard to miss that one of her windows was completely gone. His heart skipped a beat - he realized something wasn't right. He hovered to the window and took a quick peek inside the condo. The lights were out and he could sense that Carina wasn't there.

Leif flew through the opening and slowly lowered himself down to the loft. It was dark except for the glow of

LEDs from appliances by Carina's computer in a corner of the loft, and a clock showing 11:23 on a bed stand.

"Carina." Leif whispered, hoping she would just appear at the mention of her name. A pang of dread landed in the pit of his stomach at the silence in the condo. He hovered a few inches above the floor as he glided around the loft area, not wanting to make any noise himself. He couldn't sense anyone within the condo itself. As he glanced around the loft, he saw the bed broken and twisted on one side, with wood shards scattered across the floor. Several blankets and a sheet hung from the bed and dangled down onto the floor. He looked over the railing down to the work room and could see Carina's easel laying on the floor amidst the chaos that was the studio. He flew over the rail and lowered himself to the floor below.

He picked up the easel and stood it upright in the spot Carina liked to have it, and he hovered over to the couch cushion and picked it up. A small piece of paper fell to the floor. He picked it up and moved to the window where light from one of the street lamps was streaming in through a gap in the curtains. Something was scribbled in ink on the note.

5t4rb0und

Obviously it was a password of some type, with numbers substituting some of the letters. Leif knew Carina wouldn't be careless enough to leave a password written out on a piece of paper. He stuffed it in his pocket and looked around for any other clues. A flood of emotions hit him. He knew Carina had been taken. He hoped she wasn't hurt. She was an artist. No one would want to kidnap her unless they knew she was Avitorian.

He remembered the stories about the disappearance of his aunt Angela. The only thing they found was her bright yellow cassette tape player. No clues, no news, no contact - nothing. She was just gone, and now Carina was gone. It had to be the Eighteenth! His mind raced with the fear. When Angela disappeared, Georgeo changed their names, and got them away from the danger. He couldn't let it happen again. He couldn't just run away. At least he had a clue. The details of the last few days began to coalesce. The reality that he was followed. The conversations with Dr. Corellis and his assignment to the university was too coincidental. He couldn't run away. He couldn't lose Carina, just like his parents lost Angela.

The dread and anxiety he initially felt was fading, replaced by adrenaline and anger. He no longer felt the need to keep quiet. If Eighteenth was watching and listening, he didn't care. He screamed in rage as he flew out the open window and launched himself into the night sky. The neighbor's dog yelped and hid. A few people had heard the scream and cringed, but no one saw the Avitorian.

***

"Okay dear, we need you to hover." Dr. Corellis asked Carina.

Carina was wearing a harness over her clothes, with webbed straps over her shoulders, around her chest, her waist, and under her torso. Her arms were held to the torso harness just above each wrist. Ankle straps secured each of her legs. The harness was secured by high test climbers rope woven around specially designed locks that extended down to three floor mounted anchors, one for each leg and one for the harness. The ropes were loosely coiled on the floor between the anchors and Carina. Sensors were attached to her forehead, neck, arms, legs, and under her clothing to her chest and torso. Sensor leads, cabled together with ties, dangled from a gambled armature attached to the ceiling above her. Additional sensors matrixed across the surface of the floor.

Carina's long blond hair hung down over her face as she tried to examine the ropes and anchors. She took her time delaying her response. It was the only type of control she had over the situation, even though she was being held captive. They wanted something from her and she was going to do as much as she could to delay and agitate their efforts. She flicked her head back throwing her hair away from face. She looked at the doctor and finally replied. "What, doctor?"

Dr. Corellis chuckled and shook her head. "I have all day if you want to play games with me." She paced slowly around Carina. "And its Suzanne, dear. Just Suzanne."

Matt and several technicians in lab coats stood by the racks of computers and equipment surrounding Carina in a wide circle. Remote sensors mounted on the floor and others extended from tall poles merged together by cables snaking to the racks of equipment.

Carina watched the doctor pace around and she glanced at the technicians. Georgeo had told her to be very wary of the methods of The Eighteenth. Under no circumstances was any Avitorian to cooperate or submit to their demands. But, there was no ignoring they had already seen her flying in her condo. She should have stayed on her feet. “We must maintain deniability.” Georgeo had said. Easier said than done when there are intruders in your condo. She was way past deniability at this point. Her real fear was the threat of them turning their attention to Leif if she didn’t cooperate. She had to stall.

“Just Suzanne?” Carina smirked. “I’m all tied up, being measured by you and your technicians, and you want me to be on a first name basis? Sorry, doctor. But, I’m just not feeling the love here.”

“Well dear,” Suzanne stopped pacing in front of Carina. “A relationship requires cooperation. That’s all we’re asking for, a little cooperation. Just a slight hover would be great. Then you can return back to your comfortable quarters while we examine all our data. Maybe I’ll pick up some sushi for you for tonight.” She started pacing again. “And I’ll make sure Leif doesn’t have to get involved with our testing as well.”

Carina felt her face flush with anger. She already hated the fact she let herself get captured. She hated being confined and prodded like a lab rat. She especially hated being forced to do their bidding with the threats made to Leif. She wondered what they would hope to get by watching her hover. They already saw her hover. So what, if they actually measure something, she wondered. They’re not Avitorian. She knew they would never be able to fly, to experience life as an Avitorian. She couldn’t understand why they even cared. Just because some ancient ruler wanted to be a God? “Like it even really matters?” she mumbled while raising herself up off the ground slightly for a brief second.

As soon as she lifted off the floor various lights flashed in the room and the measuring equipment beeped and clicked. The equipment went silent as soon as she touched back down on the floor.

"Did you get that?" Suzanne turned and shouted to the technicians.

Matt and the techs examined the monitors with intensity, but shook their heads and responded, "Nothing. We've got nothing but video. All indicators are flat."

Suzanne turned and walked up to Carina. "How?"

Carina stared fearlessly back at the doctor. "Don't know."

"Do it again."

"It doesn't matter." Carina added while rising slightly off the floor then back down again.

The strobes flashed, the equipment clicked into measurement mode, then back off again.

"And?" Suzanne asked her team while staring at Carina.

"Nothing," stated Matt. "Same as before."

"Again, please."

Carina smirked. She lifted up several inches off the floor and hovered there while staring and smiling back at the doctor.

The strobes flashed again, the equipment flipped into measuring mode, a high pitched tone sounded from the equipment. Suzanne turned to face Matt and raised her hands, gesturing for any information they could provide. Matt and the technicians scanned their equipment and monitors, all of them shaking their heads negatively.

"There has to be something!" Suzanne shouted.

Matt shook his head. "Nothing. All the indicators are flat and zero. No radio waves, no light waves, nothing in or outside the spectrum, and amazingly, no downward force against the floor sensors."

Suzanne turned back to face Carina. "How are you doing this?"

"Don't know. I just am."

"You have to know. You've been taught. You have to make some kind of effort to cause it to happen. How is it done?"

"Do you really think you're asking these questions for the first time doctor?" Carina asked. "What about Angela? Didn't you ask her these same questions? Didn't she hover for you too?"

"Why you little…" Suzanne slapped Carina's face. "You will tell us how it's done. We WILL learn this from you! It IS our right and our destiny! You waste what you have by hiding in secret. Your race has always been weak. Which is why you'll never be the rulers. You will always be the ruled."

Carina glared at the doctor and shot straight up into the air, to the full extent of the ropes holding her. She strained against the harnesses while continuing to stare at the doctor, the right side of her face red with outline of the doctor's hand. She calmly stated, almost in a whisper, "It doesn't really matter. You will never be one of us."

The doctor walked to the side of the laboratory and picked up a beam rifle. She flipped it on, turned, and waited for the tone of the internal capacitors to reach their peak power. She pulled the trigger and unleashed an intense beam of microwave heat into Carina. Carina moaned, fell to the floor, and she shook violently from the intense pain of the beam.

Suzanne tossed down the rifle, walked over to Carina, and kicked her in the ribs. Carina groaned from the pain of the kick, closed her eyes, and started to cry - more from the frustration than from the pain.

"Take her back to her quarters and send all the data and video to my computer!" Suzanne barked the orders to her team.

Matt stepped out of her way as she stormed out of the laboratory.

***

The 78 foot white, luxury motor yacht slowly drifted along the shoreline of Lake Washington. The seats on the back deck of the boat were plush and inviting, but Dr. Corellis was in no mood for relaxing. She sat tensely on the edge of one of the seats, holding a cell phone to one ear, and gestured wildly with her other hand. The packaging of a burner phone was cast away on the decking below her seat. A muscular man in a dark suit stood quietly at deck rail, pretending not to pay any attention to the conversation or the frustration the doctor was showing. He was only there to provide assistance if called upon.

"The grants have been more than satisfactory, Naeheth. I have full use of the facilities and the equipment is the best in the country for particle measurements." Suzanne stood up and started pacing around the deck. She shook her head a few times and replied, "Yes, yes, Naeheth. I know what I promised. I am honored to have this opportunity." She stopped pacing and stood staring out at the building lights of Bellevue and their reflections on the water. “I will get results. I feel we are close to discovery.”

Matt walked from the galley section of the boat and out onto the back deck. A glass of wine in each hand. He stopped mid-deck and looked over at the dark suited body guard. The guard slightly shook his head. Matt frowned and nodded his understanding.

“I will call again. Two weeks.” Suzanne turned off the phone, pulled out the battery, and lightly tossed all the pieces into the propeller churned water behind the boat.

“Don’t you have another ninety minutes on that phone?” Matt spoke up, walked over to her, and handed her one of the glasses.

“They want more progress.” She replied, ignoring Matt’s attempt to lighten up the mood, and taking a sip. “I know I’m close - we’re close. It has to be particle related.”

Matt placed a hand on Suzanne’s shoulder. “I’m sure you’ll figure it out. It’s just a matter of time. Eighteenth will rise. No more piddly bureaucracies and failing politics. People need to be lead, as we once lead them before.”

“I fear we must take action soon.” Suzanne added. “Technologies and governments are destroying what’s left. We have to take it all back. There can only be one government. This power she has - they have!” She threw her glass of wine against the decking and leaned out over the back of the boat, shaking her fist against the night sky. “Ahhhgggh!” she screamed. “It was ours! This ability was ours.” She turned and faced Matt. “As Ahmose was our Pharaoh, I WILL make it ours again!”

THIRTEEN - FORCES OF NATURE

"Throughout history, we have lost loved ones to the Eighteenth, to medical scrutiny, scientists, witch hunters, inquisitions, and inter-marriage to humans. This is why it is so important for us to maintain our standards. We cannot lower ourselves to the barbarity of the Eighteenth, or anyone who seeks to exploit who we are. When humans finally figure out how to have peace and harmony, the Eighteenth will fade away. Then, and only then, can we make ourselves known." (Georgeo speaking to a group of young Avitorians.)

The clock on Leif's bed-stand showed 3:24 A.M. Leif paced the floor of his room in agitation. He cradled his head in his hands and pulled at his hair in frustration. A million different thoughts raced through his mind. *Where has Carina been taken. I should have done something sooner! Is this the Eighteenth? Is Dr. Corellis involved? What do I do now?* He pulled out the piece of paper with the password on it. *Someone who works with computers was involved. I work with computers.* He stared at the password.

5t4rb0und

"Starbound." Leif said it out loud - burning it into his memory. *This is someone who is into space travel, gaming, or science.* "Crap!" He quickly stood up and looked around the room. A wave of panic slugged him in his gut. *My room could be bugged and I just spoke the password.* He turned his TV on to cover up the sound of his movements and he checked the most obvious places, the light, under the bed-stand, and under the bed. *This is a waste of my energy. Focus!*

"This is CNN," sounded out from the flat screen TV on the bedroom wall.

"I have to find her." Leif whispered to himself, under the sounds of a car commercial. He changed into a full set of thermal under-layers, which he usually wore for snowboarding. He followed up with black jeans, a black hoodie, gloves, a dark blue ski jacket, and a red half face ski-mask. He now regretted buying the red one instead of the black one he had looked at. The combination of his anger and his excited energy was starting to make him sweat under the ski gear, but it was November and rainy. Flying around at 4 A.M. would be very cold. He turned off all the outside lights around his condo. He had never launched from here before, always afraid of being seen, or the possibility of being scolded by Georgeo later. CNN was showing a skirmish in the Middle East as Leif stepped into the chill of his backyard and launched into the air.

It didn't take long for Leif to reach the university campus. It was less than two miles, as a crow flies. Leif was pleased to see how dark the skies were above the campus. Most of the light sources had cut off shields, forcing the light beams downward. If anyone was out at this time in the morning, their light adapted eyes wouldn't perceive him in the darkness above. Leif hovered and tried to determine where to begin looking. He knew there were a lot of secured doors at the Physics building and there would be a few students there as well. Night time was best for quiet research into particle and wave length studies, plus the reduced traffic on the streets meant less potential for vibrations on the underground equipment.

Where would she keep Carina? Leif had already mentally implicated Dr. Corellis in Carina's abduction, even though he had no proof. It was just a gut feel. He closed his eyes and reached out with his senses. Carina's electrical signature was fresh in his memory from their many flights together. The memory of her presence tugged at his heart. "Gah," he exclaimed and opened his eyes. *Way too much electricity below. Especially at the hospital.* The electricity below was like a solid, impenetrable wall to his senses. He slowly turned and examined the buildings of the campus.

I don't even know if she's here. She could be anywhere. This is where Dr. Corellis would be. How would they get Carina here? Leif flew over and checked the street entrances into the campus. *Way too cramped and usually busy. Security cameras watch the streets.* He turned toward the water. *Portage Bay. What's that?* Like a glowing needle against a backdrop of black velvet, a white luxury yacht was anchored next to the Marine Sciences building. All the other boats, ships, and vessels parked by the university were dark, worn, and rusty. Anything looking somewhat clean and maintained was usually parked on the other side of the bay at the Seattle Yacht Club.

Gotta check this out. It is going to be tough, Leif thought. He was dressed in black and the yacht was all white. The darkest area around the boat was aft and starboard. Leif dove toward the back of the boat while scanning for any potential boat traffic. He stopped and hovered horizontally, just above the water, hoping he would blend in with the liquid darkness of the bay. He heard muffled talking near aft, from the open hatch of the yacht. Two port windows were below the deck line, a few feet above Leif's head. He did another scan of the bay and drifted up to gaze into one of the windows. He could see a slight sliver of a gap through the curtains. The light was dim, but he could see the passageway to the engine room below. He drifted left to look into the other window. There were no curtains on this one. Leif took a quick peek at an angle, to make sure no one would be looking back at him. Through this portal he had a better view of the corridor, lit dimly by a double row of LED foot lights. He could see multiple storage cabinets lining the corridor, a hallway leading off to the left, and stairs past the hallway, which lead up to the deck.

Leif flinched at the sound of a sliding door from the aft deck of the boat. He slid down below the port window and floated slightly above the water, right against the hull - just in case someone decided to peek over the deck railing. He could hear footsteps of several people and the very familiar voice of Dr. Corellis.

"I know they're getting impatient. I'm going to put him on the project and have him put his findings into the paper."

Leif felt a surge of anger rise in him at hearing the doctor's voice. He was in the right place and closer to locating Carina. He listened as the footsteps reached a metallic ramp connecting the boat to the dock. Leif drifted up the side of the boat and peeked with one eye over the edge of the gunwale. He could see the doctor holding her cellphone to her ear and two men behind her. She stopped on the middle of the ramp and turned to speak with one of the men.

Leif quickly dipped below the edge of the deck, but stayed high enough to continue listening.

"My purse," the doctor stated to one of the men. "It's on my desk."

Leif listened to the footsteps as the man fetched the purse for Dr. Corellis. She continued with her phone call while waiting on the gangplank. "It'll keep him occupied. I sense he's getting worried and he'll start snooping before long." The man hurriedly returned with the purse and handed it to the doctor.

Leif raised up slightly to get another peek as the group continued across toward the dock. He quickly glanced out over the water for any approaching boat traffic, then drifted along the back of the boat, ducked below a mooring line, and slowly raised up over the edge of the concrete dock. He watched the doctor's group walk past several parked cars and a dilapidated fishing boat propped up in a wooden dry dock. Leif shifted to his left to get a better view of the group as they walked around the boat, toward a door of a two story building. Dr. Corellis was still mumbling on her cell phone. One of the men opened the door and they all entered the building.

Leif scanned the dock and the surrounding area for any sign of movement. The entire dock was lit by flood lights mounted on the roof of the building. *Can't risk flying.* He rolled up onto the dock, stood up, brushed off his pants and quickly walked toward the building as he continued to scan the surrounding area. He creeped to the shadow of a dry docked boat and peeked around the keel toward the building door. A small square window stood empty, and a sign to the right of the door read 'Marine Sciences Building #29'. His heart pounded and felt like it was going to burst through his jacket. He shook his hands, took a deep breath, and blew it out slowly. *I can't believe I'm doing this.*

After calming himself down, he walked toward the door at a normal pace, trying to look like he belonged there. *Right!* he thought. *I'm in all black, in a hoodie, and a face mask. Perfectly normal.* Reaching the door, he looked around again and peeked into the window. No sign of anyone. All he could see were rows of aquariums, water tanks, a rack of computer equipment, tool chests, and more doors. He tried the door lever. It was locked. "Da..."

"Hey. Can I help you?"

The voice from the side of the dock made Leif jump. He glanced in the direction of the voice and was blinded by the light from a thousand lumen flashlight. He couldn't make out the details, but he was certain it was a U.W. security guard, most likely with the flashlight in one hand and a walkie-talkie in the other, instead of a gun. Leif's mind raced with the possibilities. *Jail and no chance of finding Carina.* He pushed himself off of the door and ran as fast as he could toward the white yacht.

"Stop! Police!" the security guard yelled and started running.

Leif scrambled around the old boat, almost tripping on the edge of the wood support, and headed for the edge of the cement dock.

"Halt! I'm not going to tell you again," the guard yelled.

Leif didn't even hesitate as he reached the edge of the dock. He jumped off the dock and dove for the water, using his ability to increase the speed and the range of his dive. Right before he entered the water he could hear the guard calling for backup. Leif didn't notice how cold the water was. The anger, the adrenaline, and his focus on getting out of the area took full control of his senses. Once he was below the surface there was no need to swim. He flew through the water to the middle of Portage Bay, about a hundred yards away from the dock. With all the excitement he hadn't taken a deep breath before hitting the water. His lungs burned from oxygen starvation as he raised his head above the water. Gasping for air, he turned toward the dock to see the security guard standing on the edge, shining his flashlight in the water around the yacht. Leif turned around scanning for any sign of approaching boats or even a helicopter. Nothing. He glanced back at the Marine Sciences building longingly. A pang of fear and anxiety stabbed him with the realization he failed to find and rescue Carina. He slowly lifted out of the water, watching the security guard scan the waters around the dock. He watched a UW security car drive up onto the dock and pull next to the guard with the flashlight, it's headlights almost shining toward Leif. A spotlight from the car came on and focused on the water next to the yacht. He took advantage of the guard's lack of attention and, darted into the air, gaining as much altitude as quickly as he could. Tears welled up in his eyes from the disappointment and anger, and mixed with the water on his face. They streamed down his cheeks as he flew back to his condo.

Leif landed with a thump on his back porch deck and entered through the sliding patio door. He walked past the TV still tuned to an endless stream of commercials. He started to shake uncontrollably as he peeled off his wet clothing - some of it tearing. He didn't care about the clothes. He was overwhelmed by the feeling of defeat. Stepping naked into the bathroom shower, he turned the water on full, and slammed his fist against the tiles. He slumped down into the tub and cried. It didn't matter if anyone could hear him or not.

***

The body guard hurriedly approached Dr. Corellis, Matt, and another guard as they walked down a long corridor. "Excuse me doctor. We've got a situation." Their previous conversation halted as they all stopped and stood in the middle of the hallway and stared at the bodyguard. He had one hand on an earphone and the other on a lapel clip mic on his jacket. He squeezed the mic. "Subject is missing?" The doctor and Matt gave each other a look of concern while waiting for a response. The other guard took a stance of alertness with one hand inside his jacket, on his hip, and the other hand pushing on his own earphone. "Roger. Keep me posted." He released the mic and looked at Dr. Corellis. "Someone in dark clothing and face covering was spotted on the dock by U.W. Security. They approached and the subject dove into the water and disappeared, with no further sightings. Harbor police are patrolling as well."

Matt turned, tapped the other guard on the arm. "With me." He stated while walking quickly toward the end of the corridor.

Dr. Corellis watched Matt head down the hallway then turned toward her bodyguard. "Get to the boat and enable the infrared air scanner. We have a couple hours before sunrise. If he returns, I want to be alerted immediately."

***

The elevator door slid open with a ding. Matt and the guard peered out at opposing angles, guns drawn and ready. Each held a flashlight pressed against the barrel of their guns, ready to take any target that moved. They both swept their lights across the room and declared "Clear!" almost in unison. They stepped from the elevator and Matt flipped a light switch with his elbow while continuing to scan the laboratory. There were a lot of places to hide -

desks, computer racks, and scientific equipment. Matt stuffed his flashlight in a pocket and signaled for the guard to check the rest of the lab and he would check the next room. The elevator door closed behind them as they crept in different directions.

Matt slowly edged through the room, scanning for potential danger. He reached a door for the next room and took a quick peek through the thick, square, wire reinforced glass window. Satisfied no one was on the other side waiting for him, he leaned his chest on the access scanner pad to the right of the door, allowing the RFID badge in his jacket pocket to be sensed by the pad. The door clicked, he turned the handle, and pushed it open with one foot while pointing his gun through the opening. The room was bathed in dim blue light, illuminating the person strapped down and in a drug induced sleep on the hospital bed - Carina. Matt scanned the bank of monitors fed by trails of sensor leads attached to Carina. Satisfied she was still asleep and undisturbed, Matt walked to a glass room behind her. It was dark with just the reflections of blue light from a large metal container in the middle of the room and several dimmed LED monitors to one side of it. Matt shined his flashlight into the room and directly onto a LCD panel on the circular container. It read: 'Angela 1995 : Stable : -196.02'. A reflective glimmer of movement on the glass wall caught Matt's attention. His heart almost skipped till he realized it was Dr. Corellis as she stepped through the door.

"Looks like our facility is secure." The doctor stated softly, knowing Carina was in a drug induced sleep, but still not wanting to speak loud enough to potentially wake her.

Matt turned and responded. “Do we know who it was?”

“There’s no positive ID. That dive into the water took some agility. I’m sure Georgeo is still pretty spry for his age.” She paused and grinned. Her face showed she was reflecting on some past memories of an encounter she had years ago.

“I detect a ‘but’ in there.” Matt added.

The doctor refocused on Matt. “It could have been Leif.” She looked down at Carina. “I’m sure he’s getting anxious by now. If it’s him, I want to catch him in the act. I’m certain he’ll bring help. Till then, we’ll just string him as long as we can.” She paused and her eyes looked past Matt to a distant memory. “I sense it’ll be soon. We need to be ready.”

***

Leif was almost out of breath from his jog to the Astro-Physics building on campus. He managed to rush from his shower, get dressed, drive, park, and jog to the door of the facility in under 45 minutes, and thus reduce any suspicion he was the one who dove into the water about an hour ago. During his jog he saw multiple security cars sitting in the street intersection leading to the Marine Sciences building and a helicopter slowly circled over Portage Bay, with a spotlight scanning the water. He took a couple deep breaths to calm his breathing, stepped into the building lobby, and greeted the security guard. “What’s with all the security and the chopper?” he asked.

The guard chuckled, “Some fool in a hoodie was prowling one of the buildings then dove into the bay when we saw him.”

“Ah, finally some excitement, eh?” Leif stated while walking past the guard desk.

“Well, not much. I’m sure we’ll find him at the bottom. That water’s way too cold to hang out in for long.”

“Yeah, I’m sure it is.” Leif added and stepped into an opened elevator. The door closed and he leaned back against the wall. “Wow!” he whispered to himself.

As Leif progressed toward the laboratory he didn’t come across any other staff or students. He really wanted to be noticed - the ambitious, staff programmer on campus at 5:30 a.m. - but there was no one else here yet. He logged into his work computer and tried to get his mind into writing code. A strong alibi was needed to keep him from being looked at as a possible suspect. *There’s no way someone could jump into the bay at 4:30 and be here at work by 5:30 a.m.*, he reasoned. *Focus! I gotta focus!* He pulled up his list of programming assignments on the computer screen and selected one of the many assigned by Dr. Corellis. While waiting for the assignment to be transferred to his computer, he plugged his headphones into his smartphone, selected some music to calm his nerves, then began scrolling and writing his programming code.

It didn’t take long for Leif to get into ‘the zone’ while programming. All other thoughts, concerns, or distractions were shut out. It was just him and the code. Which is also one of the worse times to interrupt a programmer. He nearly fell out of his chair when he felt the hand on his shoulder. “Whoa,” he stated while pulling the headphones off and turning to see Dr. Corellis standing there.

"I'm sorry, Leif. I didn't mean to startle you." The doctor kept her hand on his shoulder. "I just was surprised to see you logged in so early and figured I'd come down to see how it's going."

He quickly took a look at the clock to see it was 6:37 a.m. and then responded. "Good, um, I was just cranking on one of the assignments."

"So, I see." She paused and glanced at the code on the screen. "You're here pretty early. Is everything okay?"

Leif wasn't sure if she was probing due to the morning's incident, or if she was truly concerned. Even though his intuition told him she was involved with Carina's abduction, he had no evidence. "I couldn't sleep, so I decided to come in early and get some work done." He turned to look at the computer monitor and to prevent the doctor from detecting if he was telling the truth or not. *Technically, it's the truth.*

"Anxious about the new job or is it the programming assignments?" The doctor pulled out a chair and sat down next to Leif.

His mind raced with his own questions as soon as the doctor sat down. *Why is she so concerned all of a sudden? Does she know it was me this morning? Is she trying to get me to flinch? Should I see if I can get her to flinch?* The thought just occurred to him and he didn't hesitate to try. "Nah, it's just some issues with the girlfriend." He turned back to look at the doctor, hoping for a reaction.

"Really? You both looked pretty happy at the observatory. In fact, I think Jewels was a little jealous." She chuckled.

It wasn't the reaction Leif was hoping for. He decided to press on. "I thought things were good, but she's been avoiding me lately." He paused for a moment. "Almost like she just disappeared." More by unconscious action than willfully, he stared the doctor directly in the eyes when he uttered 'disappeared.' It was only for a second, but it was enough to catch a reaction.

Dr. Corellis was caught slightly off guard by Leif's directness. She paused and her gaze focused beyond him for just a second. She quickly recovered. "I'm sure it's just a small 'girl thang'. The way she was hanging on to you the other night, that's permanent."

Leif's heart raced. Now he was certain. *That look. She knows more than she's saying.* It was hard for him to maintain his composure. He stared at the screen and realized he should respond back. "Yeah. Maybe so. I hope you're right."

The doctor quickly flipped back into work mode. "I have a new assignment for you. I placed it into your list and raised it to a priority one item." She stood up, gave him a couple pats on the shoulder, and headed for the door.

"A priority 1? Must be important. What is it?" He asked while pulling up the assignment list on his monitor.

"Dark matter, Leif. It's about Dark Matter," she stated while leaving the room.

FOURTEEN - IT'S PERSONAL

Born unto air we are
Clouds among us we'll see
Flow of the life,
peace of the mind,
love of the heart
Born unto air we are

Born unto air we are
Moons gazing down on us
Stars join our dance,
birds come along,
fun for us all
Born unto air we are

Born unto air we are
We hover together
Family and friends,
games till dawn,
fog rolling in
Born unto air we are

(Ancient song of young Avitorians)

Even though it was cold and dark, Leif could hear and feel the animal life around the wooded area. The smell of the evergreens mixed with the dampness of the undergrowth was calming for him. His anxiety was so intense when he left the office, he was worried he might run someone off the road in his haste to reach the secluded spot in the mountains. But, he was here now. He could breathe deeply, feel the forest, and begin to think more clearly. Still, it was a struggle. *I need to get in there, but they're going to be expecting me now.* He took another deep breath and blew it out slowly. *I need help.*

Leif pulled his phone from his pocket and tapped the home button. The light from the screen was blinding and a startled rabbit bounded into the thick ferns. "Sorry buddy." Leif stated to the rabbit while typing his text message.

Uncle G. Need help. Can we meet?

He slid the phone back into his pocket. The woods were blacker now due to blowing his night adapted vision out with the bright phone light. It would take another fifteen to thirty minutes for his eyes to get fully dark adapted again. Closing his eyes, he reached out with his senses. The rabbit had stopped after running under the ferns and was nibbling on some leaves. Leif smiled, knowing the small animal was too curious to run completely away. Farther off he could sense more rabbits and a couple coyotes creeping toward them. He would scare them off if he could, but they were too far away, and a thrown rock wouldn't make it past the thick evergreens. His phone vibrated. He squinted his eyes to reduce the brightness from the phone as he pulled it out of his pocket.

2 hours away. Hiking spot?

Leif responded:

Ok. I'm here.

Georgeo responded within a minute.

K.

Two hours. He must be fairly close. Canada maybe, or Oregon. The two hours was going to feel like a lifetime. He was tempted to go hover over the campus and keep an eye out on activities. *It would be too dangerous. They'll be watching.* He looked up and tried to get a glimpse of the sky in between the trees. Slowly he lifted himself up till he found a sturdy branch toward the top of an evergreen. He set his weight down on the branch and held onto the center trunk. The tree swayed slightly from a breeze out of the southwest. He was flooded with the memories of flying out from his bedroom window and up to the tree in his backyard. He could feel the breeze, see the clouds drifting overhead, and sense the scurrying animals below. The coyotes had given chase, but the rabbits had found their dens and protection. He was glad to see the coyotes would go hungry for now.

The night air was cold and the breeze was giving him a chill. He decided to expend some nervous energy and swoop through the trees while waiting for Georgeo. Reaching out with his senses he released his grip from the evergreen and drifted slowly toward another tree top. He could feel the flow of life within the trees with his mind. A subtle flow of electrons could be sensed with the water climbing through the tree trunks, carrying precious minerals and oxygen to the leaves. While shifting to a horizontal position he placed his right hand out in front and gripped the next tree trunk as he approached it. He used his momentum and pulled to gain more velocity. Flinging his body past the tree he reached out with his left hand and gripped the next approaching tree trunk. It swayed slightly from the breeze and he compensated, grabbed hold, and pulled himself past the tree. Gaining more velocity, he quickly reached out with his right hand and grabbed another tree top. Pulling rapidly, he gained more speed. The next tree was slightly higher as the slope of the mountain increased. He reached it and pulled himself past it. Soon he had a rhythm to his motion. One arm and then the other. He was "swimming" among the tree tops. He swung his feet in front of him to land against a large tree trunk, bent his knees, and then pushed off toward another direction. Arms back out in front, he gripped another tree and flung himself to higher tree tops.

The chill of the night air was gone and Leif found himself sweating from the exertion. He pulled and pushed as quickly as he could. His senses were racing. The tree tops were flying past and he was dodging branches by dipping above or below them as he grabbed for tree trunks. An angry owl hooted at him as it flew off in haste when he approached it's resting spot. Various animals scattered below as they heard him whoosh through the trees. He continued to push himself, the anger, the anxiety, and the pressure of wanting to rescue Carina drove him to exert himself. No longer reaching for the tree trunks he continued to fly through the trees. They all became a blur to him as he skirted the branches and swaying tops.

A large animal caught his attention and he stopped suddenly to investigate. A large bald eagle was perched on the topmost branch of a swaying evergreen. It gazed at him briefly and looked away, as if to say 'Yeah, I see you too.' Leif's breath was almost taken away by the majestic view of the eagle. It pivoted its head around to watch for food, or danger, or both. There was no fear exhibited by the eagle. It would glance at him every few seconds while keeping a vigilant watch. The eagle extended one wing to full length and it groomed a couple feathers before retracting the wing and continuing its rotating gaze. "Wow." Leif whispered. He figured the single wing length was around three feet, which would make the total wing span of over six feet across.

"Beautiful, isn't it?" A voice next to Leif stated.

"Wha…" Leif quickly slid sideways to put a little distance between him and the other person. As quickly as he had moved, he suddenly realized the other person was Uncle Georgeo. "Wow. I didn't feel you coming."

"You were obviously distracted." Georgeo responded while gazing at the eagle. "Sorry I'm late."

"You're late?" Leif checked his watch and pressed the illuminate button. "Thirty-two minutes and I didn't even notice."

"Well, I tried to hurry. One of my most favored nephews decided to contact me. First time I've heard from him in a long time. He doesn't write, he doesn't call, and he surely doesn't send me flowers anymore."

"I'm sorry uncle." Leif replied with remorse. "I've been, as you say, distracted. By a girl."

"Carina?"

Leif was surprised by Georgeo's response.

Georgeo continued, “Her parents contacted me yesterday. They said she had been seeing someone, but they’ve been unable to reach her the past few days. I just figured it was due to being distracted by you.”

“I think it’s the Eighteenth, uncle. I think they have her, and I think I know where.”

Georgeo turned to face Leif. “What? How do you know this?”

“I’ve been followed a few times, my new employer is making me uncomfortable, and I think she’s behind Carina’s disappearance.”

“Who’s your employer?”

“Dr. Corellis, at the University. She brought me into the Astro-physics facility to do some programming on particle physics.”

Georgeo’s remained silent. He turned back to watch the eagle. He made fists with his hands and stretched his fingers. Leif could sense the tension.

It seemed the bald eagle could sense it as well. It spread its wings, screeched a piercing call, and lifted off with a massive stroke of its wings. It dove off into the distance and disappeared beyond the tops of the trees.

Georgeo’s tone of voice was cold and serious as he replied, “I need you to get me as much information as you can.” He turned back toward Leif. “You’re on the inside and they’re trying to use you for some reason. Suzanne is a pro at manipulation and she’s one of the most dangerous advocates of the Eighteenth. You must be extremely careful. Keep me updated and we’ll figure out how to get Carina out.”

“You know Dr. Corellis?”

Georgeo paused. His gaze turned inward as he answered. “Yes, unfortunately. We go a long way back. The Eighteenth is getting bolder and I’m sure she is behind this.”

“I’m sorry uncle. I should’ve contacted you sooner. What should I do?”

“Cooperate as much as you can without compromising. Find out as much as you can. I’ve got to take care of some things first.” Georgeo floated over to Leif and gently grabbed ahold of his shoulders. “This is personal, between me and Suzanne. I will take care of this.” He paused. “We, we will take care of this!” Georgeo released Leif, he turned, and rapidly launched into the night air - fading away into the clouds above.

Leif felt beads of sweat run down his back. A chill from the night air caused him to shiver as he dropped down into the trees.

***

Two nurses, a man and a woman, worked busily over Carina. They adjusted settings on the monitors, changed the bed dressings while rolling Carina onto one side and then the other, and injected drugs into the drip line. The female nurse checked the heart rate monitor and stated, “She should be responding to the L-Dopa. Heart rate has a slight increase, but she’s still not waking up.”

The male nurse lifted the sheet from Carina’s feet and rolled it back. He pinched the insole of both feet. There was no response from Carina. “Maybe we should increase the dosage?”

"I don't think that's wise. If she's sick or psychotic Dr. Corellis is not going to be able conduct testing. The pressure is on and she's not going to be happy." The female nurse added.

As if on cue, the room door clicked open and Dr. Corellis, Matt, and another lab assistant stepped in. The doctor took notice of the situation as soon as she entered the room. "Why isn't she awake?" Without looking at the nurses, she grabbed the patient clipboard from the female nurse and flipped through the topmost pages. "L-Dopa ten minutes ago?"

"Yes doctor." The female nurse responded. "A consideration for increased dosage was discussed, but I feel it could lead to nausea or slight psychosis, which would not contribute to patient testing." She stated confidently.

Dr. Corellis looked up at the nurse and paused for a few seconds while considering her options. "What about electrical stimulation?"

"We could try median nerve stimulation, but..."

Dr. Corellis interrupted with, "We don't have time for that." She walked over to the side of the room and pulled the portable defibrillator off the wall. "Matt, give me a hand with this."

The nurses, knowing what was coming, pulled back Carina's gown from below the neck to just above her breasts. Matt grabbed a conductive gel packet from a medical supply drawer and peeled open the top. Dr. Corellis laid the defib unit on a tray table next to Carina's bed. She turned it on and pulled the paddles from the unit. Her assistant set the power settings on the defib. The capacitors of the unit built up to a high pitched tone as the doctor held out one of the paddles across the bed. Matt spread a layer of gel onto the paddle.

Dr. Corellis rubbed the paddles together then placed them on Carina's exposed skin, below each shoulder blade. "Clear!"

Everyone except the doctor stepped back from Carina's bed as the doctor pressed the discharge button on one of the paddles. The hum and sound of crackling electricity filled the room as Carina's body arched against the bed straps and pulsed from the discharge. It was over in less than a second. Carina's body fell limp. Everyone looked to the cardiac monitor. A sharp spike appeared on the scrolling screen followed by a steady heart pulse.

The female nurse checked Carina and responded. "She didn't respond. She's still out."

Dr. Corellis extended one paddle over the bed. "Matt!"

He squeezed a thicker layer of gel onto the paddle and stepped back from the bed.

The doctor rubbed the two paddles together while adding, "Takc it up two morc notchcs."

Her assistant turned the dial two more clicks on the defib unit then stepped back.

Everyone held their breath as the sound of the capacitors climbed back up to a high pitch tone.

"Clear!" Dr. Corellis placed the paddles back onto Carina and she pressed the discharge button.

The sound of crackling electricity lasted longer this time as Carina's body arched and strained against the bed straps. She fell back into the bed with a gasp of air. Her eyes opened wide and she let out a groaning exhalation.

"Finally!" Dr. Corellis responded while clipping the paddles back into the defib unit.

The nurses checked the cardiac monitor. Another spike from the defib showed, followed by an increased heart rate. The female nurse turned back to Carina. She pulled out a pen light and checked Carina's eyes. "Um, doctor. She's awake, but not responsive."

The doctor grabbed the pen light from the nurse and flicked the light across Carina's eyes. There was no response from her iris. She handed the light back to the nurse and slapped Carina across the face with her hand. "Wake up!" she shouted.

Aside from the reddening skin on Carina's face, there was no other response. Dr. Corellis grabbed a round metal dish half full of water for swabbing and tossed the water onto Carina's face. Still, no further response from Carina. The right side of her face was red from the slap and her eyelids drooped halfway down her eyes. Her gaze was glassy.

Dr. Corellis threw the metal dish across the room. It bounced off a wall and crashed to the floor with a disturbing sound. Everyone else in the room remained silent, afraid to say anything.

The doctor headed for the door while stating, "Increase the L-Dopa and contact me immediately if there's any change."

***

Leif sat at his work desk and booted up his computer. He looked around to see if any of the other night-owl students or technicians were watching. Fortunately, they were all too busy with their own activities and assignments. The clock on the wall showed 3:42 a.m. - zombie time, as the programmers liked to call it back at Amzoft. It was too early for the day workers and too late for the strivers. But, the perfect time for programmers, or scientists, to be locked into the ‘zone’ - intensely focused on the task at hand with no consideration for time or other distractions. To everyone else, Leif was just another one of those programmer geeks who kept strange hours. It was also the perfect time for him to do some probing without drawing too much attention.

The computer played its start-up tune and Leif logged in. He scanned the room again then pulled a slip of paper out of his shirt pocket to remind himself of the scribbled password he found in Carina’s condo.

5t4rb0und

He stuffed the note back into his pocket and loaded his usual programming applications on the computer. Email was the first system he checked every morning. Not wanting to raise any suspicion, he stepped through his normal routine and read a few boring emails about campus policy changes, staff changes, acknowledgments for ‘special’ students, etc. After taking another quick glance around the room, he pulled up the email directory of the students and faculty staff. “Dang,” Leif mumbled to himself as the lengthy list scrolled up the screen. He scrolled the list back to the beginning and paused it.

His heart was pounding as he took another look around the room. Taking a deep breath to calm himself, he raised his cell phone and took a picture of the computer screen. He scrolled the email list and took another picture. The process of scanning the room, scrolling the list, and taking a picture, consumed ten minutes to grab all the email addresses. It seemed like an hour.

For the next two hours Leif forced himself to write code. It was hard to stay focused. He would catch himself staring at a single line of code while his thoughts drifted to Carina, how Dr. Corellis was involved, and wondering how Georgeo was going to help. With every change to the code he would re-compile and run his code. The compile process would take a few minutes and it gave him more time to think, to formulate his next plan of action. If his computer activities were being logged, the excessive number of compiles should greatly inflate the size of the log, forcing its potential readers to get bored before they would find his request for the list of email addresses.

Six-o-clock finally came around - the cafeteria would be open. Leif logged off his computer, grabbed his backpack, and he headed out for desperately needed coffee.

The cafeteria was already busy with students and faculty staff. Leif scanned the room for any familiar faces. Some he recognized from seeing them on campus, but no one from Astrophysics. He took his time stepping past the food selections behind the steam coated glass while looking for where he would plant his plate, and hide his computer hacking. A food server eyed him impatiently and sighed in relief when Leif finally pointed at his selections. He located an available corner table where he could have his back to a wall and no possibility for someone to see his tablet computer screen.

Leif pulled his tablet out of his backpack and attached a portable keyboard to it. He could see multiple wi-fi networks listed on the screen, freely available for connecting to the internet. The campus was awash in high-speed internet connections, but he wasn't interested in sending his data across the school's network. He selected a wi-fi connection through his mobile phone. Once the connection to the internet was completed, he launched his email application on the tablet and pulled up the first picture of email addresses on his phone. One by one, he attempted to log into the email accounts with the password he found in Carina's condo. It was a painfully slow process - enter the email address, enter the password, wait while the program attempted to login, wait for it to time-out and show a 'Invalid login or password' error, then move on to the next email address. At least the wait for the error message gave him time to scan the cafeteria for any probing eyes.

After an hour of probing the different email addresses Leif was wondering if he was wasting his time. It was tough controlling the inner anger he was feeling. The thoughts of what might be happening to Carina while he was just sitting here typing on his computer turned his stomach into knots. His breakfast still sat untouched on the table next to his tablet computer. He sipped on his cold coffee after entering another email address and scanning the cafeteria. Surprised, he quickly put the coffee down when a list of emails scrolled up on the screen. The top of the screen showed the email address associated with the password he had entered: 'kevinismith@uwcenpa.edu'. He took a deep breath, blew it out slowly, and scanned the list of email subject lines. Most were schedules and task assignments within the lab, a few were from someone named Melissa about dinner plans. Nothing of any significance. *Wait! I'm looking in the wrong place.* Leif looked for a folder marked 'Sent', found it and opened it. He scanned the list for emails on the same or next day he thought Carina disappeared.

Leif's heart raced as he came across an email with the subject of 'Difficult Acquisition'. He visually scanned the cafeteria first and then opened up the email.

Hey Doc. Difficulty with the acquisition, but completed on schedule. Some cleanup managed by Matt. One casualty during the activity - Andersen. Proceeding to delivery to MSB. Ks.

"Acquisition?" Leif whispered to himself. "Delivery." *She's here somewhere. I knew it!* Leif found another email from yesterday, marked with a subject 'Procedure Results'. He opened it.

Doc. Subject has refused to perform required exercises. Over-sedation may be contributing factor. Per your recommendations, the skeletal receptors have been ordered and will be arriving within the next 2 days. Surgical staff from Egypt will be arriving in 3 days. Ks.

A shudder ran through Leif's body. A mixture of anger, shock, and adrenaline. Looking up from the computer tablet made it worse. Doctor Corellis was in line at the register and she was looking back at him. *Crap!* Leif almost forgot to breathe. He forced a smile and a wave, even though hatred and disdain coursed through his veins.

He knew she would be headed his way as soon as she got through the line. He quickly logged out of Kevin's email account and logged into his own account. He loaded a virtual network connection program for accessing his computer down in the lab. With it he would be able to take over the screen and keyboard of the computer with his tablet computer. He looked up and could see the doctor standing at the register, handing her money to the cashier. The screen from his work computer popped up on his screen, with the login and password fields. He entered the information and waited for the work computer desktop to be displayed. There was always a bit of a lagging delay when accessing from a remote computer. The doctor turned and started walking toward him.

The work desktop finally displayed and Leif quickly selected the source code editor he used for writing his programming. Fortunately, it would load the last code module he was working on automatically. The code screen appeared on his tablet computer just as Doctor Corellis arrived at his table.

"May I join you?" she asked.

Leif paused for a moment, trying to look like he was wrapped up in his code. "Absolutely," he added.

"Sorry if I'm interrupting your work." She placed her tray and coffee down on the table and she sat down across the table, not able to see what Leif currently had on his screen.

"It's okay. I'm just a little stumped on a routine and I figured if I took a break up here with some food and coffee, it would clear my head enough to work on it." He turned the tablet computer around for the doctor to see.

She chuckled while taking a peek at the screen. “I really wouldn’t have the first idea about how to write any code. I can work with formulas in physics, but I’m kind of rusty since I just administrate everyone else to do it for me.”

Leif turned the tablet back around and quietly breathed a sigh of relief. “Um, okay. Well, I’m sure I’ll get it figured out soon.” He stared at the screen, not wanting to look the doctor in the eyes. She didn’t deserve his attention and he didn’t want her to get any indication of the anger he felt.

“I’m sure you will.” She added and took a sip of her coffee. “Speaking of, I wanted to commend you for the work you’ve been doing for our facility. Thanks to your routines, we have a much better grasp of particle physics in a vacuum. However,…”

Leif looked up.

“We would like to take that math and see how it applies in a normal atmosphere, especially with what we’ve recently discovered about dark matter.”

“You want me to adapt the routines for measuring dark matter in earth’s atmosphere?” Leif tried to look confused.

“Well, if dark matter exists in space, couldn’t we reason that it could exist within our planetary atmosphere, maybe within the mantel of the earth itself?

Leif gazed up at the ceiling as he contemplated a response. He knew where this was going and he really didn’t want to be the one to assist her with her agenda. “I guess,” he answered.

“Well, Leif. You’re a smart guy. I’m sure you have the ability to figure it out.” She paused and leaned toward him, lowered her volume, and gazed directly at him. "I have other options available to me. However, your work would help me to take a, um, less painful approach."

At that moment, Leif understood the doctor knew who he was and she knew he was aware of her efforts. *She might even suspect I know she has Carina.* He gazed back at her with a slight hint of his anger in his eyes. *I don't want her to know for sure.* Though he wanted to just reach out and choke the life out of her at that moment, he realized it wouldn't accomplish anything. He didn't want to give in to her prying or her efforts with Carina. "A painful approach?" he asked while changing his gaze to one of curiosity.

The doctor paused for a moment before responding. "A lot more effort is involved with my other options if you don't come up with the code for the measurements."

"Ah. Understood doctor." He paused and gazed back at his code on the computer tablet. "I'll do the best I can do."

"I know." She added. "I have the utmost of confidence in you." She stood up with her tray and coffee and added, "Because, if you can't come through with it, I'll just have to use my other option and you wouldn't be of much more use to the university." She turned and walked toward the faculty dining room, not waiting for a response from him.

In his mind, Leif picked up his tray and threw it at the doctor. He was angry! But, he knew it wouldn't accomplish anything. He was certain Carina was here and doctor Corellis was behind this. He had the information Georgeo needed to know. Leif didn't waste any more time. He texted Georgeo.

More vital info found. Need to meet.

He pressed the send button and mumbled to himself, “We’re coming Carina. Hang in there!”

FIFTEEN - NO LONGER SAFE

"My position comes with weight and responsibility no Avitorian should ever carry on their own. As long as The Eighteenth prevails, I will never rest. I will continue to fly and to carry our heritage. You can choose not to fly, to blend in with the humans, but you will never be one of them. You owe it to Carina to teach her about her heritage and to let her fly if she wants." (Georgeo speaking to Carina's parents shortly after her birth.)

Leif awoke hesitantly from the vibration of his cellphone alarm. He sat up and rubbed the sleep from his eyes and his face. The car was great for driving. It was lousy for sleeping in, especially when parked at a slight incline at the end of a dirt road in the forest. Two days of no sleep and constant anxiety was taking its toll on his mind and body. He checked his cellphone for new messages from Georgeo. Only the last message from earlier in the day appeared:

Site @ 6pm

The clock on the phone showed 5:47 pm. It was dark outside and it was hard for Leif to see out through the fogged up windows. He opened his door and quickly grabbed the keys from the ignition switch when the dinging alert of the car startled him. Stepping into the cold, crisp, night air felt refreshing and helped to shake the groggy remnant of sleep from his mind. He took a deep breath, blew it out slowly while closing his eyes, and reached out with his senses. There were some small animals hiding cautiously at a distance - no doubt startled by the car door and dinging alert. He reached out further and could sense a group of deer, bedded down for the night while one of them stood guard, possibly smelling Leif's scent. He smiled when he detected Georgeo approaching through the boughs of the evergreens overhead.

"You're early," Leif continued to stare out into the woods while Georgeo slowly settled next to him.

"I'm glad you noticed. I doubt you would've been able to see me."

Leif turned to see Georgeo was completely dressed in black. From tennis shoes, jeans, jacket, and black knitted cap. If it wasn't for his face, he would just be a shadow in the woods. "What did you find out?" Georgia asked.

"I managed to login to a email account for a Kevin Smith at the astrophysics lab. There were a couple emails to Dr. Corellis saying their subject was delivered to the MSB."

"MSB? What's a MSB?"

"It's the Marine Sciences Building. It's where the doctor's boat is docked. I did some snooping around and saw the doctor and her crew go into the building. I attempted to get in but…" Leif paused for a moment. He knew Georgeo wouldn't be happy about his being seen. He sighed and continued. "The campus cops saw me and I had to bail into the water."

Georgeo gazed up into the canopy of the evergreen trees, pulled off his knitted cap, and ran one hand through his silvery hair. He pulled the cap back on and looked back at Leif. "That's going to make it tougher. I'm guessing Suzanne suspects it was you."

"Yeah. I'm pretty certain of it." Leif added.

"Why?"

"She's blackmailing me to do some programming for their dark matter measurements in the lab. She said my work would be a less painful approach than her other options."

"Carina could be her other option, or just take you captive as well."

"There's more." Leif added. "Another email from Kevin said she's sedated and that a surgical team is arriving to insert some type of receptors."

Leif could sense the anger building up in Georgeo. It was too dark to see the details of his face. The minute of silence seemed to last forever till he finally responded.

Georgeo's voice was lower, quieter, and full of wrath. "I'll meet you here at eleven. Get more intel if you can, but be very, very careful. We go in tonight."

The whoosh of Georgeo's departure into the sky startled Leif. He felt the breeze and heard the rush of evergreen branches, all within a split second. The sudden movement made him blink and Georgeo was gone.

***

Dr. Corellis slowly paced the rear boat deck while gesturing with one hand and holding a cellphone to her ear with the other. "We have to stabilize her. The team will be here tomorrow and they're not going to be very happy if they can't get started! Understand?" She stopped pacing and waited for a response. "Keep me posted," she concluded and tossed the phone onto a padded chair.

"What's her status?" Matt asked while handing the doctor a glass of red wine.

"Vitals have improved, but she's still not responsive. I didn't anticipate this." She stood at the deck railing, stared off toward the opposite shoreline, and sipped her wine.

"So, bring in the boy. Maybe she'll respond to him."

"Matt…" she turned to face him. "If we bring him in he'll refuse to continue the math. I need him to finish. Dark Matter particle physics could be the key to understanding how it works - how they do it. No one has ever come this close to an understanding of the physics."

"If you bring him in, she'll respond. He'll do whatever you want if he thinks you'll let them go after the research." Matt paused and stood beside her at the railing. He spoke almost in a whisper. "Show him Angela."

Dr. Corellis stepped back from the railing, tossed the wine from her glass onto Matt's face, and threw the wineglass to the deck with a crash. Glass shards flew across the wood in all directions. "How dare you! How dare you question my decisions! Apparently you don't understand them as well as I thought you did."

Matt wiped his face with his shirt sleeve. "Suzanne. I…"

She interrupted him. "I don't want to hear it. You need to go!" She turned and faced the water and gripped the railing tightly with both hands.

Matt obliged, wiping wine off his face and headed for the ship's cabin. As soon as he closed the door behind him Dr. Corellis signaled the guard over.

"Make sure the infrared is still on for tonight. I don't want any more surprise visits."

"Yes, doctor. May I suggest a fresh glass of merlot?"

"Hot tea, green. The air is a bit frigid tonight."

***

The drive from Tiger Mountain to the university normally took 30 to 60 minutes depending on the traffic. Leif was in a hurry and managed to make it to the parking garage by 6:40 p.m. A little under 25 minutes. He hustled to the physics lab and his desk. As soon as he placed his backpack on his desk one of the other technicians showed up.

"Hey Leif, welcome to second shift," the technician stated with a chuckle. "It's interesting you're showing up right now."

Leif wasn't quite sure how to react to the tech's statement and he was a bit wary after Dr. Corellis' veiled threat this morning. "Um, why's that?"

"We're getting ready to run a test experiment of particle mass detection in the hydrogen bubble chamber. Dr. Corellis has suggested we incorporate a weak light source via laser and see if the detection of neutrinos matches the math you've been working on for us. Aside from collisions with hydrogen atoms, we're wanting to see if there's any fluctuation in the light source during the collision."

Leif was overwhelmed by the techno speak of the technician, but he kind of got the gist of it. "Wow. I had no idea my algorithms for the effects of gravity, light pressure, and planets could be taken down to such a minute level."

"Well, all we do is reduce the mass equation of your math. The rest of the physics still applies."

Leif nodded in agreement, not completely convinced it was that easy.

The technician continued. "Just follow me and we'll go down to the bubble chamber."

"Down?" Leif asked. "I keep forgetting there are a couple floors below."

The technician chuckled again. "Yeah, there are 2 more floors below us. The chamber is on the lowest level.

During their walk and elevator ride Leif continued to quiz the technician about the experiment. His calculations of mass and densities of material, plus the distance from the center of the planet, provided the newer calculations for the effects of gravity on their measurements. He mentioned the university conducted sound depth measurements to get a feel for the type of material densities below the university, and thus be able to adjust what they expected to see.

As they reached the bottom level, the elevator door opened to reveal a small room with a set of double doors with instruction signs for how to enter. After they exited the elevator and the doors slid closed, the technician tapped on a panel and the lights of the room dimmed to darkness with a slight red glow. They waited till their eyes adjusted, filling the time with more astro-physics speak, until they were able to read the instructions. A press of a button opened the double doors.

The entire laboratory was bathed in the same red glow as the entry room. In the center of the room was a large, oblong, circular container. It looked like a railcar gas container without the wheels and trailer. Several window ports were spaced evenly along the side. Pipes and cables hung from above the container and were attached to the top. A square tube extended from one end of the container and reached down into a long dark tunncl off to Leif's left. Technicians in lab coats hurried about the large container with their tablet computers. It reminded Leif of ants scurrying around the queen of the burrow. Equipment racks with computers and monitors lined a wall on the right side of the lab.

"This is the bubble chamber." The technician pointed to the large container. "It's filled with liquid hydrogen, highly pressurized and cooled to minus four hundred twenty three degrees, to keep the hydrogen in a liquid state."

"This way." The technician signaled Leif to follow. He continued as they walked to the left of the chamber. "As neutrinos pass through the earth at a high speed, they tend to miss most atoms. They just fly through happily along through space. But, in the slight chance one passes through our chamber, there are so many hydrogen atoms packed into the water, the odds of impact are greatly increased. If a neutrino strikes a hydrogen atom, leptons fly off from the impact, leaving a trail through the liquid. We have photo-receptors for capturing the events." He pointed at the side of the chamber, covered with a couple hundred protrusions, each with a network cable attached and coiling into a massive bundle of wires - all nicely zip-tied and dropping into a foot-wide pipe stretching into the tunnel.

"How often do the collision events happen?" Leif asked.

"The last one we saw was fourteen months ago."

"What?" Leif gasped while they continued walking into the tunnel, following the pipe and cables. "Why all the activity then?"

"Doctor Corellis has a project she's been developing, but she's being pretty quiet about it. We think it's something special for the Department of Defense, which would explain all the extra funding we're getting. Anyway, she's providing some type of particle generator in the room above us within the next day or two. We're not permitted to see the source, but we'll be down here gathering measurements and looking for collisions." The technician paused as they reached a door at the end of the tunnel. The pipe and cables passed through a foam packed opening in the wall, next to the door. He scanned his card against a black security pad next to the door and continued. "The crew is making sure all the fittings and sensors are working correctly before the big experiment."

Leif's heart sank with the realization the experiment would use Carina as the source of sub-atomic particles for impacting the hydrogen atoms. He didn't know if anything could be measured. It made him angry to think of Carina as the doctor's lab rat for experimentation. He loved her so deeply. *I've got to get her away from these maniacs.*

The door clicked, the technician pushed it open, and politely held it while letting Leif step through first. While the room did not have the dim red glow of the laboratory, it was still dimly lit. Most of the light in the room came from the rows of computer monitors and the wall of flat screen monitors, all showing measurements and status updates from the equipment in the lab. One of the wall monitors showed the dim, blue, glow from inside the bubble chamber. The fluid inside it was perfectly still, making it hard to tell it was full of liquid hydrogen. A large circular row of desks extended from one wall of the room, left of the wall monitors, and circled under the monitors to the wall on the right, almost forming three quarters of a full circle. In the middle of the circle was a recessed circular pit, with another set of circular desks, providing the occupants with a full view of the wall monitors and the monitors in the larger circle. Although there were close to fifty monitors in the large circle, only a few of the staff sat at their consoles. The senior engineers sat at the desks in the pit, engrossed in reviewing statistics on their own computers.

Leif had seen enough. “I’ve got to go.” He stated while glancing at his watch.

“What’s the hurry? We’re getting ready to grab a snapshot of the stable environment as a comparison against the actual experiment.”

“Um, I’ve got a lot of programming to do and now that I’ve seen what’s going on, I’m sure the doctor would want me to have some major features ready by tomorrow.” He turned and headed for the door. “I can find my way out. Thanks for the tour.”

Leif pushed open the door to the tunnel and was surprised to see someone preparing to enter. A mid-20ish man with spiked, short, blonde hair, and the build of a football line-backer squeezed past Leif - almost pushing him into the door frame. As Leif slid sideways, he got a peek at the man’s name tag, clipped to his brown leather jacket. The name ‘Smith, Kevin’ caught his eye. He glanced up from the tag to see Kevin frowning.

“Do you mind?” Kevin stated while stepping through the doorway.

Leif quickly raised his arm to cover his own name tag and reached out with it to pat Kevin on the shoulder. “Sorry buddy. Thought you were going to let me through first.”

Kevin turned and strode into the room, ignoring Leif’s pat on the shoulder and his comment. Leif used his foot to speed up the closing of the door. He turned and walked quickly through the tunnel, past the bubble chamber, and toward the double entry doors. No one noticed his nervous pace and glances back down the tunnel. Everyone else was too busy getting the chamber ready for the big test. He pressed a palm button next to the doors, unlocking them and switching the entryway to dim light - preventing flooding of the laboratory with bright light. As soon as he was through the doors he hit the elevator button and glanced back through the closing double doors to make sure Kevin wasn't in pursuit. He pressed the lighted elevator button again and again. "Come on!" Adrenalin was coursing through his body and his heart was racing, along with his mind. *I gotta get ahold of Georgeo. I've got to get Carina out.*

Anger and anxiety was building up inside him. Part of him wanted to storm back into the lab, find Kevin, and beat the crap out of him. It might feel good for a few seconds, but it wouldn't help him to get Carina out. Leif leaned one hand against the side of the elevator, took a deep breath, and blew it out slowly. *Calm. I have to calm down. Think clearly.*

The elevator doors opened with a ding. Leif jumped in and tapped the button for his floor, then the button for closing the elevator door. The doors started closing and Leif could see the double doors of the laboratory open. Leif stepped to one side to get a better view of the lobby before the door slid closed. He caught a glimpse of Kevin lurching toward the elevator door. Leif jumped back and slammed against the back of the elevator as the door closed. He could hear Kevin spewing profanity and hitting against the door as the elevator started moving. Leif's heart almost stopped from the shock of seeing Kevin come after him. *Maybe the technician told him who I was?* He realized the elevator's next stop was the floor where he did his work. *I have to get out of the building.* He tapped the button for the ground floor and hoped no one would want to get on from the work area.

The elevator dinged and the door opened on the work floor. Leif exclaimed a sign of relief to see no one was there wanting to go up. Then he noticed a fire alarm switch on the other side of the hallway, outside of the elevator. Barely giving it much thought, he jumped out of the elevator, pulled the fire alarm switch, and quickly stuck his arm into the path of the closing elevator door to make sure it didn't close. The screeching fire alarm echoed through the hallway, piercing his eardrums. He jumped back into the elevator and double tapped the button for the ground floor. "Come on, come on, come on." He repeated and covered his ears from the loud alarm raging from the speaker in the elevator. It seemed like an eternity before the door finally opened on the ground level. Leif darted from the elevator and ran to the security guard in the lobby.

The guard was on the phone, speaking with the fire department. "… and it just went off a couple minutes ago, but I don't see any issues on the fire panel."

Leif shouted at the guard. "There's a problem in the laboratory with the bubble chamber. You need to get the fire department and hazmat team here as soon as possible!" The guard stared back at him blankly, trying to digest the emergency as Leif ran through the lobby, out the double glass doors, and into the night.

It felt good to grab a deep breath of the cold night air. It invigorated Leif as he decided his next action. He pulled out his cell phone and quickly texted Georgeo.

Fire alarm on campus. Diversion. Need to move tonight.

Leif looked around quickly to see if anyone was in the area. The fire alarm could be heard outside the building and he knew it would attract attention. So far, no one was in the area to notice. He ran to the side of the building where most of the shadows were falling, away from the street lights. Looking up into the sky, he could see there was a low cloud layer passing slowly overhead. He could smell rain in the air. Taking another quick glance around he bounded into the air as quickly as he could and entered into the cold, damp clouds above the campus.

***

"What do you mean he was here? What's all the noise?" Doctor Corellis stated into her cell phone. She paused a few seconds to listen, then responded. "He was in the lab with the bubble chamber? Fire alarm? You fools! How could you let this happen?!" She paused again, while pacing the rear deck of her yacht. "Fire department… Can you get the wave rifles?" She paused, collecting her emotions. "You already have them. Good. Bring them to me. I expect we might have some company tonight."

SIXTEEN - GET THE GIRL

"The pain of separation for us is too great. Once the binding of love is established, it is for life, and if there's any prolonged separation, there is a chance it can become a physical health issue." (Verbal history of Avitorians, handed down by Georgeo to a group of youngsters.)

"What's with the security guard in the hallway?" The male nurse asked while picking up the clipboard from the end of Carina's bed.

"Doctor said it was extra measures to make sure nothing interrupted Carina's sleep tonight." The female intern replied. "There's a big examination tomorrow and Suzanne wants her as well rested as possible."

"Well rested?" he chuckled. "She's so well rested she almost died on us yesterday."

"Actually, she was awake for a few hours today. I really think the L-Dopa with the extra hydration helped."

"Ah, that's good." The male nurse continued to examine the charts on the clipboard.

Carina slept soundly oblivious of the feeding tube, oxygen cannula in her nose, and the straps around her hands, chest, legs, and ankles. He hung the clipboard at the end of the bed and checked the monitors. "Everything looks good. I'm sure the doctor will be pleased with her status." He checked his watch. "I have a break in another hour. I'm dying for some coffee." He sat down at a desk with a computer at the side of the room. "Maybe we can both go grab some in a bit. As long as we stay away from the astro-physics building. There's a bunch of firetrucks and police over there. Something about a hazmat spill."

***

Georgeo slowly descended from the low clouds to the end of the dirt road in the woods. Leif was already there, still wet from his flight from the university.

"You pulled the fire alarm?" Georgeo asked.

Leif wasn't sure if he was going to get scolded or praised. "It hit me at the spur of the moment. I had to get one of the doctor's goons off of my tail. I wasn't sure I was going to make it out."

Georgeo pondered for a moment and shook his head in approval. "Good thinking. The extra diversion will help." He pulled off his stuffed backpack, unzipped the top of it, and pulled out a plastic bag full of fireworks and another bag with a mason jar. "Take a look."

Leif pulled out his phone, lit up the display, and aimed it at the contents in Georgeo's hands. The mason jar was full of liquid and had a smaller glass container inside with some chunks of metal. "What's that?"

"An extra distraction. I was pretty good at chemistry as a kid." Georgeo chuckled. "The small container has sodium. I drop this into a trash dumpster, causing the glass to break, the sodium mixes with the water, and a nice fire breaks out."

"Awesome."

"But, I have something special." George reached into the backpack and pulled out some black clothing and handed it to Leif. "Here, I want you to wear this."

"I already have dark clothing."

"This is special. There's only one of these and its mine, but for tonight, I want you to wear it. It goes on under your clothes."

"I have to strip and put this on?"

"How else do you expect to get it on under your clothes?" Georgeo asked as seriously as he could. "It'll be a little tight since I'm shorter than you. It will keep you warm in the winter skies and cool in the summer. It is infrared resistant, reflects microwaves, and makes you more invisible to The Eighteenth's equipment."

"What about you? Don't you need this?"

"They're going to be looking for you. I'll create the diversion and draw them off, but if there's a chance they focus on you, these will protect you. This way, you get in, and get Carina out."

Leif nodded and added, "Okay, then. Stealth underwear." He pulled off his jacket, shirt, and jeans, and put on the special clothing. The bottoms clung to his legs like yoga pants, but was silky and smooth. They went on easily. The top was the same except it had a hoodie that fit over his head like a scuba suit. It was a little tight under his arms, but it seemed to expand a little with his body heat. Georgeo handed him a pair of matching socks, which pulled up to just under his knees, and a pair of gloves - textured on the palms and fingertips, and smooth on the back. Even though he had been wet and sweaty from the flight and adrenaline, he could feel the fabric pulling the moisture away from his skin. "You've worn this?"

"Multiple times. I'll fill you in someday." Georgeo waited while Leif finished putting on the rest of his clothes.

"Nice. I can hardly tell the difference." Leif added.

"Where are we going?" Georgeo asked.

Leif could feel Georgeo trying his best to hide his anxiety. He pulled up a graphic map on his phone, and put it into 3D satellite mode - showing the university campus as a 3D model. "Here's the view of the entire campus." He showed Georgeo and zoomed in to where only a few buildings next to the water were visible. He pointed. "This is the Marine Sciences building. The doctor's boat is parked right next to it. Carina is somewhere in the building. This…" He zoomed out slightly and pointed. "Is the Astro-Physics building, where the firetrucks and police are going to be. It's only a couple blocks away."

"May I?" Georgeo asked while reaching for Leif's phone. He scrolled around a little and zoomed in on a different building. "What building is this?"

"That's the Harris Hydraulics Lab."

"Okay. I see a dumpster in the parking lot there. I'll hover over the doctor's boat for a minute, long enough for them to pick me up on their infrared. I'll head over here…" He pointed to the dumpster. "And drop the sodium jar. Wait out over the water until you see the dumpster in flames. By that time all their attention should be in my direction. That'll buy you time to get to the building, get in, and find Carina. Get the girl and get out!"

Leif pondered over the plan for a few moments. "What if I run into complications in the building?"

"Didn't you have complications in the physics building?"

"Yeah, I guess I did."

"You figured it out. I have no doubt you'll figure it out again." Georgeo handed the phone back to Leif. "You ready?"

Leif took a deep breath, blew it out, and shook his hands a few times. "Yes. I'm ready."

***

Leif hovered barely below the cloud layer, a couple hundred feet above the waters of Portage Bay. He could sense and hear some activity behind him, in the floating houses and neighborhood of North Broadway. He figured it was around midnight, but didn't dare check his phone. The light would easily give him away if anyone happened to look his direction. Normally, with the chill in the air and the dampness of the clouds, he would either be shivering or weighted down by his heavy coat. With the special underclothes provided by Georgeo he felt warm, dry, and comfortable. He now understood why Georgeo had given them to him to wear. He looked for Georgeo, but couldn't see him from this distance. His heart was pounding with anxiety and anticipation. He could see the Harris Hydraulics Lab building to the right of the Marine Sciences building. Georgeo would be hovering somewhere above it. He looked toward Dr. Corellis yacht. It was lit up on the inside, but he couldn't tell if anyone was out on the back deck or in the upper cabin. "Come on Georgeo," he whispered to himself.

Georgeo descended toward the roof of the Marine Sciences building. There were lights shining from under the roofline down toward the dock of the building and Dr. Corellis yacht. He descended further till he was barely above the roof. Two men came out from the cabin of the yacht and pointed in his direction. They shielded their eyes from the bright lights and pointed slightly to the right of his position. "Heh. Can't see me, aye?" He chuckled to himself. One of the men looked down at a device he was holding while the other man ran back inside the cabin. The man with the device walked toward the gangplank leading to the dock, while looking down at his device. The second man came running back out with a large and fat looking rifle. Dr. Corellis stepped out onto the deck and pointed toward the dock. No doubt directing their next move.

Georgeo flew back up toward the cloud layer and leveled out just below it. He headed over to above the next building and looked for the trash dumpster in the parking lot. It was always hard to judge his angle when trying to drop something to an exact location, so he swooped down till he was around fifty feet above the dumpster. Unfortunately, he didn't count on the lids of the dumpster being closed. He looked toward the dock and saw the two men heading his direction, but they were at least a good football field away. He dropped down next to the dumpster, pulled one of the lids up, flipping it open, and accelerated back up into the air.

The two men reached the street between the buildings. Dr. Corellis was standing on the dock, looking in Georgeo's direction. She had one hand above her eyes, trying to block out lights from the buildings and she had one hand to her ear - talking on a cell phone. Georgeo hoped she thought he was Leif. He pulled the jar out of his jacket pocket and dropped it into the dumpster.

Leif saw a flash of light followed by smoke from the parking lot of the Harris Hydraulics Lab. His heart beat heavily in his chest with the realization it had begun. There was no turning back now. "Alright. Just wait for it." He whispered to himself. The distant column of smoke ascended into the air, lit up from the sodium and water fire below. The minutes of watching the smoke and fire grow seemed like an hour. He was getting anxious. A distant siren from a firetruck sounded and Leif knew it was time.

He ascended up into the cloud cover and flew toward the Marine Sciences building.

Closing his eyes and reaching out with his senses, he tried to determine the exact location of where he needed to be. The flow of electricity through the flood lights of the building and the streetlights was almost overwhelming. He dulled his senses enough to get a better sense of the layout. There was another strong electrical source coming from the yacht and something one of two men were holding as they ran toward Georgeo and the growing heat source from burning dumpster.

Leif stopped over the top of the building and slowly lowered himself while hanging upside down. He stopped as his head peeked through the bottom of the clouds. He could see the two men running toward the building across the street. One of them was holding the large rifle and was pointing it toward Georgeo.

Georgeo could sense Leif hovering over the top of the Marine Sciences building. He continued to hover around a hundred feet over the top of the dumpster. The wind blowing in from the Sound was carrying the smoke from the fire to the east. He grinned at the men approaching. “This should make things interesting.” He whispered to himself as he pulled a couple strands of firecrackers from his jacket pocket and dropped them into the burning dumpster. “Bulls eye!” Georgeo stated as he watched the strands hit the center of the fire. He ascended up into the base of the clouds as the firecrackers started firing off.

Leif could hear the sounds of gunfire coming from the direction of the burning dumpster and he smiled at the thought of Georgeo dropping the firecrackers into the fire. He saw the two men who had been running toward Georgeo drop to the street surface and cover their heads. The plan was working - all attention was being directed on Georgeo and the burning dumpster.

Leif scanned the roof of the Marine Sciences building and didn't see any vents big enough for him to get into the building. He descended and flew to the west side of the building, further away from Georgeo, and between the dock and the front of the building. Various windows stretched along the side of the second floor of the building. The echoes of men shouting, firecrackers, and sirens from approaching firetrucks and police bounced around the buildings as Leif tugged on one of the windows. Not wanting to waste any precious time, he drifted back a few feet, covered his head with his arms, and flew feet first through the window. Glass shattered and the wooden framed splintered. He fell to the floor sliding and slammed into the opposing wall and book shelf. The shelves collapsed, sending their contents cascading noisily to the floor.

“So much for a quiet entry,” he remarked while shielding his head.

He stood and paused at the room door for a moment to listen for the footsteps of security guards. It was hard to hear anything with all the commotion going on outside. He closed his eyes and reached out with his senses. There was a lot of equipment in the building churning electricity. *I need to focus.* Covering his ears and kneeling down on the floor, he forced his mind to shut out the harsh intensity of the electrical wires and equipment in the building. The power within lifeforms was softer, gentler, and living. *Below, animals, fish. More floors below. I gotta get downstairs.*

He stood and slowly opened the door. Satisfied no one was there, he ran through the hallway to a small lobby with an elevator, and a door to the stairs. Pausing for a few seconds, he took a deep breath, and blew it out slowly. He pressed the button for the elevator, as a possible distraction, and headed for the stairwell. Instead of running down the stairs he floated down and to the first floor door. He placed an ear to the door and listened while reaching out with his senses. *Tanks full of fish and plants. No one there.*

Quickly peeking through a small, square window in the door, he could see the water tanks, surrounded by equipment, and steel racks loaded with tools. A sign on a side door read 'Lockers', which peaked Leif's interest. He slowly opened the door and quickly floated into the locker room. After checking a few of the lockers he came across a white lab coat with a name tag clipped to the upper pocket, showing 'C.Anders'. The lab coat was slightly large for Leif. *It'll do.* He grabbed a clipboard off a small corner table and dug some printed reports out of a trash can, straightened the wrinkles out of them and clipped them down. "Perfect."

Leif took a quick glance out the locker room door to make sure it was clear and he stepped back into the stairwell. He floated down to the next level. The door leading out of the stairwell lead to a long hallway ending at a series of boat docks and walkways over water. Netting stretched across the fiberglass tanks, separating different species of fish, octopus, and crabs. Leif could see lights reflecting off the white hull of the doctor's yacht at the end of one of the walkways. He turned and headed back through the hallway to the stairwell.

The stairs continued down for three more levels before revealing another door leading to a long hallway. Leif slowly opened the door and drifted past an elevator door. The walls of the hallway were networked with various pipes, cables, and wires running the length of the hallway. Leif followed the path but drifted slightly above the concrete floor, completely silent. He stopped before the hallway terminated and listened/sensed for anyone in the area. A single person in the hallway, stationary, and maybe sitting down. Past him Leif could sense two more standing in a room and someone laying prone. His heart leaped with the expectation it could be Carina. He chanced taking a quick peek around the corner. There was a security guard sitting at the end of the hallway examining his phone.

Leif took a deep breath, blew it out, and lowered himself to the floor. He walked around the corner and toward the security guard, hoping his lab coat and clipboard would indicate he was supposed to be there. The guard stood up and quickly put his phone in his pocket.

Leif decided a good offense would be the best approach. "What are you doing?"

"Um, just checking my text messages." The guard responded.

Leif tried to sound as authoritative as possible. "You do understand Dr. Corellis wants the utmost of vigilance for protecting the patient, yes?"

"Of course." The guard responded while looking defensive about being dressed down by someone in a lab coat. "Can I help you?" he asked.

"Just here to do some measurements before the big experiment tomorrow." Leif responded while looking down at his clipboard.

"Ah, of course." The security guard pushed open the door behind him and pointed for Leif to enter.

Surprised the guard gave in so easily, Leif responded. "Well, make sure you stay on your toes. There are a lot of distractions going on outside and the doctor is going to expect nothing but the best from all of us."

"Yes, of course." The guard replied.

Leif stepped into the room and paused while the door slowly closed behind him. *Wow, I can't believe how easy that was.* The room was just a plain laboratory with shelves and equipment in racks on the walls. There were three stainless steel doors at the opposite wall, which looked like doors to walk-in refrigerators. There were no other doors except for the one he just came through. He ran one hand through his hair while pondering what to do next. Voices from behind one of the doors startled him and he quickly flew to the side of a tall computer equipment rack, shielding him from the view of the three doors, but not from the main door to the hallway.

The steel door closest to him opened with the hiss of an air tight seal being released. A man and a woman in hospital scrubs stepped out while talking. "Do you think she'll be ready for the implants tomorrow?" The woman asked.

"She certainly seems more stable now," the man replied as they stepped across the room toward the exit door.

Leif quietly slid backward, trying to keep himself from being seen if they turned around.

The man continued while reaching for the door handle. "The ringers drip should be done by the time we get back. We'll do another snapshot of vitals and call to update the doctor." He pulled the door open and allowed the woman to step through first.

The security guard in the hallway looked toward the man as he held the door open. Leif's heart jumped with the realization he could easily be seen by the guard. The man followed the woman through the door and greeted the security guard. Leif held his breath as the door slowly closed behind them. He shivered from the adrenaline rush with the click of the door. Not wasting any time, he hovered to the steel door and opened it with another hiss. Another steel door stood about six feet in front of him. He quickly reached for it, but it wouldn't open. There was no scanner pad next to it or a lock. He started to panic as he heard the door close behind him and a flow of cool air washed over him from above. A red LED readout next to the door showed a countdown starting from twenty and stepping down every second. Leif took a deep breath and tried to calm down till the counter reached zero. The door in front of him beeped. He grabbed the handle and pulled the door open with a hiss.

The room was bathed in red light except for a dim white light above the bed with Carina. Leif gasped in relief as he saw her - tears welling up in his eyes. "Carina," he lightly whispered as he stepped to the side of the bed and grasped her hand. It was warm to the touch, but she didn't respond. He scanned the monitors and equipment at the head of her bed. Past the equipment he noticed a glass room with a large vertical cylinder. He gave her hand another squeeze and whispered in her ear. "Carina. It's me, Leif." She didn't respond. He pulled his phone out of his pocket and quickly tapped out a text message to Georgeo.

Found her. Below MSB. Guard in hall.

He shoved the phone back in his pocket and scanned the restraining straps around Carina. No locks, just buckles. He glanced back over to the glass room. The tall metal cylinder with a window at the top and a small digital display caught his eyes again. He had to give it a quick look. He hovered over to the glass of the room and stared at the cylinder. Through the small glass window of the cylinder, he could see the face of a girl, with long, limp hair off to the sides. Her eyes were closed and her skin had a pale bluish tint to it. He could hear equipment running in the room and figured it was some type of cryonics chamber. Below the window was a steel tag with the name of the girl - Angela.

Leif's mind raced with the possibilities. *Aunt Angela?* He tugged at the door, but it was locked. "Ahhhgg!" He shouted at the door as he gave it another yank, without success. He flew back to Carina's side and patted her on the face. "Carina, wake up. Come on. Wake up!" She didn't respond. He released the buckles on the restraints and gently removed the IV to the fluids bag, the oxygen cannula in her nose, and the feeding tube down her mouth, while trying to be careful with the adhesive tape holding everything down. Tears fell down his cheeks as he raced to get her free from the equipment while trying to be gentile enough to not hurt her.

He rubbed her arms and her feet, hoping to get her blood circulating better. "Carina, wake up babe. It's me Leif. We've got to go. We have to get out of here." Stepping back up to the head of the bed, he gently stroked her cheeks and gave her a kiss on the forehead. "Carina. I'm going to carry you." He placed one arm under her knees and another arm behind her shoulders, lifted gently and used his hand to steady her head. He lifted up slightly off of the floor and glided over to the steel door. Using his left hand, under her knees, he reached for the door handle, turned it, and pushed the door open. Standing in the middle of the chamber, he waited for the door behind him to close, and for the stream of air to wash over them. "Come on, come on."

The cool air flowed over them both as Carina let out a small moan. Leif waited for the red numbers to reach zero. He pulled her face up toward his and he whispered, "Carina. It's okay. I've got you now. We're getting out of here."

The LED counter reached zero and Leif pushed on the door with one foot. He glided out through the door and paused for a moment while staring at the exit toward the hallway. *The guard.* He slowly drifted to the door, not sure how he was going to handle the guard while holding Carina. As he reached for the door handle something slammed against the other side of the door with a loud thump, startling Leif. He leapt back away from the door as it shook from another loud thump. The door opened and Georgeo gazed into the room while straddling the floored security guard, who was groaning and clutching his ribs. A can of pepper spray rolled down the hallway and the guard's cellphone was scattered into various pieces on the floor.

"Georgeo!" Leif exclaimed. "What did you…"

"It's just a couple ribs. It's what he gets for texting while on duty." Georgeo stated while holding the door open and signaling for Leif to hurry. "We need to go. It's getting busy outside."

Leif drifted through the door and followed Georgeo over the guard and down the hallway. He stopped half way down the hallway. "Georgeo."

Georgeo turned. "What? We really don't have much time."

"It's Angela. They have aunt Angela. She's in a cryo tube, back there."

"Are you sure?" Georgeo asked while checking over his shoulder.

"I saw the name tag. It's her." Leif stated in frustration.

Georgeo paused for a few seconds and gazed down at the floor. "Okay. Noted, but for now, we get you both out of here." He turned and drifted to the corner of the hallway and signaled Leif to follow. "We're clear to the next level."

They drifted up the three flights of stairs and stopped at the landing leading to a hallway and another flight of stairs. Georgeo looked up at the next flight of stairs and put his hand out to stop Leif and Carina. "It's not good. People are coming down." He turned to face Leif. "We have to split up. You've got to get out with her." He pointed down the hallway. "Head out past the yacht and then up. You're wearing the suit. They can't stop you. Meet me at the trail."

"What about…"

"No time Leif. Just go. Now!"

Leif increased his hold on Carina and flew down the hallway. He quickly peered through the window in the door, opened it, and hovered through to the area with the water tanks and catwalks suspended over the water. One of the catwalks led to an opening under the dock, next to the yacht belonging to Doctor Corellis. He really didn't want to get any closer to the doctor, but he didn't have much choice if he wanted to escape. The weight of Carina was starting to wear on his arms. *No time to hesitate.* He flew over the catwalk and stopped where it ended. He could hear voices echoing off the side of the yacht from the dock above. A distant sound of motors and spraying water reminded him of the fire Georgeo set in the trash dumpster at the next building. The water and the sky past the yacht was dark. He knew he would stick out against the night with the white lab coat, but he wasn't about to let go of Carina. "Hold on Carina. Here we go." He whispered and gave her a kiss on the cheek.

Mustering up all his strength, Leif flew off the end of the catwalk and past the yacht. He kept low to the water and circled around behind the starboard side of the boat, trying to keep the yacht between him and the people on the dock. He could hear shouts of people in the distance. He increased his speed and stayed barely above the surface of the water of Portage Bay. Once he reached the middle, he stopped, rotated around, and could see spot lights from the cabin of the yacht sweeping his direction. He looked up and rocketed into the sky as quickly as he could. It seemed like forever before he reached the safety of the cloud layer. The cool, damp mist of the cloud felt refreshing and it calmed his nerves. He held Carina as close as he could as he gained altitude and headed for Tiger Mountain. He gently kissed her on the forehead. “You’re safe now, Carina.”

Droplets from the cloud mist gathered on Carina’s skin and soaked her hair. She gasped a deep breath of the cold, night air, and slowly opened her eyes. She was barely able to let out a whisper. “Leif?”

SEVENTEEN - HANGING ON

I can only be the best when I am with you.
I can only be at peace when I am with you.
The clouds, they don't mean nothing.
The sky is never blue.
The moon will never shine.
Unless I am here with you.

I can only be air born when I am with you.
I can only be in joy when I am with you.
The stars don't dare to shine.
The songs just can't be sung.
These arms can hold no one.
Unless I am here with you.

Avitorian song of love, author unknown.

"Aaahhhhggh!" The blood curdling scream from Dr. Corellis made Matt and her security detail stop in their tracks. She ran toward the edge of the cement dock, holding a wave gun in her hands. "There they are!" She continued screaming. "They're getting away!" She stopped at the edge of the dock and engaged the charging capacitors on the gun and aimed it at a faint white dot climbing up into the clouds. A LED light in the eyesight of the rifle turned green and she pulled the trigger. The distance was too great. Throwing the gun to the ground she turned and screamed at the security personnel who were focusing their spot lights into the water near the yacht. "You idiots! The air! Not the water. Our target was in the air!"

Matt stood close, just out of arm's length from the doctor. An assistant held a parabolic dish pointed into the sky above the bay, a cable connected the dish to a computer tablet in Matt's hands. "Strange. The infrared didn't show anything." Matt muttered.

"This was deliberate and planned." She cursed at the clouds. "The fire alarm, the flier, the trash fire. All diversions. This wasn't just Leif." She pulled out her cellphone and speed-dialed. There was no answer. Grunting in disgust, she headed for the door of the Marine Sciences building. "Matt. Stay here and watch for any activity. You two..." She pointed at two security guards. "Come with me. Medical is not answering the phone."

***

Georgeo stepped back from the door leading up to the stairwell. A man and a woman in white lab coats descended the stairs and stepped through the door. A cellphone rang with a popular rock song ringtone. The female technician handed her coffee cup to the other medical tech and reached into her pocket for the phone. "I bet that's the doctor."

Georgeo took advantage of the distraction and walked up behind both of the technicians. He placed a foot in front of the male tech's leg and pushed with one hand at the man's back, causing him to fall forward and down the stairs. Hot coffee splayed out from the cups in his hands as he tried to break his fall. The startled female tech spun around toward Georgeo, giving him the opportunity to grab the ringing cellphone from her hand.

"Thank you." Georgeo smiled as he pushed the female tech backward toward the other technician sprawled out on the stairs, who was attempting to right himself just as the female technician landed on top of him. They both tumbled down the stairs with guttural exclamations. "Gravity," said Georgeo as he hurled the cell phone against the wall, shattering it to pieces - silencing the ringtone with an air of finality. He turned and pushed through the door and up the stairwell.

Georgeo reached the next floor and stepped through the door into the main warehouse of the Marine Sciences building. Water tanks stocked with fish and plant life filled the room, racks of equipment and shelves lined the walls. He could faintly hear the groaning of the technicians in the stairwell below. Apart from the gurgling of water pumps there were no sounds of anyone in the warehouse. He pulled his cellphone from his pocket and tapped out a text message while walking toward the exit door on the opposite end of the room.

As he reached the door, he could hear shouting outside. Looking through the window of the door, Georgeo saw Dr. Corellis and a couple of her staff heading toward him. "Oh, boy. Here we go." He opened the door, stepped out onto the dock, and stopped. He watched with a smile as they walked toward him.

Dr. Corellis looked up from her cellphone and stopped suddenly at the sight of Georgeo standing in front of the door. One of her guards reached inside his jacket, but she stopped him. "No, wait."

"Well, hello doctor." Georgeo stated loudly. "Long time, no see."

"Been what, a little over twenty-five years?" She raised the wave rifle, flipped a switch, and pointed it at him. The hum of capacitors charging up to a high pitch could be heard from the rifle.

He chuckled. "What? This is how you greet me after so long? By pointing one of your toys at me?" He spread out his hands and started to walk slowly toward her. "I thought we had something special."

"Just want to make sure you don't go flying off, like before." She stepped toward him and her guards walked along with her, each of them with a hand inside their jackets.

"Flying off?" Georgeo replied. "You think I can fly?" He motioned with his hands up to the sky, looked up, and gave a small jump - pretending to launch like superman.

Dr. Corellis flinched at Georgeo's posture and pulled the trigger on the rifle, but only held it for a couple seconds as she realized he wasn't going to fly. Georgeo grabbed at his chest from the intense heat. It ended as quickly as it had started.

“Wow.” Georgeo stated. “That’s a pretty fancy microwave you have there.” He knew this would be his best opportunity to catch them off guard. He dropped to his knees and placed his hands behind his head. “I give.” He lowered his head, but kept sight of the end of the rifle from the corner of one eye.

The doctor was surprised at Georgeo’s gesture and she lowered the rifle. The guards released their grip on their weapons and stepped forward to reach for Georgeo’s arms. As they reached for him he lowered his arms, grabbed an ankle of both guards, levitated slightly above the dock and flew backward quickly, raising their legs. The force literally pulled their feet out from under the them and they both landed hard on the back of their heads on the cement of the dock. He released them and he flew horizontally toward Dr. Corellis. She was startled by the sudden attack on the guards and fumbled with getting the rifle into firing position.

Georgeo reached for the business end of the rifle, using his momentum to push it up and the doctor backward. She fell back onto the dock, the impact of the hard surface caused her to release her grip on the wave rifle. Georgeo stopped flying and let himself fall to the surface of the dock, landing on his feet, with the rifle in his hands.

Two university police officers appeared from around the side corner of the building. In their immediate view of the dock, they saw a woman and two men down on the concrete, and a man with a rifle standing, facing the woman. One of the officers shouted “Freeze! Police!”

while the second officer made the split decision to react by pulling his gun and firing off three rapid rounds at the man with the rifle.

Georgeo turned toward the shout of the officer. He started to release his grip on the rifle, but was struck by one bullet in the shoulder and another bullet to the upper chest. The force of the impacting bullets spun him around and backward. He felt like he had been hit by a baseball bat at full swing.

"Noooo! Stop!" Dr. Corellis screamed at the officers. She jumped up and ran over to Georgeo.

He released the rifle, rolled over to all fours, and tried to push himself up. He couldn't understand why one arm wasn't working and he was having difficulty taking a deep breath. Dr. Corellis cursed at the officers while helping Georgeo roll over onto his back. He reached into his jacket pocket, pulled out his cellphone, and attempted to smash it against the concrete. Dr. Corellis placed her hand between the phone and the concrete and grabbed the phone out of Georgeo's hand. One of the two guards was struggling to get to his feet. The other one was out cold from his head injury.

The officers both had their guns out and were quickly moving toward the doctor and Georgeo. "Miss, step away, now! Step away!" One of the officers shouted. The other officer was talking into his shoulder mounted microphone.

The doctor stood up and stepped back, away from Georgeo. She discretely stuffed his cellphone into her pocket and she continued to walk backward. Matt and several of her crew were running toward her.

The officers reached Georgeo. One of them kept a gun trained on at him. The other officer kicked the rifle away from reach, rolled Georgeo over onto his stomach, and placed his hands into handcuffs. The officer knelt down and rolled Georgeo onto his side. “Sir! You’ve been shot. We have an ambulance on the way.” The officer patted Georgeo’s pockets, looking for a wallet, but found nothing. “Sir! What is your name? Do you have any ID on you?”

Georgeo tried to breathe, but he couldn’t get enough of a breath to respond to the officer. He felt cold and numb. All he wanted was to be left alone, to sleep. He turned his head toward the officer and whispered two words with his last breath. “Got away.”

Dr. Corellis continued to step backward while watching one of the officers start CPR on Georgeo. Matt and the rest of the crew caught up with her.

“Are you okay?” Matt asked.

She turned to him, grabbed one of his arms, and started walking briskly toward the yacht. “We have to store the gear. There are going to be a lot of questions.” The rest of her crew turned and walked along, listening intently. “We don’t know this man. He attacked us with his strange gun.” She pulled Georgeo’s cellphone out and checked the screen.

tiger mt k3 Eva

She stopped walking.

“What?” Matt asked.

“They’re pulling out. I’m guessing Leif and Carina are going to be here.” She showed the screen to Matt.

“Is the other rifle in your Jeep?”

"No. The guys have it in the next lot. They thought they had Leif before the trash…"

"No time to discuss." She turned toward the others. "Secure medical. Move Angela to base. Tell police I had to get away and safe. Make excuses. Shut down ops and pull out." She looked to Matt. "Let's get the other rifle and get out of here."

***

Leif held on as tightly to Carina as he could. She had awakened briefly, but fell back asleep. They were both soaked from the heavy moisture in the clouds. Only after he felt they were safely away from the light glow of the towns below did he rise up above the cloud layer. The air above the clouds was colder and he slowed his speed to cut down on the wind-chill. He shifted from holding her in his arms while vertical to leaning back and shifting her weight onto his chest and stomach. Flying feet first at a forty-five degree angle he could see where they were going. He shifted her head over one shoulder and hugged her tightly with one arm while letting the airflow slip his lab-coat off his other arm. Gripping her with the free arm, he repeated the process with the other arm and the coat came completely off. He managed to swing it over and on top of Carina.

The special under-suit from Georgeo kept him warm and his body heat was radiating against Carina. As she warmed up a bit she started to shiver.

"Hang on Carina. We'll be down soon." He whispered into her ear, next to his cheek. "I've got you." The sound of his words sunk deep into his being. The rescue was done. Somehow, they managed to actually do it. She was here, in his arms. He had missed her so much. "I'm sorry, Carina." He whispered. "I'm sorry I wasn't here sooner. I'm sorry I let them get to you." He choked on his words as tears began to roll down his cheeks and mix with the moisture on his skin. "I'll never let them hurt you again. Never."

"I know." Carina weakly whispered. She wrapped her shivering arms around him.

***

"You know there's only the two of us and one rifle." Matt stated while driving.

"And what else would you have me do? Sit around and wait to get interrogated." Suzanne stated while poking around on the cellphone she took from Georgeo. "The only way I can recover this project is to get Carina and or Leif. Otherwise, we'll have to shut the whole thing down and pull out." She pointed ahead. "There! Take the 520 East, then 405 South."

"I know how to get to Tiger Mountain." Matt stated defiantly.

"Well, can't you go any faster? They ARE flying."

He just looked over at her and shook his head. "Want me to get stopped by Seattle's finest?" He paused and looked ahead. "Maybe explain that rifle laying in the back seat."

She continued to search through the information on the cellphone. "Just shut-up and drive. Get us there as quick as you can, without getting pulled over."

***

Leif lowered into the trees as gently as he could. It helped that Carina was awake and she was providing a little assistance with the flight, even though she was still shivering. They gently lowered into the darkness below the trees. Leif did his best to sense where the ground was and managed to touch down without misjudging. He cursed himself for not leaving his car here. Carefully, he lowered Carina to the ground, on top of the lab-coat. "I'm glad it's dark." He stated while removing his black jeans, jacket, and shirt, revealing the protective garments from Georgeo.

"C-c-cute." Carina stated while he pulled his jeans over her legs and zipped up her jacket.

He chuckled, pulled her up off the ground, and held her close while rubbing her extremities to get her circulation going.

She hugged him and laid her weight on him while he was rubbing her back. The shivering was staring to slow as she began to get warmer.

"I wish Georgeo would hurry up." He stopped massaging Carina when he sensed a vehicle off in the distance.

He held onto Carina tightly and drifted up and to the side of the dirt road, and into the cover of the trees. The dancing beams from vehicle headlights danced through the trees as the vehicle approached. Leif drifted a little farther back into the trees as the vehicle got closer. He continued to hover while holding Carina close. The vehicle reached the end of the road and stopped. No one got out for a few minutes and the motor was still on. Leif couldn't tell what kind of vehicle it was, but he could sense there were two people inside the vehicle. The driver side door opened and someone got out.

"Leif?" A man shouted out from the side of the vehicle.

Leif instantly recognized it was his father, Ben. "Dad!" Leif shouted from the woods and then drifted with Carina in his arms to the vehicle.

"Leif. What's going on? Why the evac from Georgeo?"

Leif didn't answer, but instead focused on getting Carina to the vehicle. He lowered to the ground near the back of his dad's 4Runner. "Dad. Where can I lay her down?"

Ben opened the back door, reached in and threw some items from the seat into the back of the vehicle. "Hold on." He said as he unrolled a sleeping bag along the back seat. "Here. Put her in here."

Leif carefully laid Carina into the back seat. She hesitated when releasing her arms from around him. "It's okay. You're safe now. We're going to take care of you and get you to safety." As he covered her with the top of the sleeping bag, he overheard the car radio news which his mom was listening to.

"…And it seems the attacker has been shot and killed by university police. With fire crews and hazmat teams on-site, it's been a very busy night on the U.W. Campus. We'll be sure to bring you more information as it becomes available. This is Josh Harrison with KUSI News, Seattle."

"What?" Leif asked. "Who's the attacker? Dr. Corellis?"

"No dear." Francie, Leif's mother answered from the passenger side of the front seat. "They said it was an older man with grey hair."

Leif stumbled out from the vehicle and fell backwards to the ground. "No." He cried. "Not Georgeo." He slammed a fist into the dirt. "No. It can't be. He was there with me. He told me he would meet me here."

Ben reached down to help Leif stand up. "I'm sorry son. He texted us and gave us the evac signal."

"It can't be." Leif stated. "I've got to go and get him. Help him get out of there."

"Leif, no!" Ben held onto Leif's arm. "You can't. You have to go with us, and keep Carina safe. We have to evac. That's the order from Georgeo."

Leif was stunned. He knew Ben was right, but he was having a tough time accepting it. "How can Georgeo be dead. He's…" Leif paused. "He's Georgeo. He's always been there for us."

"Leif." Ben added. "I'm sorry, but…" He paused. "We have to go."

The thoughts were racing through Leif's mind. "Georgeo sent you here? With an evac message? From his phone."

"Um, yes." Ben answered. "Leif, we…"

Leif interrupted. "Dad." He turned and looked down the dirt road. "If Georgeo's gone, someone else has his phone." He looked back at his dad, his mom, and Carina in the back seat. In a whisper he stated. "I've got to fix this."

"What?" Ben asked. "How can you even expect to fix this? It's the Eighteenth!"

"Dad." Leif turned and faced Ben. "It's Dr. Corellis! She's the one I have to deal with." He paused. "She has Angela."

"What?" Ben stepped back in disbelief. "Angela? Are you sure?"

"I saw her. She's frozen. They have her in a cryonic tube." He stepped toward his dad. "I have to do this." He looked in at Carina and reached in to take her hand. "Carina. Our spot. Take them to our spot and I'll meet you there. At dawn."

Carina squeezed his hand and faintly responded. "But, Leif. What…?"

He leaned in further and kissed her on the forehead, caressed her face with one hand, and kissed her gently on the lips. "Carina. I love you. I'll be back for you. I promise. I have to fix this. I have to deal with Dr. Corellis. I have to buy us time and a life. Don't you want that with me? A life?"

Carina paused before answering. Tears welled up in her eyes. "Yes, Leif. I want a life with you!" She squeezed his hand firmly. "You better come back."

"I will. I promise." He stood up, gave his dad a hug, and reached into the vehicle to give Francie a hug and kiss. He stood and closed the back door, gave his dad a firm pat on the arm. "You've got to get going."

Ben got into the vehicle. "Leif." He paused. "Be safe. We'll see you at dawn." He closed the door and maneuvered the vehicle around while Leif watched from the side of the dirt road.

Leif gave a wave as they drove off past him. He watched as the tail lights faded into the distance. Raising up into the trees, he pulled out his cellphone, selected a number from the address book, and made a call.

***

Dr. Corellis was surprised by the vibrating of Georgeo's phone. The display on the phone showed a number, but no name. She decided to answer. "Who's this?" There was no response then the call disconnected.

"What was the number?" Matt asked.

Dr. Corellis showed him the number. "It's Leif. I recognize the number from our traces.

"He knows." Matt added.

"Yes. Keep driving."

***

Leif, now convinced, formulated a plan as he hovered in the shadow of the tree tops.

EIGHTEEN - BEGINNINGS

The crow is gone.
Blackness has fallen upon us.
Another will fly from the storm.
We await the storm.
(Message sent to all known Avitorians.)

The clouds were low and moving fast across the tops of the trees on Tiger Mountain. Every now and then the whip of a lower cloud would pass through the trees, enveloping Leif in a wet fog. He stood on a thin branch with one arm against the thick vertical trunk, two thirds the height up on a massive evergreen tree. His senses were alert as he noticed where the local wildlife grazed, moved, or bedded down in the area. While it was comforting to be among the trees and the wildlife, especially after the frantic rescue from the university, he placed most of his focus down the dirt road. Part of him felt strong and confident. Carina was safe. *We did it!* Another part of him was tired of the struggle. *Why is the Eighteenth so set on hunting us?* He thought about his last moments with Georgeo. Maybe he could've stayed and helped, or at least convince Georgeo to come along with him and Carina. Georgeo had said, "this is personal." *Did he want to confront the doctor? Did he try to go back for Angela?* Too many questions poured through his mind. He had almost drowned in thought when he sensed a vehicle turning onto the dirt road.

"Road K3." Matt turned onto the dirt road then continued, "This is crazy Suzanne." He flipped on the high beams and a secondary set of halogen spot lights, bathing everything within a hundred feet with intense white and yellow light.

"Just keep your eyes open. They could be anywhere along this road." Doctor Corellis replied and put Georgeo's cellphone in her jacket pocket. She reached into the back seat and grabbed the wave rifle. Flipping the charge switch on, the capacitors in the rifle whistled up in pitch while she lowered the window and rested the rifle on the window frame.

Leif's heart raced with anticipation. He could sense a single vehicle and two people in it. *Is that all?* He had expected the doctor to bring a small army. He waited patiently for the vehicle to appear.

Small flashes of light penetrated through the trees and brush as the Jeep slowly crept along the road. The flashes of light increased as the vehicle got closer, turning one direction, and then another, on the angled switchbacks of the road.

Leif took a deep breath and blew it out as six pinpoints of light swung around and faced toward him. He quickly drifted back behind a thick trunk of an evergreen. The lights bobbed up and down with the dips and ruts in the dirt road. Leif didn't want to ruin his night adapted vision from the light beams. He flew up through the tops of the trees, just below the base of the clouds, and followed the dirt road until he was behind the Jeep. As he lowered himself he kept pace with the Jeep and hovered a few feet above the back.

"It's a dead end." Matt stated as then slowly approached the end of the dirt road.

"Stop here." Doctor Corellis stated when the end of the road was twenty feet away. A half dozen parking slots radiated around the end of the road, surrounded by ferns and evergreens. "Keep the lights on." She stepped out of the vehicle, gripping the wave rifle tightly, and scanned the forest in front of the Jeep.

"Looking for me?" Leif asked.

Dr. Corellis swung around rapidly and pointed the rifle at Leif. She was tempted to fire and try to drop him to the ground, but she lowered the rifle. “You know; I knew a while ago you were an Avitorian.”

Matt stepped out of the Jeep and was surprised to see Leif hovering above the back of the vehicle, only a few feet away.

“Yeah,” Leif replied. “and I figured you were with the Eighteenth. So,” he paused. “where does that leave us now?”

She chuckled. “Well, Georgeo is gone. Looks like you don’t have much in the way of leadership. I suppose we just continue to hunt you down. We’re close to understanding.”

Leif felt anger at the statement about Georgeo. He did his best to suppress the anger. *I need to stay calm. Think clearly.* “Can’t happen.” He stated. “You’re not us. You never will be. You’ve been trying for thousands of years and you still haven’t figured it out.”

“We’re close. We have the technology for measuring, and we have this.” She patted the rifle. “If this can impede your flight, I’m certain we’re close to understanding how it works.” She pointed the rifle at Leif. “We are the lineage. We have the right. We will regain our rulership and it will be with the power of flight. It has been decreed ever since Ahmose.”

“Give me Angela.” Leif asked boldly.

Dr. Corellis laughed. “Right. Like that’s going to happen.”

“You can either give her back or I’ll take her from you.”

"No chance." Dr. Corellis stated. She pulled the trigger on the rifle, sending invisible beams of microwave energy into Leif.

He felt the heat of the rifle beam in his face, but nowhere else. Quickly pondering his options, he decided to let her think he was affected and dropped to the top of the Jeep, rolled off the back, and onto the ground with a groan.

"Matt, get a tranq." Dr. Corellis stated. She kept the rifle active and pointed at Leif while walking toward him. As soon as she was close enough, she gave him a kick and rolled him across the dirt.

Leif continued to groan and he rolled with the kick.

"You think you're superior than the Eighteenth?" She gave him another kick. "You're sadly mistaken. We'll just take you back to our lab and continue our experiments. We already have a wealth of information from your girlfriend, Carina. It'll be a real pleasure continuing with you." She gave him another kick, rolling him across the ground.

Leif grunted from the painful kick. He let the momentum roll him across the ground. Out of the corner of an eye, he could see Matt approach with a syringe. His face hurt from the intense heat of the microwaves and his ribs stabbed at him, but it wasn't enough to impede his ability. Curling up into a ball, he waited for the doctor to get closer. As soon as she was close enough he kicked up with one foot and knocked the end of the rifle up toward the sky. She stumbled back, startled, but managed to keep one hand on the rifle. Matt paused for a second, stunned that Leif was able to move. The doctor stepped backward, letting the weight of the rifle fall back into shooting position.

Leif wasn't about to let her get another shot off. He jumped up from the ground, gave the end of the rifle another kick, flinging it completely out of the doctor's hands and off the side of the road. He flew into the doctor, knocking her off her feet, grabbed her by the waist with one arm, pulled her close, and lifted off into the air.

Matt lunged and grabbed one of Leif's legs as he lifted off, halting Leif's flight into the air. Gripping the syringe with the tranquilizer with his fingers wrapped around the barrel and with one thumb on the plunger he swung it toward the back of Leif's leg. Leif kicked out with his other foot and made contact with Matt's face, causing Matt to release his grip and fall to the ground, missing his stabbing swing with the syringe. Doctor Corellis slammed her hands into each side of Leif's neck as he lifted up toward the trees. Leif intentionally brushed the doctor against branches of the evergreens, halting her attack, and giving her a bit of a much deserved beating as he accelerated. Clearing the trees and entering the base of the clouds, he increased his speed and used both arms to grip the doctor and draw her tighter to him. He didn't want to drop her and she didn't want to be dropped. She wrapped both arms around him and gripped his jacket into her balled up fists.

He grimaced from pain in his ribs as she gripped him tightly. "Easy on the ribs doctor. You gave me some nasty kicks down there."

Stunned with the realization she was gaining in altitude and was now at the mercy of Leif's grip, she slightly loosened her arms. They were fully in the clouds, it was dark, and she couldn't see. The moisture of the clouds soaked them as he continued to climb.

Dr. Corellis finally regained her composure enough to speak. "Where are you taking me? Are you going to drop me?"

Leif didn't answer. He continued to climb through the dense clouds.

"If I die, it will not stop. The Eighteenth will continue to hunt you, and with my death they'll be more determined to find you. A balance has to be found. We will learn the secret and we will become the rulers this planet needs. We can bring peace. We will rise above and establish the government to rule over mankind. With the ability of flight, we will be the Gods of royalty, in control, once again."

Leif laughed. "Really?"

They cleared the top of the clouds and Leif continued to climb up into the sky. The moon and the stars were bright against the clear night sky. The light reflected on the tops of the clouds below. Leif headed toward Mount Rainer as he continued to gain altitude. "You've got it all wrong doctor. As a human, you will never be able to learn the ability of the Avitorians. We are not the same as you. We do not have the hatred, the anger, or the desire of power you have. We do not seek to rule. All we want is peace, to exist with the natural life forces of this planet, and to coexist with humanity. We do not know why we are here. We do not know if we came from somewhere else or if we adapted our skills from ancient humans. There are many of us, all around the world, and you will never be able to have what we have."

Doctor Corellis knew she was at the complete mercy of Leif and she felt certain he would eventually drop her to get back for the death of Georgeo. "It wasn't my fault."

She stated and paused for a minute. "Georgeo. It was an accident. The police thought he was a danger to us and they shot him."

Leif pondered this and a mix of anger and sadness welled up inside him. It took a moment for him to regain his composure enough to reply. "He will be missed, but we will continue." He stated. "We will wait for humanity to figure it out. As long as you hate. As long as you seek power over others. As long as you think you are better than others. You will never be able to find the balance needed. You will never be Avitorian. You will never find peace." He hovered over Mount Rainer and then slowly started to descend. "We have balance. You do not. When you find the balance, then, and only then will we reveal ourselves."

He descended to a level spot on the southeast side of the mountain. It was cold and they were still above the cloud layer. Releasing the doctor, he hovered back from her and paused. He removed his jacket and handed it to the doctor.

"I have a jacket."

"Take it. You're going to need both."

"Is that how you avoided the rifle beam?" She asked while nodding at his all black under garments.

Leif didn't answer. He waited for the doctor to start slipping on his jacket over hers. As she got one arm into the jacket, he reached in and grabbed for the two cell phones from each of her jacket pockets. She tried to resist, but he pulled her closer while he dug out the phones. He gazed at both of the phones and drifted backward, out of arms reach.

Doctor Corellis shivered in the coldness of the altitude as she finished putting the jacket on. "So, you're just going to take my phone and leave me here? Why didn't you just drop me and get it over with?"

He drifted forward slightly and handed her personal cell phone back. "Amazing. It looks like you still have coverage. One bar. I'm sure it'll improve as you get lower down the mountain."

"You're letting me go." She stated. "Why not just take me down the mountain then?"

"You need some time to think. To enjoy the hike. Just follow that trail off to your left." He pointed to where a narrow, flattened, but snow covered path angled downward. Drifting farther back and hovering in the air, he continued. "Maybe we'll meet up again. In fact…" He shook his head knowingly, looked at Georgeo's cell phone, and stuffed it into a pocket. "I'm sure of it. We will meet again. Goodbye doctor." He lifted up into the air and flew off into the distance.

***

Leif circled around Mt. Rainer and reached the spot where he had originally met Carina. He hovered slightly above the clouds and slowly rotated, scanning the tops of the clouds. His ribs ached from the pounding he had taken from Doctor Corellis, he felt an inner pain from the loss of Georgeo, and now his whole family was on the run, having to relocate. At least Carina was safe. *Angelia.* Another pang of anxiety and anger rose up with the thought of Angela still being held by the Eighteenth. He stopped his spin and just hovered stationary, staring at the glow of the moonlight against the snow cap of the mountain. His hope for a normal life was shattered. He pulled out Georgeo's cell phone and he flipped through the address book. There were a lot of numbers, but most only had first names. He found Georgeo's notepad application and there was an entry titled 'For Leif'.

"What cha doing?" The soft voice of Carina came up behind him.

Leif smiled, put the phone back in his pocket, and he spun around to face her, but she wasn't there. "What?" Slowly rotating around again, he looked up and then down. As he looked down to where his feet touched the top of the clouds, a hand came up from the clouds and grabbed his foot. He laughed and let himself get pulled down into the clouds.

Carina wrapped both arms around him and hugged him tightly. He grimaced from the pain in his ribs, but tried not to show it. He hugged her as well, placed a hand against her cheek, and gently kissed her.

"I missed you." He added.

"Leif." She paused. "I knew you would come for me." She took his hand in hers. "Yes, I will go with you. Wherever you choose to go, I will go. Whatever you decide to do, I will be there with you. The Eighteenth will never come between us again." Her grip on his hand tightened.

"I promise you, I will never let them harm you again."

***

"Hello, Matt?" Doctor Corellis spoke into her cell phone. "Pull the team. We need to regroup. I have a new angle." She listened as Matt replied to her. "Yes. Leif and

Carina are gone, but now I know how to get his cooperation. Oh, and come get me at Mt. Rainer, the Paradise trail-head."

The End

Look for the upcoming book in the Air Born series, “Air Storm”.

HOW AIR BORN BEGAN

Since a young age, I've had dreams of being able to fly. Not like a super hero or from some kind of mutation. It always seemed to be a part of me, a natural, peaceful ability to hover and float throughout my house. Sometimes I would venture outside, but mostly I was indoors. Why? I have no idea. It was like this ability was my own little secret in my dreams.

I've always wanted to put this feeling into a story. I just never could come up with an approach that felt right. Then in the summer of 2013, in preparation for the Edmonds Write On the Sound Writers Conference, an idea for the story hit me. The idea excited me so much, I had to get it in down in writing. Within the span of a week I had a short story called, Love Is in the Air. Okay, yeah. A little cheesy. But it hit the mark of the feeling of natural, anti-superhuman, flight.

The story didn't win anything or even receive any kind of a mention from the judges at the conference. Slightly disappointed, but still excited about the story, I decided to share it with my editor, Azy. She was in the middle of correcting my blunders with Zegin's Abduction. Her response was, "You have to stop everything you're doing with Zegin's and turn this into a novel!" While this greatly excited me, I couldn't let go of Zegin. In between edits, I started plotting the story, created the backstory encyclopedia, and gave it a title - Air Born.

While I could've cleaned it up and edited, I decided to leave it in its original state. For your enjoyment and a peek at the quickly hatched draft of an excited writer, here it is:

Love Is in the Air

A short story by Timothy Trimble

1490 words

Leif never considered that he could be thought of as a stalker. This was different. It was only a few days ago when he first saw her - hovering barely above the clouds on a full moon night. It was her hair that caught his eye. Clouds didn't have long, flowing blond hair. It was all he could see that first night, being too shy to get any closer, and when she sank down to disappear into the cloud he felt like he could die of stupidity - for not saying hello.

When he returned to the same spot the following night, she was nowhere to be found. The clouds were thicker and interspersed with fog rising up from the forest below. His gut ached with the thought that he had lost her forever - that she would never return to give him the chance that he had thrown away the night before. That night seemed like it would never end as he hopped from cloud to cloud, searching for any sign that she had been there. He looked for the slightest wisp of cloud and fog streaking in a direction contrary to the wind. He looked into every gap with the hope that she had just passed through, leaving a trail for him to follow. As the horizon started to glow he returned home, feeling devastated and tired. It would be hard to appear normal throughout the following day - working his job, mingling with the chaotic world, and not knowing if he would ever meet up with the blond haired flier.

When he was young, Leif's parents had told him that he would eventually meet up with other fliers. At the first sign of his ability to fly they inculcated into him the teachings necessary for survival. He was not to be seen by "normal" humans. Other fliers had disappeared when they became too careless. The humans couldn't be trusted to understand what their life was like or how to coexist peacefully. Their biggest fear was the existence of fliers could become public knowledge, which would lead to capture, study, and maybe even extinction. It was too great of a risk. Maybe when the world learned to be more peaceful and compassionate - maybe then they could safely reveal themselves.

Throughout Leif's young life he had only met one other flier aside from his parents. Georgeo was his name and he was a traveler who would bring news from other fliers around the world. At that time there were only seventy other fliers Georgeo was aware of. He was certain there were more, but due to their discreteness they wouldn't make themselves known. Some even chose to live a grounded life - never to take flight, even in the privacy of their own homes. Georgeo had paused at that comment and shook his head in shame.

Regardless of the lack of sleep and stress from his work, Leif had a hard time waiting for the darkness to settle over Seattle. He thought about trying other locations, thinking that maybe she would fly to other remote spots to enjoy the peace and serenity of the night. There were too many places to look. The forests and mountains outside of Seattle were too vast to cover by a single flier. He had considered enlisting the help of his parents, but felt too embarrassed by his lack of initiative on that first night, and his excuse of their advancing age made it easy to not include them; at least, not yet.

I'm panicking, he thought to himself while driving to a secluded spot at the base of Mt. Rainier, close to where he had seen her several nights before. *I have my favorite spots. Remote and away from prying eyes. She has to have her favorite spots as well.* Leif waited for the darkness to settle. He knew he would have some time of complete darkness before the moon showed itself over the horizon. When the time was right he quickly launched into the cool night air. Distant city lights painted a faint glow against the clouds around Mt. Rainier. Fog was starting to form and drift through the thick forests below. Stars were peeking through openings in the clouds. There was a slight wind bringing more clouds in from the Puget Sound. Leif flew to his best approximation of where he had seen the long, flowing blond hair in the clouds. He slowly rotated while rising above the clouds, scanning every possible nook, wisp, crevice, and gap in the clouds. It was difficult with the darkness, but he knew the moon would be adding a radiant glow soon.

Leif took a deep breath to calm his nerves. *I have to see her again. Patience. I can do this.* He stopped gaining altitude and continued to slowly turn while scanning for any sign of a flier. The crispness of the air was helping him to relax. He always enjoyed the serenity of the mountains and the forests. Even when he was grounded - walking through the many trails and along the rivers, he found that he was most at peace and happiest when he was here. He stopped turning and gazed at the distant glow of light on the peaks of the Cascades. The moon was rising and would soon provide more light.

Leif heard a sudden rush of air above him. He looked up, expecting to see a flock of birds, or a stray seagull. There was nothing. He slowly turned around, looking up, hoping to catch a glimpse of flapping wings against the backdrop of the mountains or the distant city lights. Another rush of air passed under him, startling him to a verbal, “Whoa.” He quickly flipped upside down trying to see what had flown under him. He thought he made out the movement of a something rapidly flying away, but it was too dark to tell. He quickly followed in the same direction, but stopped when he couldn’t detect any further movement.

His heart was beating rapidly. Not sure if it was the excitement or fear of not knowing what was happening. Something or someone was out here with him. *Could it be her?* He slowly turned around looking for any possible movement while listening for any change in the light wind. The moon was starting to crest the top of the Cascade mountain range to the east. Clouds continued to move below him, coming in from the northwest.

"I've been watching you." The soft whispered voice came from above and to the south.

Leif quickly turned to look in the direction of the voice. There she was - hovering in the distance and being softly caressed by the clouds surrounding Mt. Rainier. Leif could hardly contain the beating of his heart. He could hear it in his ears and was afraid that it would just fall out of his chest and kill him before he could utter a single word. He could tell that she was smiling as she hovered among the clouds. The glow of the rising moon washed over her. She was wearing jeans and a flowing loose jacket over a t-shirt. Her hair moved with the wisps of the clouds and would occasionally land at her elbows as she hovered with her hands on her hips. Her posture seemed to imply that it was now Leif's turn to respond.

Leif took a deep breath and blew it out slowly. He smiled with a bit of a chuckle, realizing that while he was hoping to sneak up on her that she had, in fact, done the same to him. He paused and took another breath before responding. "You've been watching me?"

She drifted closer as she responded, “Yea. For like two months.” She paused and looked off toward the lights of Seattle and continued. “I had to strike a pose for you before you saw me.”

“Wow. I’ve been so blind for two months, eh?” Leif responded with embarrassment. “And here I was feeling guilty about stalking you.”

She let out a small laugh. “Well, I guess I’ve been stalking you, Leif.” She replied.

“What? You even know my name? I admit, you really have me at a great disadvantage.” Leif responded as he started to slowly drift closer to her.

“Sorry. I’m Carina.” She looked down as she drifted closer.

“Carina.” He paused while approaching her. He decided to stop at around 10 feet. Close enough to see her and not too close to be intimidating. For who, he wasn’t sure.

Carina had stopped her approach as well. She looked up at Leif and smiled.

Leif reached out with his hand, open, and ready for an introductory handshake.

Carina drifted closer and took his hand. “Nice to meet you.”

"Would you like to talk awhile over a cup of coffee?" Leif asked.

"I would love to."

ACKNOWLEDGMENTS

Special thanks to Azaliah, who told me I had to stop everything I'm doing and turn my short story into a novel. To the Air Born beta readers, who's invaluable feedback kept me going through the three years it took to write this story.

Hugs and love to my 8318 family, especially those in S.E. You've endured my readings and continue to treat me like just another bro.

Huge thanks to Walnut Street Coffee in Edmonds and Red Cup Coffee in Mukilteo - my favorite writing hangouts, and the greatest coffee in the Pacific Northwest. To the crew at Averetek - your support and friendship means more than you know.

My heart to Richard and Joycelynn, who introduced me to the love of reading.

Lastly, thanks to Mr. McFarland, who told me I would find a purpose for algebra.

OTHER BOOKS BY TIMOTHY TRIMBLE

Zegin's Adventures in Epsilon
ISBN/EAN13: 1-50326-243-X/9781503262430

Adventures in Flight Simulator, Microsoft Press
ISBN: 1-55615-582-4

FileMaker Pro Design & Scripting for Dummies, Wiley Publications
ISBN: 0-471-78648-9

THE MUSIC OF AIR BORN

Even though I started writing as a teenager, I was sidetracked by music. My creative outlet for many, many, years was through writing music and performing. Brain surgery in 2006 brought an end to the performing due to the loss of hearing in one ear. Don't feel bad. It also brought me back to creative writing of stories.

Air Born is my new song and an epic one at that! This doesn't mean that music is no longer a part of my life. Even with one functioning ear, I still greatly enjoy listening to music.

During the journey of writing Air Born, I listened to a lot of music. I found various songs that helped me to set the tone for each chapter of Air Born. Originally, I had the idea of embedding a QR code at the top of each chapter, which when scanned, would launch the reader's browser, go to a site with the song, and play it. While this seemed a great idea, and everyone I spoke with about it thought it was a great idea, I ran into many legal roadblocks. It seems, if you're going to publish something for money, if you use someone's art, you have to have permission, and you have to compensate the artist. I totally get it and I would expect the same if someone wanted to use something from Air Born.

So, if you so happen to stop by Spotify, and perform a search for Air Born, I'm sure you'll come across my personal listening list, thrown together, while I was writing. I hope you enjoy listening as much as you enjoy reading. Again, thank you for your support of my bringing this story to life.

Timothy Trimble

Reader Notes:

Air Born

Made in the USA
San Bernardino, CA
03 April 2017